Switched

by

Amanda Hocking

Third Paperback Edition: January 2011

For information:
http://amandahocking.blogspot.com/

Switched — Book I
ISBN 978-1453688939

For Pete — fellow Aardvark, comrade, and former cover model.

Table of Contents

Prologue:
Eleven Years Ago

A few things made that day stand out more than any other: it was my sixth birthday, and my mother was wielding a knife. Not a tiny steak knife, but some kind of massive butcher knife glinting in the light like a bad horror movie. She definitely wanted to kill me.

I try to th0ink of the days that led up to that one to see if I missed something about her, but I have no memory of her before then. I have some memories of my childhood, and I can even remember my dad who died when I was five, but not her.

When I ask my brother Matt about her, he always answers with things like, "She's batshit, Wendy. That's all you need to know." He's seven years older than I am, so he remembers things better, but he never wants to talk about it.

We lived in the Hamptons when I was a kid, and my mother was a lady of leisure. She' d hired a live-in nanny to deal with me, but the night before my birthday, the nanny had left for a family emergency. My mother was in charge of me, for the first time in her life, and neither of us were happy.

I didn't even want the party. I liked gifts, but I didn't have any friends. The people coming to the party were my mother's friends and their snobby little kids. She had planned some kind of princess tea party I didn't want, but Matt and our maid spent all morning setting it up.

By the time the guests arrived, I already ripped off my shoes and plucked the bows from my hair. My mother came down in the middle of opening gifts, surveying the scene with her icy blue eyes.

Her blond hair had been smoothed back, and she had on bright red lipstick that only made her appear paler. She still wore my father's red silk robe, the same way she had since the day he died, but she added a necklace and black heels, as if that would make the outfit appropriate.

No one commented on it, but everyone was too busy staring at my performance. I had complained about every single gift I had gotten. They were all dolls or ponies or some other thing I would never play with.

My mother came into the room, stealthily gliding through the guests to where I sat. I had torn through a box wrapped in pink teddy bears, containing yet another porcelain doll. Instead of showing any gratitude, I started yelling about what a stupid present it was.

Before I could finish, her hand slapped me sharply across the face.

"You are not my daughter," my mother said, her voice cold. My cheek stung from where she had hit me, and I gaped at her.

The maid quickly redirected the festivities, but the idea percolated in my mother's mind the rest of the afternoon. I think when she said it, she meant it the way parents do when their child behaves appallingly. But the more she thought, the more it made sense to her.

After an afternoon of similar tantrums on my part, someone decided it was time to have cake. My mother seemed to be taking forever in the kitchen, and I went to check on her. I don't even know why she was the one getting the cake instead of the maid, who was far more maternal.

On the island in the kitchen, a massive chocolate cake covered in pink flowers sat in the middle. My mother stood on the other side, holding a gigantic knife she used to cut and serve the cake onto tiny saucers. Bobby pins were coming loose from her hair.

"Chocolate?" I wrinkled my nose as she tried to set perfect pieces onto the saucers.

"Yes, Wendy, you like chocolate," my mother informed me.

"No, I don't!" I crossed my arms over my chest. "I hate chocolate! I'm not going to eat it, and you can't make me!"

"Wendy!"

The knife happened to point in my direction, some frosting sticking on the tip, but I wasn't afraid. If I had been, everything might've turned out different. Instead, I wanted to have another one of my tantrums.

"No, no, no! It's my birthday, and I don't want chocolate!" I shouted and stomped my foot on the floor as hard as I could.

"You don't want chocolate?" My mother looked at me, her blue eyes wide and incredulous.

A whole new type of crazy glinted in them, and that's when my fear started to kick in.

"What kind of child are you, Wendy?" She slowly walked around the island, coming towards me. The knife in her hand looked far more menacing than it had a few seconds ago.

"You're certainly not my child. What are you, Wendy?"

Staring at her, I took several steps back. My mother looked maniacal. Her robe had fallen open, revealing her thin collarbones and the black slip she wore underneath. She took a step forward, this time with the knife pointed right at me. I should've screamed or run away, but I felt frozen in place.

"I was pregnant, Wendy! But you're not the child I gave birth to! Where is my child?" Tears formed in her eyes, and I just shook my head. "You probably killed him, didn't you?"

She lunged at me, screaming at me to tell her what I did with her real baby. I darted out of the way just in time, but she backed me into a corner. I pressed up against the kitchen cupboards with nowhere to go, and she wasn't about to give up.

"Mom!" Matt yelled at her from the other side of the room.

Her eyes flickered with some recognition, the sound of the son she actually loved. For a moment, I thought it might stop her, but it only made her realize she was running out of time, so she raised her knife.

Matt dove at her but not before the blade tore through my dress and slashed across my stomach. Blood stained my clothes as pain shot through me, and I sobbed hysterically. My mother fought hard against Matt, unwilling to let go of the knife.

"She killed your brother, Mathew!" my mother insisted, looking at him with frantic eyes. "She's a monster! She has to be stopped!"

1. Home

Drool spilled out across my desk, and I opened my eyes just in time to hear Mr. Meade slam down a textbook. I'd only been at this high school a month, but I'd figured out that was his way of waking me up from my naps during his History lecture. I always tried to stay awake, but his monotone voice lulled me into sleeping submission every time.

"Miss Everly?" Mr. Meade snapped. "Miss Everly?"

"Hmm?" I murmured.

I lifted my head and discreetly wiped away the drool. I glanced around to see if anyone had noticed. Most of the class seemed oblivious, except for Finn Holmes. He'd been here a week, so he was the only kid in school newer than me. Whenever I looked at him, he always seemed to be staring at me in a completely unabashed way, as if it was perfectly natural to gawk at me.

There was something oddly still and quiet about him, and I had yet to hear him speak, even though I had him in four of my classes. He wore his hair smoothed back, and his eyes were a matching shade of black. His looks were rather striking, but he weirded me out too much for me to find him attractive.

"Sorry to disturb your sleep." Mr. Meade cleared his throat so I would look up at him.

"It's okay," I said.

"Miss Everly, why don't you go down to the principal's office?" Mr. Meade suggested, and I groaned. "Since you seem to be making a habit of sleeping in my class, maybe he can come up with some ideas to help you stay awake."

"I am awake," I insisted.

"Miss Everly, now." Mr. Meade pointed to the door, as if I had forgotten how to leave and that's what was holding me back.

I fixed my gaze on him, and despite how stern his gray eyes looked, I could tell he'd cave easily. Over and over in my head, I kept repeating *I do not need to go the Principal's office. You don't want to send me down there. Let me stay in class.* Within seconds, his face went lax and his eyes took on a glassy quality.

"You can stay in class and finish the lecture," Mr. Meade said groggily. He shook his head, clearing his eyes. "But next time, you're going straight to the office, Miss Everly." He looked confused for a moment, and then launched right back into his history lecture.

I wasn't sure what it was that I could do exactly – I tried not to think about it enough to name it. About a year or so ago, I'd discovered that if I thought about something and looked at somebody hard enough, I could get them to do what I wanted.

As awesome as that sounded, I avoided doing it as much as possible. Partially because I felt like I was crazy for really believing I could do it, even though it worked every time. But mostly, I didn't like it. It made me feel dirty and manipulative.

Mr. Meade went on talking, and I followed along studiously, my guilt making me try harder. I hadn't wanted to do that to him, but I couldn't go to the principal's office. I had just been expelled from my last school, forcing my brother and aunt to uproot their lives again so we could move closer to my new school.

When class finally ended, I shoved my books in my bookbag and left quickly. I didn't like hanging around too long after I did the mind control trick. Mr. Meade could change his mind and send me to the office, so I hurried down to my locker.

Bright colored fliers decorated battered lockers, telling everyone to join the Debate team, try out for the school play, and not to miss the fall semi-formal this Friday. I wondered what a "semi-formal" consisted of at a public school, but I hadn't bothered to ask anyone.

I got to my locker and started switching out my books. Without even looking, I knew Finn was behind me. I glanced back over my shoulder to see him, getting a drink from the drinking fountain, but almost as soon as I looked at him, he lifted his head and looked at me. Like he could sense me too.

This guy was just looking at me, nothing more, but it freaked me out somehow. I'd put up with his stares for a week, trying to avoid confrontation, but I couldn't take it anymore. *He* was the one acting inappropriately, not me, and I couldn't get in trouble for just talking to him. Right?

"Hey," I said to him, slamming my locker shut. I readjusted the straps on my bookbag and walked across the hall to where he stood. "Why are you staring at me?"

"Because you're standing in front of me," Finn replied simply. He looked at me, his eyes framed by dark lashes, without any hint of embarrassment or even denial. It was definitely unnerving.

"You're *always* staring at me," I persisted. "It's weird. You're weird."

"I wasn't trying to fit in."

"Why do you look at me all the time?" I rephrased my original question, since he kept avoiding it.

"Does it bother you?"

"Answer the question." I stood up straighter, trying to make my presence more imposing so he wouldn't realize how much he was rattling me.

"Everyone always looks at you," Finn said coolly. "You're very attractive."

That sounded like a compliment, but his voice was emotionless when he said it. I couldn't tell if he was making fun of a vanity I didn't even have, or he was simply stating facts. Was he flattering me or mocking me? Or maybe something else entirely?

"Nobody stares at me as much as you do," I said as evenly as I could.

"If it bothers you, I'll try and stop," Finn offered.

That was tricky. In order to ask him to stop, I had to admit that he got to me, and I didn't want to admit that anything got to me. If I lied and said it was fine, then he would just keep on doing it.

"I didn't ask you to stop. I asked you why," I amended.

"I told you why."

"No, you didn't," I shook my head. "You just said that everyone looks at me. You never explained why *you* looked at me."

Almost imperceptibly, the corner of his mouth moved up, revealing just the hint of a smirk. It wasn't just that I amused him; he was pleased with me. Like he had challenged me somehow and I passed.

My stomach did a stupid flip thing I had never felt before, and I swallowed hard, hoping to fight it back.

"I look at you because I can't look away," Finn answered finally.

I was struck completely mute, trying to think of some kind of clever response, but my mind refused to work. My jaw slacked, and I imagined that I looked like an awestruck school girl, and I hurried to collect myself.

"That's kind of creepy," I said at last, but my words came out weak instead of accusatory.

"I'll work on being less creepy then," Finn promised.

I had called him out on being creepy, and it didn't faze him at all. He didn't stammer an apology or flush with shame. He just kept looking at me evenly. Most likely, he was a damn sociopath, and for whatever reason, I found that endearing.

I couldn't come up with a witty retort, but the bell rang, saving me from the rest of that awkward conversation. Finn just nodded, thus ending our exchange, and turned down the hall to go to his next class. Thankfully, it was one of the few he didn't have with me.

True to his word, Finn wasn't creepy the rest of the day. Every time I saw him, he was doing something inoffensive that didn't involve looking at me. I still got that feeling that he watched me when I had my back to him, but as it turned out, I couldn't seem to do much about feelings.

When the final bell rang at three o'clock, I tried to be the first one out. My older brother Matt picked me up from school, at least until he found a job, and I didn't want to keep him waiting. Besides that, I didn't want to deal with anymore contact with Finn Holmes.

I walked quickly over to the parking lot at the edge of the school lawn. Scanning quickly for Matt's Prius, I absently started to chew my thumbnail. I had this weird feeling, almost like a shiver running down my back. I turned around, half-expecting to see Finn staring at me, but there was nothing.

I tried to shake it off, but my heart raced faster. This felt like something more sinister than a boy from school. I was still staring off, trying to figure out what had me freaked out, when a loud honk startled me, making me jump. Matt sat a few cars down, looking at me over the top of his sunglasses.

"Sorry," I opened the car door and hopped in, but he looked at me for a moment. "What?"

"You looked nervous. Did something happen?" Matt asked, and I sighed. He took his whole big brother thing way too seriously.

"No, nothing happened. School sucks," I brushed him off. "Let's go home."

"Seatbelt," Matt commanded, and I did as I was told.

Matt had always been quiet and reserved, thinking everything over carefully before making a decision. He was a stark contrast to me in every way, except that we were both relatively short. I was small with a decidedly pretty, feminine face. My brown hair was an untamed mess of curls that I kept up in loose buns.

He kept his sandy blond hair trim and neat, and his eyes were the same shade of blue as our mother's. Matt wasn't overtly muscular, but he worked out a lot. He had a sense of duty, like he had to make sure he was strong enough to defend us against anything.

"How is school going?" Matt asked.

"Great. Fantastic. Amazing."

"Are you even going to graduate this year?" Matt had long since stopped judging my school record. A large part of him didn't even care if I graduated high school.

"Who knows?" I shrugged.

Everywhere I went, kids never seemed to like me. Even before I said or did anything. I felt like I had something wrong with me, and everyone knew it. I tried getting along with the other kids, but I'd only take getting pushed for so long before I pushed back. Principals and deans were quick to expel me, but I think they sensed the same things the kids did.

I just didn't belong.

"Just to warn you, Maggie's taking it seriously," Matt said. "She's set on you graduating this year, from this school."

"Delightful," I sighed. Matt could care less about my schooling, but my aunt Maggie was a different story. And since she was my legal guardian, her opinion mattered more. "What's her plan?"

"Maggie's thinking bedtimes," Matt informed me with a smirk. As if sending me to bed early would somehow prevent me from getting in a fight.

"I'm almost eighteen!" I groaned. "What is she thinking?"

"You've got four more months until you're eighteen," Matt corrected me sharply, and his hand tightened on the steering wheel. He suffered from serious delusions that I was going to run away as soon as I turned eighteen, and nothing I could say would convince him otherwise.

"Yeah, whatever," I waved it off. "Did you tell her she's insane?"

"I figured she'd hear it enough from you," Matt grinned at me.

"So did you find a job?" I asked tentatively, and he shook his head.

He'd just finished an internship over the summer, working with a great architecture firm. He'd said it didn't bother him, moving to a town without much call for a promising young architect, but I couldn't help but feel guilty about it.

"This is a pretty town," I said, looking out the window.

We approached our new house, buried on an average suburban street amongst a slew of maples and elms. It actually seemed like a boring, small town, but I'd promised I'd make the best of it. I really wanted to. I don't think I could handle disappointing Matt anymore.

"So you're really gonna try here?" Matt asked, looking over at me. We had pulled up in the driveway next to the butter colored Victorian that Maggie had bought last month.

"I already am," I insisted with a smile. "I've been talking to this Finn kid." Sure, I'd talked to him only once, and I wouldn't even remotely count him as a friend, but I had to tell Matt something.

"Look at you. Making your very first friend." Matt shut off the car and looked at me with veiled amusement.

"Yeah, well, how many friends do you have?" I countered, and he just shook his head and got out of the car, so I quickly followed him. "That's what I thought."

"I've had friends before. Gone to parties. Kissed a girl. The whole nine yards," Matt said as he went through the side door into the house.

"So you say." I kicked off my shoes as soon as we walked in the kitchen, which was still in various stages of unpacking. After as many times as we'd moved, everyone had gotten tired of the whole process, so we tended to live mostly out of boxes. "I've only seen one of these alleged girls."

"Yeah, cause when I brought her home, you set her dress on fire! While she was wearing it!" Matt pulled off his sunglasses and looked at me severely.

"Oh come on! That was an accident and you know it!"

21

"So you say." Matt opened the fridge.

"Anything good in there?" I asked and hopped onto the kitchen island. "I'm famished."

"Probably nothing you'd like." Matt started sifting through the contents of the fridge, but he was right.

I was a notoriously picky eater. While I had never purposely sought out the life of a vegan, I seemed to hate most things that either had meat in them or man-made synthetics. It was odd and incredibly irritating for the people who tried to feed me.

Maggie appeared in the doorway to the kitchen, flecks of paint stuck in her blond curls. Layers of multi-colored paint covered her ratty overalls, proof of all the rooms she had redecorated over the years. She had her hands on her hips, so Matt shut the fridge door to talk to her.

"I thought I told you to tell me when you got home," Maggie looked at him.

"We're home?" Matt offered.

"I can see that." Maggie rolled her eyes, and then turned her attention to me. "How was school?"

"Good," I said. "I'm trying harder."

"We've heard that before." Maggie gave me a weary look.

I hated it when she gave me that look. I hated knowing that I made her feel that way, that I had disappointed her that much. She did so much for me, and the only thing she asked of me was that I at least *try* at school. I had to make it work this time.

"Well, yeah... but..." I looked to Matt for help. "I mean, I actually promised Matt this time. And I'm making a friend."

"She's talking to some guy named Finn," Matt corroborated my story.

"Like a *guy* guy?" Maggie smiled too broadly for my liking.

The idea of Finn being a romantic prospect hadn't crossed Matt's mind before, and he suddenly tensed up, looking over at me with a new scrutiny. Fortunately for him, that idea hadn't crossed my mind either.

"No, nothing like that," I shook my head. "He's just a guy, I guess. I don't know. He seems nice enough."

"Nice?" Maggie gushed. "That's a start! And much better than that anarchist with the tattoo on his face."

"We weren't friends," I corrected her. "I just stole his motorcycle. While he happened to be on it."

Nobody had ever really believed that story, but it was true, and it was how I figured out how I could get people to do things just by thinking it. I had just been thinking that I really wanted his bike, and then I was looking at him and he was listening to me, even though I hadn't said anything. Then I was driving his motorcycle.

"So this really is gonna be a new start for us?" Maggie couldn't hold back her excitement any longer. Her blue eyes had started to well with happy tears. "Wendy, this is just so wonderful! We can really make a home here!"

I wasn't nearly as excited about it as she was, but I couldn't help but hope she was right. It would be nice to feel like I was home somewhere.

2. If You Leave

Our new house had also supplied us with a large vegetable garden, which thrilled Maggie endlessly. Matt and I were much less thrilled. While I loved the outdoors, I'd never been a big fan of manual labor.

Autumn was settling in, and Maggie insisted that we had to clear the garden of its dying vegetation to prepare it for planting in the spring. She used words like "rototiller" and "mulch," and I hoped Matt would deal with them. When it came to work, I usually just handed Matt the necessary tools and kept him company.

"So when are you hauling out the rototiller?" I asked, watching as Matt tore up dead vines. I'm not sure what it used to be, but it reminded me of grapevines. While Matt pulled things up, my job was to hold the wheelbarrow so he could throw them in.

"We don't have a rototiller." He gave me a look as he tossed the dead plants into the wheelbarrow. "You know, you could be helping me with this. You don't need to physically hold that at all times."

"I take my job very seriously, so I think it'd be better if I did," I said, and he rolled his eyes.

Matt continued grumbling, but I tuned him out. A warm fall breeze blew over us, and I closed my eyes, breathing it in. It smelled wonderfully sweet, like fresh cut corn and grass and wet leaves. A nearby wind chime tinkled lightly, and I was dreading winter would come and take this all away.

I'd been lost in the moment, enjoying the perfection, but something snapped me out of it. It was hard to describe exactly what it was, but the hair on the back of my neck stood up. The air suddenly felt chillier, and I knew somebody was watching us.

I looked around, trying to see who it was, and this weird fear ran over me. We had a privacy fence on the back of the yard, and a thick row of hedges blocking our house on either side. I scanned both of them, searching for any signs of crouching figures or spying eyes. I didn't see anything, but the feeling didn't go away.

"If you're gonna be out here, you should at least wear shoes," Matt said, pulling me from my thoughts. He stood up, stretching his back, and looked at me. "Wendy?"

"I'm fine," I answered absently.

I thought I saw movement around the side of the house, so I went over there. Matt called my name, but I ignored him. When I rounded the house, I stopped short. Finn Holmes stood on the sidewalk, but oddly enough, he wasn't looking at me. He was staring at something down the street, something out of my sight.

As strange as it sounds, as soon I saw him, the anxiety I'd felt started to subside. My first thought should've been that it was him, since he was the one that always stared at me in such a creepy fashion, but it wasn't.

Whatever I'd felt in the backyard, that wasn't him. When he stared, he made me self-conscious. But this... this made my skin crawl.

After a second, Finn turned to look back at me. His dark eyes rested on me a moment, his face expressionless as always. Then, without saying a word, he turned and walked off in the direction he'd been staring.

"Wendy, what's going on?" Matt asked, coming up behind me.

"I thought I saw something," I shook my head.

"Yeah?" He looked at me hard, concern etched in his eyes. "Are you okay?"

"Yeah. I'm fine," I forced a smile at him and turned to the backyard. "Come on. We've got a lot of work to do if I'm gonna make it to that dance."

"You're still on that kick?" Matt grimaced.

Telling Maggie about the dance may have been the worst idea I've ever had, and my life is made up almost entirely of bad ideas. I hadn't wanted to go, but as soon as she'd heard about it, she decided it would be the most fantastic thing ever. I'd never gone to a dance before, and she was so excited about it, I let her have this small victory.

With the dance at seven, she figured she had enough time to finish the coat of paint in the bathroom. Matt started to voice his complaints, but Maggie shut him down. To keep him from getting in her way, she commanded him to finish the yard work. He complied only because he knew that there was no stopping Maggie anymore.

Despite Matt's attempts to slow us down, we finished the garden in record time, and I went inside to get ready. Maggie sat on the bed and watched me as I rummaged through my closet, offering suggestions and comments on everything. This included an endless stream of questions on Finn, and Matt would grunt or scoff every now and then at my answers, so I knew he was listening nearby.

Once I had decided on a simple blue dress that Maggie insisted looked amazing on me, I let her do my hair. My hair refused to listen to anything I tried to do it, and while it wasn't exactly obedient for Maggie, she outwitted it. She left some of it down, so the curls would frame my face, and pulled the rest of it back.

When Matt saw me, he looked really pissed off and a little awed, so I knew that I must look pretty awesome.

Maggie gave me a ride to the dance, because we both weren't convinced that Matt would let me out of the car. He kept insisting on a nine o'clock curfew, even though the dance went until ten, even as Maggie and I walked out the door. I thought I'd be back well before that, but Maggie told me to take all the time I wanted.

My only experience with dances was what I had seen on TV, but it really wasn't that far off. The theme appeared to be "Crepe Paper in the Gymnasium," and they had mastered it perfectly.

The school colors were white and navy blue, so white and navy blue streamers covered everything, along with matching balloons. For romantic lighting, they had strung everything with white Christmas lights.

Refreshments covered a table on the side, and the band playing on the makeshift stage under the basketball hoop wasn't that bad.

Their set list appeared to include only songs from the films of John Hughes, and I came in the middle of a "Weird Science" cover.

The biggest difference between real life and what films had taught me is that nobody actually danced. A group of girls stood directly in front of the stage, swooning at the lead singer, but otherwise, the floor was mostly empty.

People sat scattered all over the bleachers, and I attempted to fit in, so I sat on the first row. I kicked off my shoes immediately, because for the most part, I hate shoes. With nothing else to do, I resorted to people watching. As the night wore on, I found myself feeling increasingly lonely and bored.

Kids had actually started dancing as the gymnasium filled up, and the band moved onto some kind of Tears For Fears medley. I had decided that I'd been here long enough, and I planned on making my escape when Finn finally pushed through the doors.

Wearing a slim-fitting black dress shirt and dark jeans, he looked good. He had the sleeves rolled up and an extra button undone on his shirt, and I wondered why I had never realized how attractive he looked before.

His eyes met mine, and he walked over to me, surprising me with his obvious attempts at interaction. As often as he seemed to be watching me, he never initiated contact with me. Not even today, when he'd walked past my house.

"I didn't peg you for the dancing kind," Finn commented when he reached me.

"I was thinking the same thing about you," I said, and he shrugged.

Finn sat down on the bleachers next to me, and I sat up a bit straighter. He glanced over at me but didn't say anything. Already, he looked annoyed and he'd just gotten here. An awkward silence settled over us, and I hurried to fill it.

"You arrived awfully late to the dance. Couldn't decide what to wear?" I teased.

"I had stuff with work," Finn explained vaguely

"Oh? Do you work somewhere near my house?" I asked, plundering on ahead with this failed conversation.

"Something like that," Finn sighed. Eager to change the subject, he looked over at me. "Have you been dancing?"

"Nope," I said. "Dancing is for suckers."

"Is that why you came to a dance?" Finn looked down at my bare feet. "You didn't wear the right shoes for dancing. You didn't even wear the right shoes for walking."

"I don't like shoes," I told him defensively. My hem landed above my knees, but I tried to pull it down, as if I could get it to cover my bare feet embarrassment.

Finn gave me a look I couldn't read at all, then went back to staring at the people dancing out in front of us. By now, the floor was almost entirely covered. Kids still dotted the bleachers, but they were mostly the headgear kids and the ones with dandruff.

"So this is what you're doing? Watching other people dance?"

Finn asked.

"I guess," I shrugged.

Finn leaned forward, resting his elbows on his knees, and I moved so I sat up straighter. My dress was strapless, and I rubbed at my bare arms, feeling naked and uncomfortable.

"You cold?" Finn glanced over at me, and I shook my head. "I think it's cold in here."

"It's a little chilly," I admitted. "But nothing I can't handle."

Finn would barely look at me, which was a complete 180 from his constant creepy staring. Somehow, I found this worse. I don't know why he had even come to the dance if he hated it so much, and I was about to ask him that when he turned to look at me.

"You wanna dance?" Finn asked me flatly.

"Are you asking me to dance with you?"

"Yeah," Finn shrugged.

"Yeah?" I shrugged sarcastically. "You really know how to sweet talk a girl."

His mouth crept up in his hint of a smile, and that officially won me over, the way it always did. I hated myself for it.

"Fair enough." Finn stood up and extended his hand to me. "Would you, Wendy Everly, care to dance with me?"

"Sure." I placed my hand in his, trying to ignore how warm his skin felt and the rapid beating of my own heart, and got to my feet.

Naturally, the band had just started playing "If You Leave" by OMD, making me feel like I had walked into a perfect movie moment. Finn led me to the dance floor, and he placed his hand on the small of my back. I put one hand on his shoulder, and he held my other hand.

I was so close to him, I could feel the delicious heat radiating from his body. His eyes were the darkest eyes I had ever seen, and they were looking at only me. For one unspoiled minute, everything in life felt perfect in a way that it never had before. Like there should be a spotlight on us and we were the only two people in the world.

Then something changed in Finn's expression, something I couldn't read, but it definitely got darker.

"You're not a very good dancer," Finn commented in that emotionless way he did.

"Thanks?" I said unsurely. We were mostly just swaying in a small circle, and I wasn't sure how I could screw that up, and we seemed to be dancing the exact same way as everyone else. Maybe he was joking, so I tried to sound playful when I said, "You're not that great yourself."

"I'm a wonderful dancer," Finn replied matter-of-factly. "I just need a better partner."

"Okay." I stopped looking up at him and stared straight ahead over his shoulder. "I don't know what to say to that."

"Why do you need to say anything to that? It's not necessary for you to speak incessantly. Although, I'm not sure you've realized that yet." Finn's tone had gotten icy, but I still danced with him because I couldn't come up with enough sense to walk away.

"I've barely said anything. I've just been dancing with you." I swallowed hard and didn't appreciate how crushed I felt. "And you asked me to dance! It's not like you're doing me a favor."

"Oh come on," Finn disparaged me with an exaggerated eye roll. "The desperation was coming off you in waves. You were all but begging to dance with me. I *am* doing you a favor."

"Wow." I stepped back from him, feeling confused tears threatening and this awful pain growing inside of me. "I don't know what I did to you!" His expression softened, but it was too late.

"Wendy-"

"No!" I cut him off. I had started shouting, and everyone around us had stopped dancing to stare at us, but I didn't care. "You are a total dick!"

"Wendy!" Finn repeated, but I turned and hurried through the crowd.

There was nothing in the world I wanted more than to get out of there. Patrick, a kid from biology class, stood by the punch bowl, and I rushed over to him. We weren't friends, but he'd been one of the few kids here that had been nice to me. When he saw me, he looked confused and concerned, but at least I had his attention.

"I want to leave. *Now*," I hissed at Patrick.

"What-" Before Patrick could ask what happened, Finn appeared at my side.

"Look, Wendy, I'm sorry," Finn apologized sincerely, which only pissed me off more.

"I don't wanna hear anything from you!" I snapped and refused to look at him. Patrick looked back and forth between the two of us, trying to decipher what was going on.

"Wendy," Finn floundered. "I didn't mean-"

"I said I don't want to hear it!" I glared at him, but only for a second

"Maybe you should let the guy apologize," Patrick suggested gently.

"No, I shouldn't." Then, like a small child, I stomped my foot. "I want to go!"

Finn stood just to the side of us, watching me intently. I clenched my fists and looked at Patrick directly in his eyes. I didn't like doing this when people watched, but I had to get out of here. I kept chanting what I wanted over and over in my head. *I want to go home, just take me home, please, please, just take me home. I can't be here anymore.*

Patrick's expression started to change. His face relaxed and got faraway. Blinking, he just stared blankly at me for a minute.

"I think I should just take you home," Patrick said groggily.

"What did you just do?" Finn asked, narrowing his eyes.

My heart stopped beating, and for one terrifying second, I was certain he'd know what I'd done. But then I realized that'd be impossible, so I shook it off.

"I didn't do anything!" I snapped and looked back at Patrick. "Let's get out of here."

"Wendy!" Finn asked, giving me a hard look. "Do you even know what you just did?"

"I didn't do anything!" I insisted, and I refused to talk about it anymore.

I grabbed Patrick's wrist, dragging him towards the exit, and much to my relief, Finn didn't follow. In the car, Patrick tried to ask me what had happened with Finn, but I wouldn't talk about it. He drove around for awhile so I was reasonably calm by the time I went home, and I couldn't thank him enough for it.

Matt and Maggie were waiting by the door for me, but I barely said a word to them. That freaked out Matt, who started threatening to kill every boy at the dance, but I managed to reassure him that I was fine and nothing bad had happened. Finally, he let me go up to my room, where I proceeded to throw myself onto the bed and not cry.

The night swirled in my head like some bizarre dream. I couldn't get a read on the way I felt about Finn. Most of the time, he seemed weird and bordering on creepy. But then we had that glorious moment where we danced together, before he completely shattered it.

Even now, after the way he'd treated me, I couldn't shake how wonderful it had felt being in his arms like that. In general, I never liked being touched or being close to people, but I loved the way I had felt with him.

His hand strong and warm pressing on the small of my back and

35

the soft heat that flowed from him. When he had looked at me then, so sincerely, I had thought…

I don't know what I thought, but it turned out to be a lie.

Strangest of all, he seemed to be able to tell that I had done something to Patrick. I didn't know how anyone could know. I wasn't even sure that I was doing it. But a normal, sane person wouldn't even suspect that I could do that.

I could suddenly explain all Finn's odd behavior; he was completely insane.

What it came down to is that I knew nothing about him. I could barely tell when he was mocking me and when he was being sincere. Sometimes I thought he was into me, and other times he obviously hated me.

There wasn't anything I knew about him for sure. Except that despite everything, I think I was starting to like him.

Sometime in the night, after I had changed into sweats and a tank top, and after I had spent a very long time tossing and turning, I must've finally fallen asleep. When I woke up, it was still dark out, and I had drying tears on my cheeks. I had been crying in my sleep, which seemed unfair since I never let myself cry when I was awake.

I rolled over and glanced at the alarm clock. Its angry numbers declared it was a little after three in the morning, and I wasn't sure why I was awake. I flicked on my bedside lamp, casting everything in a warm glow, and I saw something that scared me so badly, my heart stopped.

3. Stalker

A figure was crouched out my window, my *second story* window. Admittedly, a small roof is right outside of it, but that's not exactly the thing I expected to see. On top of that, it wasn't just anybody.

Finn Holmes looked hopeful, but not at all ashamed or frightened at having been caught peeping into my room. In fact, he knocked gently at the glass, and belatedly, I realized that's what had woke me up.

He hadn't been peeping intentionally; he'd been trying to sneak into my room. So that was *slightly* less creepy, I supposed.

For some reason, I got up and went over to the window. I caught sight of myself in my mirror, and I did not look good. My pajamas were of the sad, comfy variety. My hair was a total mess, and my eyes were red and puffy.

I knew I shouldn't even let Finn in my room. He was probably a sociopath and he didn't make me feel good about myself. Besides, Matt would kill us both if he caught him in here.

So, I stood in front of the window, my arms crossed, and glared at him. I was pissed off and hurt, and I wanted him to know it. Normally, I prided myself on not getting hurt, let alone telling people if they had hurt me. But this time, I thought it would be better if he knew that he was a dick.

"I'm sorry!" Finn talked so his voice would carry through the glass, and his eyes echoed the sentiment. He looked genuinely remorseful, but I wasn't ready to accept his apology yet. Maybe I never would.

"What do you want?" I demanded as loudly as I could without Matt hearing me.

"To apologize. And to talk to you." Finn looked earnestly at me. "It's important." I chewed my lip, debating between what I knew I should do and what I really wanted to do. "Please."

Against my better judgment, I opened the window. I left the screen in so he could deal with that, and took a step back so I was sitting on the end of my bed. Finn pulled the screen out easily, and I wondered how much experience he had with sneaking in girls' windows.

Carefully, he climbed into my room, shutting the window behind him. He glanced over my room, making me feel self-conscious. It was rather messy, with clothes and books strewn about, but most of my stuff sat in two large cardboard boxes and a trunk on one side of my room.

"So what did you want?" I said, trying to drag his attention back to me instead of inspecting my things.

"I'm sorry," Finn repeated, with that same sincerity he had outside. "Tonight I was cruel." He looked away thoughtfully before continuing. "I don't want to hurt you."

"So why did you?" I asked sharply.

Licking his lips, he shifted and exhaled deeply. He had

intentionally been mean to me. It wasn't some accident because he was cocky or unaware of how he treated people. Everything he did felt meticulous and purposeful.

"I don't want to lie to you, and I promise you that I haven't," Finn answered carefully. "And I'll leave it at that."

"I think I have a right to know what's going on," I snapped, and then remembered that Matt and Maggie were sleeping down the hall and hastily lowered my voice.

"I came here to tell you," Finn assured me. "To explain everything. This isn't the way we normally do things, so I had to make a phone call before I came to see you. I was trying to figure things out. That's why it's so late. I'm sorry."

"Call who? Figure out what?" I took a step back.

"It's about what you did tonight, with Patrick," Finn said gently, and the pit in my stomach tightened.

"I didn't do anything with Patrick." I shook my head. "I have no idea what you're talking about."

"You really don't?" Finn eyed me suspiciously, unable to decide if he believed me or not.

"I-I don't know what you're talking about," I stumbled. A chill ran over me and I started feeling vaguely nauseous.

"Yeah, you do." Finn nodded solemnly. "You just don't know what it is."

"I'm just very… persuasive," I said without any real conviction. I didn't want to keep denying it, but talking about it, giving credibility

39

to my own private insanity, scared me even more.

"Yeah, you are," Finn admitted. "But you can't do that. Not like this."

"I didn't do anything! And even if I did, who are you to try and stop me?" Something else flashed in my mind, and I looked at him. "Can you even stop me?"

"You can't use it on me now." Finn shook his head absently. "It's really not that major, especially the way you're using it."

"What is it?" I asked quietly, finding it hard to make my mouth work. I let go of any pretense I had that I didn't know what was going on, and my shoulders sagged.

"It's called *persuasion*," Finn said emphatically, as if that were somehow much different from what I had been saying. "Technically, it would be called psychokinesis. It's a form of mind control."

I found it disturbing how matter-of-factly he talked about all of this, as if we were talking about biology homework instead of the possibility that I possessed some kind of paranormal ability.

"How do you know?" I asked. "How do you know what I have? How did you even know I was doing it?"

"Experience," he shrugged.

"What does that mean?"

"It's complicated." He rubbed the back of his head and stared at the floor. "You're not going to believe me. But I haven't lied to you, and I never will. Do you believe that at least?"

"I think so," I replied tentatively. Considering we'd only spoken a handful of times, he hadn't much of an opportunity to lie to me.

"That's a start." Finn took a deep breath, and I nervously pulled at a strand of my hair as I watched him. Almost sheepishly, he said, "You're a changeling." He looked expectantly at me, waiting for some kind of dramatic reaction.

"I don't even know what that is," I shrugged. "Isn't it like a movie with Angelina Jolie or something?" I shook my head. "I don't know what it means."

"You don't know what it is?" Finn smirked. "Of course you don't know what it is. It would make it all too easy if you had even the slightest inclining about what is going on."

"It would, wouldn't it?" I agreed.

"A changeling is a child that has been secretly exchanged for another."

The room got this weird, foggy quality to it. My mind flashed onto my mother, and the things she had screamed at me. I had always known I didn't belong, but at the same time, I'd never consciously believed it was true.

But now, suddenly, Finn confirmed all the suspicions I had been harboring. All the horrible things my mother had told me were true.

"But how…" Dazedly, I shook my head and realized one important fact. "How would you know that? How could you possibly know that? Even if it were true?"

"Well…" Finn watched me as I struggled to let everything sink in and decided to continue. "You're Trylle. It's what we do."

"Trylle? Is that like your last name or something?" I asked.

"No," Finn smiled. "Trylle is the name of our 'tribe,' if you will." He rubbed the side of his temple. "This is hard to explain. We are, um, trolls."

"You're telling me that I'm a *troll?*" I raised my eyebrow, and finally decided that he must be insane.

Nothing about me resembled a pink-haired doll with a jewel in its stomach or a creepy little monster that lived under a bridge. Admittedly, I was kind of short, but Finn was at least six feet tall.

"You're thinking of trolls the way they've been misrepresented, obviously," Finn hurried to explain. "That's why we prefer Trylle. You don't get any of that silly 'Billy Goats Gruff' imagery. But now I have you staring at me like I have totally lost my mind."

"You have lost your mind." I trembled, out of shock and fear, and I didn't know what to think. I should've thrown him out of my room, but then again, I never should've let him in.

"Okay. Think about it, Wendy." Finn moved on to trying to reason with me, as if his idea had real merits. "You've never really fit in anywhere. You have a quick temper. You're very intelligent and a picky eater. You hate shoes. Your hair, while lovely, is hard to control. You have dark brown eyes, dark brown hair."

"What does the color of my eyes have to do with anything?" I retorted, focusing on the things that I felt like I could disagree with. In fact, none of the things he said were all that conclusive.

"Earth tones. Our eyes and hair are always earth tones," Finn

42

answered. "And often times, our skin has almost a greenish hue to it."

"I'm not green!" I looked at my skin anyway, just to be sure, but it didn't look green.

"It's very faint, when people do have it," Finn said. "But no, you don't. Not really. Sometimes it gets more predominant after you've been living around other Trylle for awhile."

"I am not a troll," I insisted fiercely. "That doesn't even make any sense. It doesn't... So I'm angry and different. Most teenagers feel that way. It doesn't mean anything." I combed through my hair, as if to prove it wasn't that wild. My fingers got caught in it, proving his point rather than mine, and I sighed. "That doesn't mean anything."

"I'm not just guessing here, Wendy," Finn informed with a wry smile. "I know who you are. I know you are Trylle. That's why I came looking for you."

"You're looking for me?" My jaw dropped. "That's why you stare at me all the time in school. You're stalking me!"

"I'm not *stalking*," Finn looked at me defensively. "I'm a tracker. It's my job. I find the changelings and bring them back."

Of all the major things that were wrong with this situation, the thing that bothered me the most is when he said it was his job. There hadn't ever been any attraction between us. He had just been doing his job, and that meant following me.

He was stalking me, and I was only upset about it because he was doing it because he had to, not because he wanted to.

"I know this is a lot to take in," Finn admitted. "I'm sorry. We usually wait until you're older. But if you're already using persuasion, then I think you need to head back to the compound. You're developing early."

"I'm what?" I just stared up at him.

"Developing. The psychokinesis," Finn said as if it should be obvious. "Trylle have varying degrees of abilities. Yours are clearly more advanced."

"They have *abilities*?" I swallowed "Do you have abilities?" Something new occurred to me, twisting my insides. "Can you read my mind?"

"No, I can't read minds."

"Are you lying?"

"I won't lie to you," Finn promised.

If he hadn't been so attractive standing in front of me in my bedroom, it would've been easier to ignore him in the first place. If I hadn't felt this ludicrous connection with him, I would've thrown him out right away.

As it was, it was hard to look into his eyes and not believe him. But after everything he had been saying, I couldn't believe him. If I believed him, that meant my mother was right. That meant that I was evil and a monster, and I didn't want to be. I had spent my whole life trying to prove her wrong, trying to be good and do the right things, and I wouldn't let this be true

"I can't believe you."

"Wendy," Finn sounded exasperated. "You know I'm not lying."

"I do," I nodded. "After what I went through with my mother, I'm not ready to let another crazy person into my life. So you have to go."

"Wendy!" He was in complete disbelief.

"Did you really expect any other reaction from me?" I stood up, keeping my arms crossed firmly in front of me, and I tried to look as confident as I possibly could. "Did you think you could treat me like shit at a dance, then sneak into my room in the middle of the night and tell me that I'm a troll with magical powers, and I'd just be like, yeah, that sounds right?

"And what did you even hope to accomplish with this?" I asked him directly. "What were you trying to get me to do?"

"You're supposed to come with me back to the compound," Finn said, defeated.

"And you thought I would just follow you right out?" I smirked to hide the fact that I was really tempted to do that. Even if he was insane.

"They usually do," Finn replied in a way that completely unnerved me.

Really, that answer is what completely lost me. I might have been willing to follow his delusions because I liked him more than I should, but when he made it sound like there had been lots of other girls willing to do the same thing before me, it was kind of a turn off.

Crazy, I could deal with. Slutty, not so much.

"You need to go," I told him firmly.

"You need to think about this. This is obviously different for you than it is for everyone else, and I understand that. So I'll give you time to think about it." He turned and opened the window. "But there is a place that you belong. There is a place where you have family. So just think about it."

"Definitely," I gave him a plastic smile.

He started to lean out the window, and I walked closer to him so I'd be able to shut the window behind him. Then he stopped and turned to look at me. He felt dangerously close to me, his eyes full of something smoldering just below the surface.

When he looked at me like that, he took all the air from my lungs, and I wondered if this is how Patrick felt when I persuaded him.

"I almost forgot," Finn said softly, his face so close to mine I could feel his breath on my cheeks. "You looked *really* beautiful tonight." He stayed that way a moment longer, completely captivating me, then abruptly he turned and climbed out the window.

I stood there, barely remembering to breathe, as I watched him grab onto a branch of the tree next to my house and swing down to the ground. A cool breeze fluttered in, so I closed the window and pulled my curtains shut tightly.

Feeling very dazed, I staggered back to my bed and collapsed on it. I had never felt more bewildered in my entire life.

I barely got any sleep. What little I had was filled with dreams of little green trolls coming to take me away. I lay in bed for hours after I woke up. Everything felt muddled and confusing.

I couldn't let myself believe that anything Finn had said made sense, but I couldn't discount how badly I wanted it to be true. I had never felt like I belonged anywhere. Until recently, Matt had been the only person I had ever felt any connection with.

Lying in bed at six-thirty in the morning, I could hear the morning birds chirping loudly outside my window. Quietly, I got up and crept downstairs. I didn't want to wake Matt and Maggie this early. Matt got up with me every day to make sure that I was awake and drove me to school, so this was his only time to sleep in.

For some reason, I felt desperate to find something to prove we were family. All my life I had been trying to prove the opposite, but as soon as Finn had mentioned that it might be a real possibility, I felt oddly protective.

Matt and Maggie had sacrificed everything for me. I had never been that good to either of them, but they had loved me unconditionally. Wasn't that evidence enough?

I crouched on the floor next to one of the cardboard boxes behind the couch in the living room. Maggie's pretty cursive had scrawled across it the word "memorabilia." She never actually unpacked any of the pictures or anything, because the last time she had Matt had smashed all the picture frames. That had been almost ten years ago, but I was betting that his reaction now would have

47

only lessened slightly.

Underneath Matt and Maggie's diplomas and lots of Matt's graduation photos, I found several photo albums. Based on the covers, I could tell which ones had been Maggie's purchases. Maggie picked albums covered in flowers and polka dots and happy things. My mother had only had one with a faded brown non-descript cover.

Below the oldest photo album, there was a damaged blue baby book. Carefully, I pulled it out, along with my mom's photo album.

My baby book had been blue because all the ultrasounds had said I was a boy. Tucked in the back of the book there was even a cracked ultrasound photo where the doctor had circled what they had incorrectly assumed was my penis.

Most families would have made some kind of joke about that, but not mine. My mother had just looked at me with disdain and said, "You were supposed to be a boy."

Most mothers start out filling the beginning of the baby book, but then forget as time went on. Not mine. She'd never written a thing in it. The handwriting was either my father's or Maggie's.

My foot prints were in there, along with my measurements and a copy of my birth certificate. I touched it delicately, proving that my birth was tangible. I had been born in this family, whether my mother and I liked it or not.

"What are you doing, kiddo?" Maggie asked softly from behind me, and I jumped a little. "Sorry. I didn't mean to scare you." Wrapped in her house coat, Maggie yawned and ran a hand through her sleep disheveled hair.

"It's okay." I tried to cover up my baby book, feeling as if I had been caught doing something naughty. "What are you doing up?"

"I could ask you the same thing," Maggie replied with a smile. She sat down on the floor next to me, leaning against the back of the couch. "I heard you get up." She nodded to the pile of albums on my lap. "You feeling nostalgic?"

"I don't know really."

"What are you looking at?" Maggie leaned over so she could peer at the photo album. "Oh, that's an old one. You were just a baby then."

I flipped open the book and it went chronologically, so the first few pages were of Matt when he was little. Maggie looked at it with me, making clucking sounds at my dad. She gently touched his picture once and commented on how handsome he was.

Even though everyone agreed that my father had been a good guy, we rarely talked about him. It was our way of not talking about my mother and not talking about what happened. Nothing before my sixth birthday mattered, and that just happened to include every memory of Dad.

Most of the pictures in the album were of Matt, and there were many with my mother, my dad, and Matt looking ridiculously happy. All three of them had blond hair and blue eyes. They looked like something out of a Hallmark commercial.

Towards the end of the book, everything changed. As soon as

pictures of me started to appear, my mother began looking surly and sullen. In the very first picture, I was only a few days old. I wore an outfit with blue trains all over it, and my mother glared at me.

"You were such a cute baby!" Maggie laughed. "But I remember that. You wore boys' clothes for the first month because they were so sure you were going to be a boy."

"That explains a lot," I mumbled, and Maggie laughed. "Why didn't they just get me new clothes? They had the money for it."

"Oh, I don't know," Maggie sighed, looking far away. "It was something your mother wanted." She shook her head. "She was weird about things."

"What was my name supposed to be?" I couldn't remember. When I was younger, people had talked about it, but nobody reminisced about my childhood anymore.

"Um... Michael!" Maggie snapped her fingers when she remembered. "Michael Conrad Everly. But then you were girl, so that ruined that."

"How did I get Wendy from that?" I wrinkled my nose. "Michelle would make more sense."

"Well..." Maggie looked up at the ceiling, thinking. "Your mother refused to name you, and your father... I guess he couldn't think of anything. So Matt named you."

"Oh yeah." I faintly remembered hearing that before. "But why Wendy?"

"He liked the name Wendy," Maggie shrugged. "He was a big

Peter Pan fan, which is ironic because *Peter Pan* is the story of a boy who never grows up, and Matt was a boy who was always grown up." I smirked at that. "Maybe that's why he's always been so protective of you. He named you. You were his."

A picture of me from when I was about two or three with Matt holding me in his arms. I lay on my stomach with my arms and legs outstretched, while he grinned like a fool. He used to run me around the house like that, pretending that I was flying, and call me "Wendy Bird," and I would laugh for hours.

As I got older, it became more and more apparent that I looked nothing like my family. My dark eyes and frizzy hair contrasted completely with them.

In every picture with me, my mother looked completely exasperated, as if she had spent the last half hour fighting with me before the picture. But then again, she probably had. I had always been contrary to everything she was.

"You were a strong-willed child," Maggie admitted, looking at a picture of me covered in chocolate cake at my fifth birthday. "You wanted things the way you wanted them. And when you were a baby, you were colicky. But you were always an adorable child, and you were bright and funny." Maggie gently pushed a strand of hair back from my face. "You were *always* worthy of love. You did nothing wrong, Wendy. She is the one with the problem, not you."

"I know," I nodded.

But for the first time, I truly believed that this all might be entirely my fault. If Finn was telling the truth, as these pictures seemed to confirm, I wasn't their child. I was exactly what my mother accused me of being, and she was just more intuitive than everybody else. It was my fault because I wasn't even human.

"What's wrong?" Maggie asked, looking concerned. "What's going on with you?"

"Nothing," I lied and closed the photo album.

"Did something happen last night?" Her eyes were filled with love and worry, and it was hard to think of her as not being my family. "Did you even sleep?"

"Yeah. I just... woke up, I guess," I answered vaguely.

"What happened at the dance?" Maggie leaned back against the couch, resting her hand on her chin as she studied me. "Did something happen with a boy?"

"Things just didn't turn out the way I thought they would," I said honestly. "In fact, they couldn't have turned out more different."

"Was that Finn boy mean to you?" Maggie asked with a protective edge to her voice.

"No, no, nothing like that," I assured her. "He was great. But he's just a friend."

"Oh." Understanding flashed across her eyes, and I think she had gotten the wrong idea from that, but whatever kept her from asking more questions. "Being a teenager is hard, no matter what family you come from."

"You're telling me," I muttered.

Upstairs, I heard the sound of Matt getting up and moving around. Maggie shot me a nervous look, so I hurried to pack up the photo albums. He wouldn't exactly be mad at me for looking at them, but he definitely wouldn't be happy either. And first thing in the morning, I did not want to deal with a fight with my brother, on top of worrying about whether or not he was really even my brother.

"You know, you can talk to me about this stuff whenever you want," Maggie whispered as I slipped the albums back in the cardboard box. "Well, at least whenever Matt isn't around."

"I know," I smiled at her.

"I suppose I should make you breakfast." Maggie stood up and stretched, then looked down at me. "What do you even eat for breakfast?"

"Nothing, usually. I barely wake up in time for school," I said.

"Hmm," Maggie thought for a minute. "How about plain oatmeal with fresh strawberries? Those are things you eat, right?"

"Yeah, that sounds great," I nodded.

Something pained me when she asked that. There were so many things I wouldn't eat and I was constantly hungry. It had been a struggle just to feed me. When I was a baby, I wouldn't even drink breast milk. Which only added more fuel to the idea that I wasn't my mother's child.

Maggie had turned to walk into the kitchen, but I called after her. "Hey, Mags. Thanks for everything. Like… making me food and stuff."

"Yeah?" Maggie looked surprised and smiled. "No problem."

Matt came downstairs a minute later, deeply confused by the fact that both Maggie and I were up before him. We ate breakfast together for the first time in years, and Maggie was overly happy thanks to my small compliment. I was subdued, but I managed to play it off as something resembling happiness.

I don't know if they were my real family or not. There were so many signs pointing to the contrary. But they had raised me and stood by me the way no one else had. Even my own mother had failed me, but not Matt or Maggie. They were unfailing in their love for me, and most of the time, they had gotten next to nothing in return.

But maybe that last part was the proof. They only gave, and I only took.

4. Changeling

The weekend was turbulent. I kept expecting Finn to appear at my window again, but he didn't, and I wasn't sure if that was good or bad. I wanted to talk to him, but I was terrified. Terrified that he might be lying, and terrified that he might be telling the truth.

I kept looking for clues in everything. Like, Matt is pretty short and so am I, so he must be my brother. Then a minute later, he would say he prefers winter to summer, and I hate winter, so he must not be my brother.

These weren't clues one way or another, and deep down I knew that. My whole life had been one giant question, and I had gotten desperate for answers.

There was also that burning unanswered question about what exactly Finn had wanted with me. Sometimes, he treated me like I was nothing more than an irritant. Then there were other times, when he looked at me and took my breath away.

I hoped that school would bring some kind of resolution to all of this. When I got up Monday morning, I took extra care to look nice, but I tried to pretend like it wasn't for any particular reason. That it wasn't because this was the first time I'd see Finn since he had come into my room, and that I still wanted to talk to him. I still wanted to impress him.

When the first period bell rang and Finn still hadn't taken his place a few rows behind me, a knot started growing in my stomach. I looked around for him all day, half expecting him to be lurking around some corner. He never was, though.

I barely paid attention to anything all day in school, and I felt incredibly defeated when I walked to Matt's car. I had expected to gain something today, but in the end, I was left with even more questions.

Matt noticed my surly demeanor and tried to ask about it, but I just shrugged him off. He had been growing increasingly concerned since I had come home from the dance, but I had been unable to put his mind at ease.

I already felt the sting of Finn's absence. Why hadn't I gone with him? I was more attracted to him than I had ever been to anyone, and I don't mean just physically. In general, people didn't interest me, but he did.

He promised me a life where I fit in, where I was special, and maybe most importantly, a life with him. Why was I staying here?

Because I wasn't convinced yet that I was evil. I wasn't ready to give up on the good I had worked so hard for in my life.

I knew of one person that had always seen through my façade and knew exactly what I was. She'd be able to tell me if I had any good in me, or if I should just give in, give up and run off with Finn.

"Hey, Matt?" I stared down at my hands. "Are you busy this afternoon?"

"I don't think so…" Matt answered tentatively as he turned on the block towards our house. "Why? What's on your mind?"

"I was thinking... I'd like to go visit my mother."

"Absolutely not!" Matt was livid. "Why would you even want that? That's so completely out of the question. No way, Wendy. That's just obscene."

Staring directly in his eyes, I repeated the same thoughts over and over. *I want to see my mother. Take me to see her. Please. I want to see her.* His expression was hard, but eventually, it started to soften around the edges. It took longer than it had with Patrick or Mr. Meade.

"I'll take you to see our mother." Matt sounded like he was talking in his sleep.

I instantly felt guilty for what I was doing. It was manipulative and cruel. But I wasn't just doing it to see if I could. I needed to see my mother, and this was the only way I could.

I felt nervous and sick, and I knew Matt would be irate once he figured out what was going on. I didn't know how long this persuasion would last. We might not even make it to the hospital where my mother lived, but I had to try.

Matt drove me to see my mother for the first time in over eleven years.

There were several times throughout the long car ride that Matt seemed to become aware that he was doing something he would never do. He would start ranting about how terrible my mother was and that he couldn't believe he'd let me talk him into this.

Somehow, it never occurred to him to turn around, but maybe it *couldn't* occur to him.

"She's a horrible person!" Matt said as we approached the state hospital.

I could see the internal battle waged underneath his grimace and his tortured blue eyes. His hand was locked tightly on the steering wheel, but it looked like he was trying to pull it away and he couldn't.

Guilt flushed over me again, but I tried to push it away. I didn't want to hurt him, and controlling him like this was reprehensible.

The only real comfort I had was that I wasn't doing anything wrong. I wanted to see my mother, and I had every right to. Matt was just being overzealous about his protective duties, once again.

"She can't do anything to hurt me," I reminded him for the hundredth time. "She's locked up and medicated. I'll be fine."

"It's not like she's going to strangle you or anything," Matt allowed, but there was an edge to his voice where he hadn't completely ruled out that possibility. "She's just... a bad person. I don't know what you hope to gain from seeing her!"

"I just need to," I said softly and looked out the window.

I had never been to the hospital, but it wasn't exactly as I imagined. My entire basis for it was Arkham Asylum, so I had always pictured an imposing brick structure with lightning always flashing just behind it.

It was raining lightly and the skies were overcast as we pulled up, but that was the only thing similar to the psychiatric hospital of my fantasies. Nestled in thick pine forest and rolling grassy hills, it was a sprawling white building. It looked more like a resort than a hospital.

After my mother had tried to kill me and Matt had tackled her in the kitchen, someone had called 911. She was hauled off in a police car, still screaming things about me being monstrous, and I was taken away in an ambulance.

Charges were brought against my mother, but the case never went to trial. She plead out, claiming she was not guilty by insanity. They had originally given her cross diagnosis of latent postpartum depression and temporary psychosis brought on by the death of my father.

With medication and therapy, there had been the general expectation that she would be out in a relatively short amount of time.

Cut to eleven years later where my brother is talking to the security guard so we can get clearance to get inside the hospital. From what I understand, she refused to admit any remorse for what she'd done.

Matt went to visit her once, five years ago, and what I got out of it is that she didn't know she did anything wrong. It was inferred, but never actually spelled out, that if she got out, she'd do it again.

There was a great deal of bustling about once we finally got inside. A nurse had to call a psychiatrist to see if I would even be able to see her. Matt paced anxiously around me, muttering things about everyone being insane.

We waited in a small room filled with plastic chairs and magazines for 45 minutes until the doctor came to meet with me. We had a brief conversation where I told him that I only wished to speak with her, and he seemed to think it might be beneficial for me to have some closure.

Matt wanted to go back with me to see her, afraid that she would damage me in some way, but the doctor assured him that orderlies would be present and my mother wasn't prone to violence. Matt eventually relented, much to my relief, because I had just been about to use persuasion on him.

He couldn't be there when I talked to her. I wanted an honest conversation.

A nurse led me back to an activity room. A couch and a few chairs filled the room, along with a few small tables, some with half-completed puzzles on them. On one wall, a cabinet overflowed with beat up games and battered puzzles. Plants lined the windows, but otherwise it was deserted.

The nurse told me that my mother would be here soon, so I sat down at one of the tables and waited.

A very large, very strong looking orderly brought her into the room. I stood up when she came in, as some kind of misplaced show of respect. She was older than I had expected her to be. In my mind she had stayed frozen the way I saw her last, but she had to be in her mid-forties by now.

Her blond hair had turned into a frizzy mess thanks to the years of neglect, and she had it pulled back in a short pony tail. She was thin, the way she had always been, in a beautifully elegant borderline-anorexic way. A massive blue bathrobe hung on her, frayed and worn, the sleeves hung long down over her hands.

Her skin was pale porcelain, and even without any makeup, she was stunningly beautiful. More than that, she carried this regality with her. It was clear that she had come from money, that she had spent her life on top, ruling her school, her social circles, even her family.

"They said you were here, but I didn't believe them," my mother gave me a wry smirk.

She stood a few steps away from me, and I wasn't sure what to do. The way she looked at me was the same way someone might inspect a particularly heinous looking bug just before they squashed it under their shoe.

"Hi, Mom," I offered meekly, unable to think of anything better to say.

"Kim," she corrected me coldly. "My name is Kim. Cut the pretense. I'm not your mother, and we both know it." She gestured vaguely to the chair I had pushed out behind me and walked over to the table. "Sit. Take a seat."

"Thanks," I mumbled, sitting down. She sat down across from me, crossing her legs and leaning back away from me, like I was contagious and she didn't want to get sick.

"That's what this is about it, isn't it?" She waved her hand in front of her face, then laid it delicately on the table. Her nails were long and perfect, recently painted with a clear polish. "You've finally figured it out. Or have you always known? I never could tell."

"No, I never knew," I said quietly. "I still don't know."

"Look at you. You're not my daughter," my mother gave me a contentious look and clicked her tongue. "You don't know how to dress or walk or even speak. You mutilate your nails." She pointed her manicured hand at my chewed down fingernails. "And that hair!"

"Your hair isn't any better," I countered. My dark curls had been pulled up in their usual bun, but I had actually tried this morning when I was getting ready. I thought it looked pretty good, but apparently, I was wrong.

"Well..." She smiled humorlessly. "I work with what I got." She looked away for a moment, then turned back to me, her icy gaze resting on me. "But what about you? You must have all the styling products in the world. Between Matthew and Maggie, I'm sure you're spoiled rotten."

"I get by," I allowed sourly. She made it sound like I should feel ashamed for the things I had, like I had stolen them. Although, I suppose in her mind, I kinda had.

"Who brought you here anyway?" The idea had just occurred to her, and she glanced behind her, as if she expected to see Matt or Maggie waiting in the wings.

"Matt," I answered.

"Matthew?" She looked genuinely shocked. "There is no way he would condone this. He doesn't even..." Sadness washed across her face and she shook her head. "He's never understood. I did what I did to protect him too. I never wanted you to get your claws into him." She touched at her hair and tears welled in her eyes, but she blinked them back and her stony expression returned.

"He thinks he has to protect me," I informed her, mostly because I knew it would bother her. Disappointingly, she didn't look that upset. She just nodded understanding.

"For all his sense and maturity, Matthew can be incredibly naive. He thought of you as some lost, sick puppy he needed to care for." She brushed a frizzy stand of hair from her forehead and stared off at a spot on the floor. "He loves you because he's a good man, like his father, and that has always been his weakness." Then she looked up hopefully. "Is he going to visit me today?"

"No." I almost felt bad about telling her that, but she smiled bitterly at me and I remembered why she was here.

"You've turned him against me. I knew you would. But..." She shrugged emptily. "It doesn't make things easier, does it?"

"I don't know." I leaned in towards her. "Look, M-... Kim. I am here for a reason. I want to know what I am." I backtracked quickly. "I mean, what you think I am."

"You're a changeling," she said matter-of-factly. "I'm surprised you didn't know that by now."

My heart dropped, but I tried to keep my expression neutral. I pressed my hands flat on the table to keep from them shaking. It was just as I had suspected, and maybe I had always known.

63

When Finn told me, it had instantly made sense, but I don't know why hearing it from her made things feel so different.

"A changeling?" I fought to keep my voice even. "What does that mean?"

"What do you think it means?" She snapped, looking at me like I was an idiot. "Changeling! You were changed out for another child! My son was taken and you were put in his place!"

Her cheeks reddened with rage, and the orderly took a step closer to her. She held up her hand and fought to keep herself contained.

"Why?" I asked, realizing that I should've asked Finn this question days earlier. "Why would anyone do that? Why would they take your baby? What did they do with him?"

"I don't know what kind of game you're playing." She smiled painfully at me and fresh tears stood in her eyes. Her hands trembled when she touched her hair, and she all but refused to look at me. "You know what you did with him. You know far better than I do."

"No, I don't! What are you talking about?" I demanded in a hushed voice. The orderly gave me a hard look, and I had to at least look like I wasn't freaking out.

"You killed him, Wendy!" My mother snarled, that sad smiled plastered on her face. She leaned in towards me, her hand clenched into a fist, and I knew she was using all her will power to keep from hurting me. "You *killed* him!"

"Mom…Kim, whatever!" I closed my eyes and rubbed my

temples. "That doesn't make any sense. I was just a baby! How could I kill anything?"

"How did you get Matthew to drive you here?" she demanded through gritted teeth, and an icy chill ran down my spine. "He would never drive you here. He would never let you see me. But he did. What did you do to him to make him do it?" I lowered my eyes, unable to even pretend to be innocent. "Maybe that's exactly what you did to Michael!" Her hands were clenched so tightly that her nails were digging into her, creating little half-moon cuts on her palms.

"I was just a baby," I insisted without any real conviction. "I couldn't have... Even if I did, there had to be more people involved. It doesn't explain anything! Why would anybody take him or hurt him and put me in his place?"

"You were always evil," she ignored my question. "I knew it from the moment I held you in my arms." She had calmed herself a bit and leaned back in her chair. "It was in your eyes. They weren't human. They weren't kind or good."

"Then why didn't you just kill me then?" I asked, growing irritated.

"You were a baby!" Her hands shook, and her lips had started to quiver. She was losing the confidence she had come in with. "Well, I thought you were. You know I couldn't be sure." She pressed her lips together tightly, trying to hold back tears.

"What made you so sure?" I asked. "What made you decide that day? On my sixth birthday. Why that day? What happened?"

"You weren't mine. I knew you weren't." She brushed at her eyes to keep the tears from spilling over. "I had known forever. But I just kept thinking about what the day should've been like. With my husband, and my son. Michael should've been six that day, not you. You were a horrible, horrible child, and you were alive. And he was dead. I just... it didn't seem right anymore." She took a deep breath and shook her head. "It still isn't right."

"I was six years old." My voice had started quavering, and I was surprised that this had gotten to me so hard. I had never thought this had bothered me. I had never felt anything about her or what happened.

"*Six-years-old*. Do you understand that? I was a little kid, and you were supposed to be my mother!" Whether she really was or not was irrelevant. I was a child, and she was in charge of raising me. "I had never done anything to anyone! I still haven't! I never even met Michael!"

"You are *lying*!" my mother hissed. "You were always a liar! You're a monster! And I know you're doing things to Matthew! Just leave him alone! He's a good boy!" She reached across the table and grabbed my wrist painfully, and the orderly came up behind her. "Take what you want! Take anything! Just leave Matthew alone!"

"Kimberly, come on." The orderly put his strong hand on her arm, and she tried to pull away from him. "Kimberly!"

"Leave him alone!" she shouted again, and the orderly started pulling her up. She fought against him, screaming at me. "Do you hear me, Wendy? I will get out of here someday! And if you've hurt that boy, I will finish the job I started!"

"That's enough!" The orderly bellowed, dragging her out of the room.

"You're not human, Wendy! And I know it!" That was the last thing she yelled before he carried her out of my sight.

I sat in the room long after she'd gone, trying to catch my breath and get myself under control. Matt couldn't see me like that. I really, really thought I was going to throw up, but I managed to keep it down.

Everything was true. I was a changeling. I wasn't human. She wasn't my mother. She was just Kim, a woman who had lost her grasp on reality when she realized I wasn't her child. I had been switched out for her son, Michael, and I had no idea what had happened to him.

Maybe he was dead. Maybe I really had killed him, or someone else had. Maybe someone like Finn.

She was convinced that I was a monster, and I had nothing to argue that with. In my life, I had caused nothing but pain. I had ruined Matt's life, and I was still.

Not only did he constantly have to uproot himself for me and spend every minute worrying about me, but I was manipulating and controlling him, and I couldn't say for sure how long that had been going on. I didn't know the long-term effects of it either.

Maybe it would've been better if she had killed me when I was six. Or better yet, when I was still a baby. Then I wouldn't have been able to hurt anybody.

When I finally went out to the waiting room, Matt rushed over to hug me. I stood there, but I didn't hug him back. He inspected me to make sure I was alright. He had heard there was some kind of scuffle and was petrified that something had happened to me. I just nodded and got out of there as fast as I could.

5. Insanity

"So…" Matt began on the drive home. I rested my forehead against the cold glass of the car window and refused to look at him. I had barely even spoken since we left. "What did you say to her?"

"Things," I replied vaguely.

"No, really," he pressed. "What happened?"

"I tried talking to her, she got upset," I sighed. "She said I was a monster. You know, the usual."

"I don't know why you even wanted to see her. She is a terrible person."

"Oh, she's not that bad." My breath fogged up the window, and I started drawing stars in the mist. "She's really worried about you. She's afraid I'm going to hurt you."

"Oh," Matt scoffed. "That woman is insane! She obviously is since she lives there, but… You can't listen to her, Wendy. You aren't letting anything she said get to you, are you?"

"No," I lied. Pulling my sleeve up over my hand, I erased my drawings on the window and sat up straighter. "How do you know?"

"What?"

"That she is insane. That… I'm not a monster." I twisted nervously at my thumb ring and stared at Matt, who just shook his head. "I'm being serious. What if I am bad?"

Matt suddenly put on his turning signal and pulled his car over

69

to the shoulder. Rain pounded down on the windows as other cars sped by us on the freeway. He turned to face me completely, putting an arm on the back of his seat.

"Wendy Luella Everly, there is nothing bad about you. *Nothing*," Matt emphasized solemnly. "That woman is completely insane. I don't know why, but she was never a mother to you. You can't listen to her. She doesn't know what she's talking about."

"Be serious, Matt," I shook my head. "I've gotten expelled from every school I've ever gone to. I'm unruly and whiny and stubborn and so picky. I know that you and Maggie have to struggle with me all the time."

"That doesn't mean you're bad. You've had a *really* traumatic childhood, and yeah, you're still working through some things, but you are not bad," Matt insisted. "You are a strong-willed teenager who isn't afraid of anything. That's all."

"At some point that has to stop being an excuse! Sure she tried to kill me, but I have to take responsibility for who I am as a person." What I was saying was true, and the painful knot in my stomach only seemed to grow larger.

"You are!" Matt actually smiled at that. "Since we've moved here, you have shown so much promise. Your grades are going up, and you're making friends. And even if that makes me a little uncomfortable, I know it's a good thing for you. You're growing up, Wendy, and you're going to be okay."

"Okay," I nodded, unable to think of an argument for that.

"I know I don't say it enough, but I'm proud of you, and I love you." Matt bent over so he could kiss the top of my head. He hadn't done that since I was little, and it stirred something inside me. I closed my eyes and refused to cry. He straightened back up in his seat and looked at me seriously. "Okay? Are you okay now?"

"Yeah, I'm fine," I forced a smile at him.

"Good." He pulled back out in traffic, continuing the drive home.

As much as I had inconvenienced Matt and Maggie, it would break their hearts if I left. Even if going with Finn would be more promising, it would hurt them too much. Leaving would put my needs in front of theirs. So if I stayed, I put them before me.

Staying would be my only proof that I wasn't evil.

When we got home, I went up to my room before Maggie could try to talk to me. My room felt too quiet, so I went over to my iPod and started scrolling through songs. A light tapping sound startled me from my search, and my heart skipped a beat.

I walked over to my window, and when I pulled back the curtain, there was Finn, crouched on the roof outside. I considered closing the curtain and ignoring him, but his dark eyes were too much. Besides, this would give me a chance to say a proper goodbye.

"What are you doing?" Finn asked as I soon as I opened the window. He stayed out on the roof, but I hadn't moved back so he could come in.

"What are *you* doing?" I countered, crossing my arms on my

71

chest.

"I came to make sure you're alright," he asked, looking at me seriously.

"Why wouldn't I be alright?" I asked.

"It was just a feeling I had." He avoided my gaze and glanced behind him at a man walking his dog on the sidewalk, then looked at me. "Mind if I come in so we can finish this conversation?"

"Whatever."

I took a step back and tried to seem as indifferent as possible, but when he slid in the window past me, my heartbeat sped up. He stood right in front of me, looking down in my eyes, and he made the rest of the world disappear. I shook my head and stepped away from him, so I wouldn't let myself get mesmerized by him anymore.

"Why did you come in the window?" I asked.

"I couldn't very well come to the door. That guy would never let me in here to see you," Finn reasoned, and he was probably right. Matt had decided he hated Finn ever since the dance.

"That *guy* is my brother, and his name is Matt." I felt incredibly defensive and protective of him, especially after the way he reacted after we saw Kim.

"He's not your brother. You need to stop thinking of him like that." Finn cast a disparaging look around my room. "Is that what this is all about? This is why you won't leave?"

"You couldn't possibly understand my reasons." I went over and sat on my bed, trying to make a physical point of laying claim to this space.

"What happened tonight?" Finn asked, ignoring my attempts at defiance.

"How are you so certain something happened?"

"You were gone," he said, without any fear that I might find it disturbing that he knew about my comings and goings. It didn't, and it shouldn't even have surprised me that he knew.

"I saw my mother. Er, well... the woman who is supposed to be my mother." I shook my head, hating the way this all sounded. I considered lying to him, but he already knew more about all of this than anyone. "What do you call her? Is there a name for her?"

"Usually, her name will suffice," Finn replied, and I felt like an idiot.

"Yeah. Of course." I took a deep breath. "Anyway I went and saw Kim." I looked up at him. "Do you know about her? I mean... how much do you really know about me?"

"Honestly, not that much." Finn seemed to disapprove of his own lack of knowledge. "You were incredibly elusive. It was rather disconcerting."

"So you don't..." I trailed off, realizing with dismay that I was on the verge of tears. "She knew I wasn't her daughter. When I was six, she tried to kill me. She had always told me that I was a monster, that I was evil. And I guess I had always believed her."

"You're not evil," Finn insisted earnestly, and I smiled thinly at him, swallowing back my sadness. "You can't possibly stay here,

Wendy."

"It's not like that anymore," I shook my head, looking away from him. "She doesn't live here, and my brother and my aunt would do anything for me. I can't just leave them. I won't."

Finn eyed me up, trying to decide if I was serious. I hated how attractive he was and whatever power it was he held over me. Just the way he looked at me made my heart race and my stomach flip.

"Do you realize what you're giving up?" Finn asked softly. "There is so much that life has to offer you. More than anything they can give you here. If Matt understood what was in store for you, he would send you there himself."

"You're right. He would, if he thought it was what's best for me," I admitted. "Which is why I have to stay."

"You think I don't want what's best for you?" Finn questioned with an underlying affection that shivered through me. "Do you really believe I would encourage you to do this if it would adversely affect you?"

"I don't think you know what's best for me," I replied as evenly as I could.

He had thrown me off guard by hinting at caring about me, and I had to remind myself that that was part of his job. All of this was. He needed to make sure I was safe and convince me to get home. That wasn't the same as actually caring about *me*.

"You are sure this is what you want?" Finn asked gently.

"Absolutely." But I sounded more confident than I really was.

74

"I'd like to say that I understood, but I don't." Finn sighed resignedly. "I can say that I am disappointed."

"I'm sorry," I said meekly.

"You shouldn't be sorry." He ran a hand through his black hair and looked at me again. "I won't be going to school anymore. It seems unnecessary, and I don't want to disturb your studies. You should at least get an education."

"What? Don't you need one?" My heart dropped to the pit of my stomach as I realized that this might be the last time I saw Finn.

"Wendy," Finn gave a small humorless laugh. "I thought you knew. I'm twenty-years-old. I'm done with my education."

"Why were you..." I trailed off, already figuring out the answer to my question.

"I was only there to keep track of you, and I've found you." Finn dropped his eyes and sighed. "When you change your mind..." He hesitated for a moment. "I'll find you."

"You're leaving?" I asked, but it made sense.

"You're still here, so I am too. At least for awhile," Finn explained.

"How long?"

"It depends on things." Finn shook his head. "Everything about your situation is so different. It's hard to say anything with certainty."

"You keep saying that I'm different. What does that mean? What are you talking about?"

"We usually wait until changelings are a few years older, and by then, you've already figured out that you're not human," Finn explained. "When the tracker comes to find you, you're relieved and eager to go."

"So why did you come for me now?" I asked.

"You moved so much." Finn gestured to the house. "We were afraid that something might be the matter. So I was here, monitoring you until you were ready, and I thought you might be." He exhaled deeply. "I guess I was wrong."

"Can't you just 'persuade' me to go along?" I asked, and some part of me hoped he could. I really did want to go with him.

"I can't," Finn shook his head. "I can't force you to come with me. If this is your decision, then I'll have to respect it."

I was turning down any chance at getting to know my real parents, my family history, and spending more time with Finn. Not to mention my abilities, like persuasion, which Finn had promised there would be more of as I got older. On my own, I'm sure I'd never be able to master or understand them.

We looked at each other, and I wished he wasn't so far away from me. I was wondering if it would be appropriate if we hugged when the door to my bedroom opened.

Matt had come in to check on me. As soon as he saw Finn, his eyes burned. Quickly, I jumped up, moving in front of Finn to block any attempts that Matt would have at killing him.

"Matt! It's okay!" I held up my hands.

"It is not okay!" Matt growled coming into my room. "Who the hell is this?"

"Matt, please!" I put my hands on his chest, trying to push him back away from Finn, but it was like trying to push a brick wall. He reached over my shoulder, pointing at Finn as he yelled. I glanced back at Finn, and he just stared blankly at my brother.

"You have some nerve!" Matt shouted.. "She is seventeen-years-old! I don't know what the hell you think you're doing in her room, but you're never doing anything with her again!"

"Matt, please, stop!" I begged. "He was just saying goodbye! *Please!*"

"Perhaps you should listen to her," Finn offered calmly.

His composure really pissed Matt off. He was yelling at Finn, and he wanted him to react. Matt's night had been horrible, too, and he didn't want some kid in here defiling me. Finn's only reaction was to stand there, cool and collected, and Matt wanted him too scared to ever go near me again.

Matt actually knocked me out of the way, and I fell backwards onto the floor. Finn's eyes flashed darkly at that, and when Matt pushed him, Finn didn't move an inch. He just glared down at my brother, and I knew that if they fought, Matt would be the one with a serious injury.

"Matt!" I jumped to my feet.

Already, I had started chanting *Leave my room. Leave my room. You need to calm down and get out of my room. Please.* I wasn't sure how effective it would be if I weren't looking at him, so I grabbed his arm and forced him to turn to me.

He tried to look away instantly, but I caught him. I kept my eyes focused and just kept repeating it over and over in my head. Finally, his expression softened and his eyes glazed.

"I'm going to leave your room now," Matt said robotically.

Much to my relief, he actually turned and walked out into the hall, closing the door behind him. I'm not sure if he walked any farther than that, or how much time I had, so I turned to Finn.

"You have to leave," I insisted breathlessly, but his expression had changed to one of concern.

"Does he do that often?" Finn asked.

"What?" I had no idea what he was talking about, and I just wanted him to go before somebody got hurt. "What are you talking about?"

"He pushed you. He clearly has an anger problem." Finn glared at the door Matt had left through. "He's unstable. You shouldn't stay here with him."

"Yeah, well, you guys should be more careful who you leave babies with," I muttered and went to the window. "I don't know how much time we have so you need to go."

"He probably won't ever be able to come into your room again," Finn said absently. "I'm serious, Wendy. I don't want to leave you with him."

"You don't have much of a choice!" I felt exasperated and ran a hand through my hair. "Matt's not usually like that, and he would never hurt me. He's just had a *really* hard day, and he blames you for upsetting me, and he's not wrong." The panic was wearing away, and I realized that I had just used persuasion on Matt again, and I felt nauseous. "I *hate* doing that to him. It's not fair and it's not right."

"I am sorry," Finn looked at me sincerely. "I know you did that to protect him, and that's my fault. I should've just backed down, but when he pushed you…" He shook his head. "My instincts just kicked in."

"He's not going to hurt me," I promised.

"I'm sorry for the trouble I've caused you."

Finn glanced back at the door, and I could tell he really didn't want to leave. When he looked back at me, he sighed heavily He was probably fighting the urge to throw me over his shoulder and take me with him. Instead, he climbed out the window and swung back down to the ground.

With that, he turned around the neighbors' hedges and I couldn't see him anymore. I kept looking after him, wishing that this didn't mean I had to say goodbye to him. There were still doubts about what I'd be giving up, but I couldn't do that to Matt.

The awful truth was that I was more than a little sad to see Finn go. Eventually, I shut the window and closed my curtains.

After Finn left, I found Matt sitting on the steps, looking bewildered and pissed off. He wanted to yell at me about Finn, but he couldn't seem to understand exactly what had happened. The best I could get out of it is that he vowed to kill Finn if he ever came near me, and I pretended like I thought that was a reasonable thing to do.

The next day, school dragged on and on. It didn't help that I found myself constantly looking around for Finn. Part of me kept insisting that the last few days had been a bad dream, and that Finn should still be here, staring at me like he always did.

On top of that, I kept feeling like I was being watched. My neck got that scratchy feeling it did when Finn stared at me for too long, but whenever I turned around, there wasn't anybody there. At least not anybody worth noting.

At home, I felt distracted and ill at ease. I excused myself from supper early and went up to my room. I peered out my curtains, hoping to find Finn lurking around somewhere nearby, but no such luck. Every time I looked for him and didn't find him, my heart hurt a little more.

I tossed and turned all night, trying to decide what to do. I didn't know how much longer Finn would hang around. There could only be so much time he could devote to tracking me. Eventually, he'd have to move on and find someone else.

I wasn't ready for that. I didn't like the idea of him moving on when I hadn't.

Around five in the morning, I gave up entirely on sleep. I looked out the window again, and this time I thought I saw something. He was out there, hiding nearby. I just needed to go out and talk to Finn, to make sure he was still there. I didn't even bother changing out of my pajamas or fixing my hair.

Hastily, I climbed out onto the roof. I tried to grab onto the branch and swing to the ground like Finn had. As soon as my fingers grabbed the branch, they slipped off and I fell to the ground, landing heavily on my back. All the wind had been knocked out of me, and I coughed painfully.

I would've loved to lie on the lawn for ten more minutes and try to ease the pain, but I was afraid that Matt or Maggie had heard something. I scrambled to my feet and rounded the hedges towards the neighbors' house.

The street was completely deserted. I wrapped my arms tightly around myself to ward off the cold that seeped in and looked around. I *knew* he had been out here. I had seen something. Maybe my fall had scared him away, like he thought it was Matt or something.

I decided to walk a little farther down the street, investigating everyone's lawn for a hidden tracker. My back ached from the fall, and my knee felt a little twisted and weird. That left me hobbling down the street in my pajamas at five in the morning. I had truly lost my mind.

Then I heard something. Footsteps? Somebody was definitely following me, and based on the dark chill running down my spine, it wasn't Finn. It was hard to explain how exactly I knew it wasn't him, but I knew it just the same. Slowly, I turned around.

6. Monsters

A girl stood a few feet behind me. In the glow from the streetlamp, she looked ravishing. Her short brown pixie cut spiked up all over. Her skirt was short and her black leather jacket went down to her calves. A wind came up, blowing back her coat a bit, and she reminded me of some kind of action star, like she should be in *The Matrix*.

But the thing that caught my attention the most was that she was barefoot.

"Okay... um, I'm going to go home now," I announced. She just stared at me, so I felt like I had to say something.

"Wendy Everly, I think you should come with us," she said with a sly smile.

"Us?" I asked, but then I felt him behind me.

I don't know where he had been before that, but suddenly, I felt his presence behind me and I looked over my shoulder. A tall man with dark, slick-backed hair stared down at me. He wore the same jacket as the girl, and I thought it was neat that they had matching outfits, like a crime fighting duo.

He smiled at me, and that's when I decided that I was in trouble.

"That's a really nice invitation, but my house is like three houses down." I pointed towards it, as if I didn't think they already knew exactly where I lived. "So I think that I should probably just get home before my brother starts looking for me."

"You should've thought of that before you left the house," the guy suggested wickedly.

I wanted to take a step forward so I'd be away from him, but I thought that would only make him pounce on me. I could probably take the girl, but I wasn't so sure about him. He was like a foot taller than me.

"You guys are trackers?" I asked. Something about them reminded me of Finn, the way they stared at me and insisted that I come with them.

"You're a quick one, aren't you?" the girl smiled wider at me, and it didn't set right with me.

They might be trackers, but not the same kind as Finn. Maybe they were bounty hunters or kidnappers or just big fans of chopping up girls into little pieces and disposing of them in a ditch. Fear crept through me, but I tried not to let on.

"Well, this has been a blast, but I have to get ready for school. Big test and all that." I started taking a step away, but the guy's hand clamped painfully on my arm.

"Don't damage her!" the girl insisted, her eyes flashing wide. "She's not to be hurt!"

Not to be hurt. Okay. That's a good thing. I can work with that, at least.

"Yeah, ease up!" I tried to pull my arm from him, but he refused to let go.

I had already decided that I wasn't going wherever they wanted to take me. Since they were under some kind of instruction not to hurt me, I thought I might have some leeway with fighting them. I only had to get a few houses down, then I'd be at home, and Matt kept a gun under his bed.

I elbowed the guy in the stomach as hard as I could. He made a coughing sound and doubled over but didn't let go of my arm. I kicked him in the shin and raised my arm so I could bite his hand that was gripping me.

He yowled in pain, and then the girl was in front of me. He had let go of me, and she tried to grab me, so I punched her. She dodged it, so my fist just connected with her shoulder.

Then I was off balance, and the guy grabbed me around the waist. I screamed and kicked at him as hard as I could. Apparently, he got tired of that, so he dropped me on the ground.

I was on my feet instantly, and he grabbed my arm again and turned me so I was facing him. He raised his hand and slapped me harder than I had ever been hit before. Everything went white, and my ear started ringing. He let go of me, and I collapsed backwards on the grass behind me.

"I said not to hurt her!" the girl hissed.

My neck ached from the force of his hit, and my jaw screamed painfully. The back of my eye had a spreading pain, but. I tried to stagger to my feet. She kicked me, not hard enough to really hurt, but enough so I'd fall back.

I lay on my back, staring up at the sky, and realized that I didn't stand a chance against them.

"I didn't! I was subduing her!" the guy growled and looked down at me. "And if she doesn't knock it off, I'll subdue her again, but harder this time!"

"Let's just get her to the car," she sounded exasperated.

He bent down to try to pick me up, but I hit away his hands. I was lying on my back, and I lifted up my legs. I wasn't really trying to kick him, but I was going to use my legs to push him back if he came near me.

In response, he hit my calf hard enough to give me a Charlie horse, which I gritted my teeth through. He put his knee on my stomach, holding me down so I couldn't fight as much.

When he tried to grab me, I pushed him back with my hands, so he grabbed my wrists, pressing them tightly together with one hand.

"Stop!" he commanded. I tried to pull my hands free, but he just squeezed tighter and my bones felt like they were about to snap. "Just stop! We're going to take you no matter what!"

"Like hell you are!" Finn barked, his voice coming from out of nowhere.

I swiveled my head, trying to see around the guy that had me pinned to the ground. The girl stood just to the side of us, but between the two of them, I could see Finn, and I had never been so happy to see anyone.

"Oh, dammit," the girl sighed. "If you hadn't spent so much

time fighting with her, we'd be out of here by now."

"She was the one fighting with me!" the guy insisted.

"Now I'm the one fighting with you!" Finn growled, glaring at him. "Get off her! *Now!*"

"Finn, can't we just talk about this?" She tried to sound sultry and flirty when she took a step closer to Finn, but he didn't even look at her. "I know how you feel about duty, but there's got to be some kind of arrangement we can come to."

She took another step closer to him, and he pushed her back, so hard she stumbled and fell backwards.

"I hate fighting with you, Finn." The guy let go of my hands and took his knee off my stomach. I took the opportunity to try to kick him in the nuts, and reflexively, he whirled on me and smacked me hard again.

Before I could even curse him for hitting me again, Finn was on him. I had rolled onto my side, cradling my injured face, so I could only see part of what was going on.

My attacker had managed to get to his feet, but I could hear the sounds of Finn punching him. The girl leapt on his back to stop him, but Finn elbowed her in the face, so she collapsed to the ground, holding her bleeding nose.

"Enough!" The guy had cowered down, putting his arms over his face to protect himself form anymore blows. "We're done! We'll get out of here!"

"You better fucking get out of here!" Finn shouted. "If I see you anywhere near her again, I will kill you!"

The guy walked over to the girl and helped her to her feet, and then they both turned and headed down the street to a black Porsche parked nearby. Finn stood on the sidewalk in front of me, watching them until they got in the car and sped off down the road. When he was certain they were gone, he smoothed out his hair and turned to me.

I was still lying on the ground, and he knelt down next to me. Gently, he placed his hand on my cheek where I had been slapped, and the skin was tender, so it stung a little, but I refused to show it. His hand felt too good to push away.

His dark eyes were pained when he looked me over, and as terrible as everything had been up until this moment, I wouldn't have traded it for anything because it led to this, to him touching me and looking at me like that.

"I'm sorry it took me so long." He pursed his lips tightly, blaming himself for not getting here sooner. "I was sleeping, and I didn't wake up until you were completely panicked."

"You sleep in your clothes?" I asked, looking at his usual dark jeans and button-up shirt combo.

"Sometimes." Finn pulled his hand from my face. "I knew something was up today. I could feel it, but I couldn't pinpoint it because I couldn't stay as close to you as I would've liked. I never should've slept at all."

"No, you can't blame yourself. It was my fault for coming out of my room."

"What were you doing out here?" Finn looked at me curiously, and I looked away, feeling embarrassed.

"I thought I saw you," I admitted quietly, and his face went dark.

"I should've been here," he said, almost under his breath, and then he got to his feet. He held out his hand to me and pulled me to my feet. I grimaced a little but tried not to show it. "Are you alright?"

"Yeah, I'm fine." I forced a smile. "A little sore, but fine."

He touched my cheek again, just with his fingertips, sending flutters through me. He looked at my injury very seriously, and then his eyes met mine, dark and wonderful. It was at that moment that I knew that I had officially fallen for him.

"You're going to have a bruise," Finn murmured dropping his hand. "I'm sorry."

"It's not your fault," I insisted. "It's mine. I was being an idiot. I should've known…" I trailed off. I had been about to say that I should've known it was dangerous, but how would I have possibly known that? I had no idea who those people were. "Who were they? What did they want?"

"Vittra," Finn growled, glaring down the road as if they would appear at the sound of their name. He tensed up as he scanned the horizon, then put his hand on the small of my back so he could usher me away. "Come on. I'll explain more in the car."

"The car?" I stopped where I was, making him press his hand harder on my back until he realized I wasn't going anywhere. His hand stayed there, and I had to ignore the small pleasure of it so I could argue with him. "I'm not going in the car. I have to go home before Matt realizes I'm gone."

"You can't go back there," Finn was apologetic but firm. "I'm sorry. I know this is directly against your wishes, but it's not safe for you there anymore. The Vittra have found you. I will not leave you here."

"I don't even understand what this Vittra is, and Matt is…" I shifted uncomfortably and looked backed towards my house.

Matt was tough, as far as people went, but I wasn't sure what kind of match he would be for the guy that attacked me. And even if he could take him, I didn't want to bring that element into the house. If something happened to Matt or Maggie because of me, I could never forgive myself.

"Wendy, we must hurry," Finn insisted urgently. Reluctantly, I nodded and let him take me away.

Apparently, he'd run to my rescue this morning, because his car was still parked at his house two blocks away. The sky really started to lighten, and I knew that Matt would be getting up any minute, so I quickened my pace.

"It's going to break his heart." I swallowed hard.

"He'd want you to be safe," Finn assured me, and he was right. But Matt wouldn't know I was safe. He wouldn't know anything about me.

"Do you have a cell phone?" I asked.

"Why?" Finn kept glancing around as we approached his car. He pulled his keys from his pocket and used the keyless entry to unlock it.

"I need to call Matt and let him know that I'm okay," I said. Walking in front of me, Finn held the passenger door open for me and I got inside. As soon as he got in the driver's seat, I turned to him. "Well? Can I call him?"

"You really want to?" Finn seemed surprised about my question as he started the car.

"Yes! Of course I do!"

Finn threw the car in gear and sped off down the road. The whole town was still asleep, except for us. He glanced over at me, debating. Finally, he dug in his pocket and pulled out his cell phone.

"Thank you," I smiled gratefully at him.

When I started dialing the phone, my hands shook, and I felt sick. This was going to be the hardest conversation of my life. I held the phone to my ear, listening to it ring, and I tried to slow my breathing.

"Hello?" Matt answered the phone groggily. He hadn't woken up yet, and he didn't know I was gone. I wasn't sure if that was a good thing or not. I closed my eyes and took a deep breath. "Hello?"

"Matt?" I said, afraid he would hang up if I didn't say something soon.

"Wendy?" Matt instantly woke up, panic thick in his voice. "Where are you? What's going on? Are you alright?"

"Yeah, I'm fine." My cheek still hurt, but I was fine. Even if I wasn't, I couldn't tell him that. "Um, I'm calling because… I'm leaving, and I wanted you to know that I was safe."

"What do you mean you're leaving?" Matt was up moving around. I could hear him open his door, and then the bang as he threw open my bedroom door. "Where are you, Wendy? You need to come home right now!"

"I can't, Matt!" I rubbed my forehead and let out a shaky breath.

"Why? Does somebody have you? Did Finn take you?" Matt demanded. In the background, I could hear Maggie asking questions. He'd woken her up with his commotion of looking for me. "I'll kill that little bastard if he lays one hand on you."

"Yeah, I'm with Finn, but it's not like you think," I said thickly. "I wish I could explain everything to you, but I can't. He's taking care of me though. He's making sure I'm safe."

"Safe from what?" Matt snapped. "I take care of you! Why are you doing this?" He took a deep breath and tried to calm down. "If we're doing something wrong, we can change it, Wendy. You just need to come home, right now." His voice was cracking, and it broke my heart. "Please, Wendy."

"You're not doing anything wrong." Silent tears started sliding down my face, and I tried to swallow down the lump in my throat. "You didn't do anything. This isn't about you or Maggie, honest. I love you guys, and I would take you with me if I could. But I can't."

"Why do you keep saying 'can't?' Is he forcing you?" Matt

growled. "I'll call the police! We'll come get you!"

"No, he's not forcing me!" I sighed and wondered if this phone call had been a bad idea. Maybe I just made it worse for him. "Please don't try and find me. You won't be able to, and I don't want you to. I just wanted you to know that I'm safe and that I love you and you never did anything wrong. Okay? I just want you to be happy."

"Wendy, why are you talking like that?" Matt sounded more afraid than I had ever heard him before, and I couldn't be certain, but I think he'd started to cry. "You sound like you're never coming back. You can't leave forever. You... Whatever is going on, I can take care of it. I'll do whatever I have to do. Just come back, Wendy."

"I'm so sorry, Matt, but I can't." I wiped at my eyes and shook my head. "I'll call you again if I can. But if you don't hear from me, don't worry. I'm okay."

"Wendy! Stop talking like that!" Matt shouted. "You need to come back here! Wendy!"

"Goodbye, Matt." I hung up to the sound of him yelling my name.

I took a deep breath and reminded myself that this was the only thing I could do. It was the only way that I could keep them safe, and it was the safest thing for me, which is exactly what Matt would want.

If he knew what was going on, he would agree with this completely. It didn't change the fact that it was absolute torture to say goodbye to him like that. Hearing his pain and frustration so evidently over the phone....

"Hey, Wendy. You did the right thing," Finn assured me, but I just sniffled.

He reached over and took my hand, squeezing it lightly. Ordinarily, I would've been delighted by that, but right now it took everything I had to keep from sobbing or throwing up. I wiped at my tears, but I couldn't seem to stop crying.

"Come here," Finn said gently. He put his arm around my shoulders and pulled me closer to him. I rested my head against his shoulder, and he held me tightly to him.

7. Förening

Taking a deep breath, I finally managed to stop crying. Even though Finn had retracted his arms, he was still close to me in the front seat of his car. When I looked at him, he seemed to become aware of this and moved his arm further away.

"What's going on?" I asked. "Who were those people? Why did we have to run away?"

Finn looked at me for a moment, then took a breath. "That is a very long answer, one that is best explained by your mother."

"My mother?" I had spent so long thinking of Kim as my mother and I didn't understand what more she would know about this, then I realized he meant my *real* mother. "We're going to see her? Where is she? Where are we going?"

"Förening," Finn explained. "It's where I live – where you'll live." He gave a small smile, meant to ease my concerns, and it did, a little. "Unfortunately, it's about a seven-hour drive."

"Where is it?"

"It's in Minnesota, along the Mississippi River in a very secluded area," Finn said.

"So what is this Förening place we're going to?" I asked, watching him.

"It's a town, sort of," Finn said. "They consider it to be more of a compound, but in the way the Kennedy's have a compound. It's just a glorified gated community, really."

"So do people live there too?" I asked, already wondering if I could bring Matt along with me.

"Not in the sense you're talking about." He hesitated before he continued and glanced at me out of the corner of his eye. "It's entirely Trylle, trackers, and mänsklig. There's about five thousand that live there in total, and we have gas stations, a small grocery store, and a school. It's just a very small, quiet community."

"Holy hell." My eyes widened. "You mean there's just a whole town of... trolls? In Minnesota? And nobody ever noticed?"

"We live very quietly," Finn reiterated. "And there are ways to make people not notice."

"You sound like you're in the mafia," I commented, and Finn smiled crookedly. "Do you guys make people sleep with the fishes or something?"

"Persuasion is a very powerful ability," he said, and his smile disappeared.

"So you have persuasion?" I asked carefully. Something about it seemed to upset him, and as I expected, he shook his head. "Why not?"

"I'm a tracker. Our abilities are different." He glanced over at me, and sensing that I would just ask more questions, he went on. "They're more suited for tracking, obviously. Persuasion isn't that useful in that arena."

"What is useful?" I pressed, and he sighed wearily.

"It's hard to explain. They're not even real abilities in the sense of the word." He stared out the windshield and shifted in his seat. "It's more instinct and intuition. Like the way a bloodhound follows a scent, except it's not actually something I can smell. It's just something I know." He looked over to see if I was getting it, but I just stared at him blankly.

"For example, when you went to visit that woman the other night-" (that woman being someone who I had thought was my mother my entire life) "-I knew you were far away, and I knew something was distressing you."

"You can tell when I'm upset? Even when you're not around me?" I asked.

"As long as I'm tracking you, yes," Finn nodded.

"I thought you said you weren't psychic," I muttered.

"No, I said I couldn't read minds, and I can't." Then with an exasperated sigh, he added. "I never have any idea what you're thinking.

"I can't tell everything you're feeling." He noticed my discomfort, so he continued "Just distress and fear. I need to be alert to situations when you're in danger so I can help you. My job is to keep you safe and bring you home."

"How do you know how to track me? Before you find me, I mean."

"Your mother has things from when you were a baby. A lock of hair usually," Finn elaborated. "I get a vibe from that, and your parents usually have a general idea about where you are. Once I'm around you, I start to get a real scent of you, and that's it."

I felt an odd warm feeling inside. My mother had things from me. Kim had never treasured anything about me, but someone out there had. She had taken a lock of hair when I was born and kept it safe all these years

"Is that why you stared at me all the time?" I thought of the way his eyes were always on me, and the way I could never make sense of his expression.

"Yes." There was something about his answer. He wasn't lying exactly, but he was holding something back. I thought about pressing him further but there were so many other things I wanted to know.

"So... how often do you do this?" I asked.

"You are my eleventh." He looked at me to gauge my response, so I kept my face as expressionless as possible.

I was a little surprised by his answer. It seemed like an incredibly time consuming process, for one thing. For me, he had lived in the same town as me for over two weeks and somehow enrolled in high school. He seemed fairly young to have done that eleven times. Plus, it was unnerving to think there were that many changelings out there.

"How long have you been doing this?"

"Since I was fifteen," Finn answered, further shocking me.

"Fifteen?" I shook my head. "No way. You're trying to tell me that at fifteen-years-old, your parents sent you out into the world to track and find kids? And these kids, they trusted you and believed you?"

"I am very good at what I do," Finn replied matter-of-factly.

"Still. That just seems... unreal." I couldn't wrap my mind around it. "Did they all come back with you?"

"Yes, of course," he said simply.

"Do they always? With everyone, I mean?" I continued.

"No, they don't. They usually do, but not always."

"But they always do with you?" I persisted.

"Yes." Finn looked over at me again. "Why do you find it so hard to believe?"

"I find this all hard to believe." I tried to think about what was bothering me. "Wait. You were fifteen? That means that you were never... you weren't a changeling. Is everyone? How does this work?"

"Trackers are never changelings." He rubbed the back of his neck and pursed his lips. "I think it's best if your mother explains the changelings to you."

"How come trackers aren't ever changelings?" I questioned.

"We need to spend our lives being trained to be a tracker," Finn said. "And our youth is an asset. It's much easier to get close to a teenager when you are a teenager than it is when you're forty."

"A big part of what you do is building trust," I remarked, eyeing him up with new suspicions.

"Yes, it is," Finn admitted.

"So at the dance, when you were being a total dick to me. That was you building trust?" I asked him pointedly. For a split second, he looked pained, but his normal emotionless expression returned.

"No. That was me putting a distance between us." His eyes were too fixed on the road and his expression hardened. "I shouldn't have asked you to dance. I was trying to correct the error. I needed you to trust me, but anything more would be misleading."

Everything that had transpired between us had just been because he was trying to get me to the compound. He had been keeping me safe, getting me to like him, and when he noticed my crush developing, he had tried to put me in my place. It stung painfully, so I just swallowed hard and stared out the window.

"I'm sorry if I've hurt you," Finn said quietly, noticing my distress.

"Don't worry about it," I replied icily. "You were just doing your job."

"I know that you're being facetious, but I was." He paused. "I still am."

"Well, you're very good at it." I crossed my arms and stared out the window.

I didn't feel much like talking anymore. There were still a million questions I had about everything, but I'd rather wait and talk to somebody else, anybody else. I thought I would be too anxious and excited to sleep, but after about an hour into the drive, I started nodding off. I fought to stay awake until I realized it would just be quicker if I slept.

When I opened my eyes, the sun shone brightly above us. I had curled up on the seat with my knees pressed against my chest, so my whole body felt sore and ached. Looking around, I sat up and stretched, trying to work the kinks out of my neck.

"I thought you were going to sleep the whole ride," Finn said.

"How far away are we?" I yawned and slouched low in the seat, resting my knees against the dashboard.

"Not far."

The scenery had started giving way to tall tree-lined bluffs. The car rolled up and down through the hills and valleys, and it really was stunningly beautiful. Eventually, Finn slowed and we turned, driving steeply to the top of a bluff. The road curved down, winding through the trees, and through them, I could see the Mississippi River cutting through the bluffs.

A large metal gate blocked our path, but when we got to it, a guard nodded at Finn and waved us on. Once we were through, I saw beautiful houses dotted along the bluffs, mostly obscured by the trees.

It was an odd sensation. I felt like there were more homes than what I could actually see. Every one of them appeared luxurious and perfectly poised to make the best of the view.

We pulled up in front of an opulent mansion perched precariously on the edge of the bluff. It was pure white, with long vines growing up beautifully over it. The back, which faced the river, was made entirely of windows, and it seemed to be held up by weak supports. While stunningly gorgeous, the house looked as if it would fall off the edge at any moment.

"What's this?" I took a break from gaping at the house to look back at Finn. He smiled at me in the way that sent shivers through me.

"This is it. Welcome home, Wendy."

I had come from money, but it had never been anything like this. This was aristocratic. Finn walked me to the house, and I couldn't believe that I'd truly come from this. I had never felt so small or ordinary in my entire life.

With a house like this, I had expected a butler to answer the door. Instead, it was just a kid. He looked about my age, with sandy hair cascading across his forehead. He was very attractive, but that made sense, because I couldn't believe that anything ugly ever came from a house like this. It was too perfect.

He seemed confused and surprised at first, but when he saw Finn, an understanding came to him and he smiled broadly.

"Oh my god. You must be Wendy." He opened the massive front door so we could come in.

Finn let me go in first, which made me nervous, and I felt embarrassed with the way this kid smiled at me, especially considering I had on my pajamas and a bruise on my cheek. He dressed like any other normal kid I had gone to school with, at least in the private schools, and I found that weird. As if he would run around in a tuxedo first thing in the morning.

"Um, yeah," I mumbled awkwardly.

"Oh, sorry, I'm Rhys." He touched his chest, gesturing to himself, and turned back to Finn. "We weren't expecting you this soon."

"Things happen," Finn explained noncommittally.

"I'd really love to stay and talk, but I just came home for lunch, and I'm already running late on getting back to school." Rhys glanced around and looked apologetically at us. "Elora is down in the drawing room. You can get yourself there, right?"

"I can," Finn nodded.

"Alright. Sorry to rush out like this." Rhys smiled sheepishly and picked up his messenger bag lying by the front door. "It was really nice meeting you, Wendy. I'm sure I'll be seeing a lot more of you."

Once he hurried out the door, I took a moment to take in my surroundings. The floors were marble, and a giant, crystal chandelier hung above us. From where I stood, I could see the breathtaking view through the windowed back wall of the house. It was all floor to ceiling glass, and all I could see were the tops of trees and the river plummeting below us. It was enough to give me vertigo, and I was on the other side of the house.

"Come on." Finn walked ahead of me, turning down a decadently furnished hall, and I scampered after him.

"Who was that?" I whispered, as if the walls could hear me. They were lined with pictures, a few of which I recognized as being painted by master painters.

"Rhys."

"Yeah, I know but... is he my brother?" I asked. I had already decided that he was foxy, so I really hoped that he wasn't.

"No." That was all Finn would say on the subject.

Abruptly, he turned into a room. It was the corner of the house, so two of the walls were entirely glass. One interior wall had a fireplace, and hanging above it was the portrait of an attractive, older gentleman. Books lined the other interior wall. Elegant, antique furniture filled the room, and a velvet chaise lounge sat poised in front of the fireplace.

A woman sat on the stool in a corner, her back to us. Her dress was dark and flowing, just like her hair that hung down her back. A large canvas was set on the easel before her. It was only partially finished, but it appeared to be some kind of fire, with dark smoke filtering over broken chandeliers.

She continued painting for several minutes while we stood there. I glanced over at Finn, but he just shook his head, trying to quiet me before I voiced a complaint. His hands were clasped behind his back, and he stood rigidly straight, reminding me of a soldier.

"Elora?" Finn said cautiously, and I got the sense that she intimidated him. This was as unnerving as it was surprising. He didn't seem like he could be intimidated by anyone.

When she turned to look at us, I forgot to breathe. She was much older than I had expected, in her fifties probably, but there was something stunningly elegant and beautiful about her. Her eyes were dark and large, and in her youth, she had probably been unbearably attractive. As it was, I could hardly believe that she was real.

"Finn!" Her voice was angelic and clear, and her surprise was endearing. With a graceful move, she swiftly stood up, and Finn did a small bow to her. It confused me, but I clumsily tried to copy it, and this caused her to laugh. She looked at Finn, but gestured to me. "This is her?"

"Yes. It is." There was a hint of pride in his voice. He had brought me here, and I was starting to realize that must have been a very special request.

When she moved, she looked even more poised and regal, and she was captivating. The length of her skirt swirled around her feet making it seem more as if she floated than actually walked.

Once in front of me, she inspected me carefully. Her gaze seemed to disapprove of my pajamas, especially the dirt stains on my knees I had sustained from the fight, but when she caught the bruise on my face, she pursed her lips.

"Oh my." Her eyes widened with surprise, but her expression lacked anything resembling concern. "What happened?"

"Vittra," Finn answered with the same contempt he had before.

"Oh?" Elora raised an eyebrow. "Which ones?"

"Jen and Kyra," Finn said.

"I see." Elora stared off for a minute, smoothing out the non-existent wrinkles in her dress. Sighing tiredly, she looked to Finn. "You're sure it was only Jen and Kyra?"

"I believe so," Finn said, thinking hard. "I didn't see any signs of others, and they would've called for backup, had there been any to call. They were quite insistent on taking Wendy. Jen got violent with her."

"I can see that," Elora looked back at me. "Just the same, you are lovely." She sounded almost awed by me, and I felt a blush redden my cheeks. "It's Wendy, isn't it?"

"Yes, ma'am," I smiled nervously at her.

"What an ordinary name for such an extraordinary girl." She looked displeased for a moment, and then turned to Finn. "Excellent work. You may be excused while I talk to her. Stay close by, though. I'll call when I need you."

Finn did another small bow before leaving the room. His level of reverence made me uncomfortable. I wasn't sure how to act around her.

"I'm Elora, and I won't expect you to call me any different. I know this is so much to get accustomed to. I remember when I first came back." She smiled and gave a light shake of her head. "It was a very confusing time." I nodded, unsure of what else to do, and she gestured expansively to the room. "Sit. We have much to talk about."

"Thanks." Uncertainly, I took a seat on the edge of the sofa, afraid that if I really sat down on it I would break it or something.

Elora went to the chaise lounge where she laid on her side, letting her dress flow around her. She held her head up with her hand and watched me with intense fascination. Her eyes were dark and beautiful, but there was something familiar about them in a weird way. They reminded me of a wild animal trapped in a cage.

"I'm not sure if Finn has explained it to you, but I am your mother," Elora said.

8. Family

It was impossible. I wanted to correct her. There must be some mistake. Nothing as stunning and elegant as that could spawn me. I was awkward and impulsive. Her hair was like silk, and as it had been pointed out to me before, my hair was like a Brillo pad. I couldn't be related to her.

"Ah. I see he did not," Elora said. "From your bewildered expression, I take it you don't even believe me. But let me assure you, there is no mistaking who you are. I personally chose the Everly family for you and delivered you to them myself. Finn is the best tracker we have, so there is no way you could be anyone else but my daughter."

"I'm sorry," I stumbled out an apology. "I didn't mean to question you. I just…"

"I understand. You're still used your to normal human way of being. That will all change soon," Elora promised. "Did Finn explain anything to you about Trylle?"

"Not really," I admitted carefully, afraid that I might get him in trouble.

"I'm certain you have many questions, but let me explain everything to you, and if you still have questions, you can ask me when I'm done." Elora had a coldness to her voice, and I doubted I'd ever be able to question her on anything.

"Trylle are, to the layman, a troll, but that term is antiquated and demeaning, and as you can tell, it doesn't do us justice at all." Elora gestured to the expanse of the room, with all its grace and luxury, and I nodded. "We are beings closely related to humans, but more in tune with ourselves. We have abilities, intelligence, and beauty that far surpass that of humans.

"There are two important distinctions to our lifestyle as Trylle that separate us from the humans," Elora continued. "We want to live a quiet life communing with the earth and ourselves. We work to strengthen our abilities and use them to better our lives, to protect ourselves and the things around us. We devote our entire lives to this. Förening exists only to preserve and enhance the Trylle way of life.

"The other distinction is how we maintain this lifestyle, although it isn't that different really." She looked thoughtfully out the window. "Human children have their boarding schools, but they prepare them for a life of servitude. That's not what we want. We want a life of complete and total freedom. That is why we have changelings.

"Changelings are a practice that dates back hundreds, maybe thousands of years." Elora looked at me gravely, and I gulped back the growing nausea in my belly. "Originally, we were more forest dwellers, less … industrialized than you see now. Our children were prone to starvation and medical problems, and we did not have an adequate educational system. So, we'd leave our babies in place of human children so they would have the benefits that only a human childhood could offer, then when they were old enough, they would come back to us.

"That practice evolved because we evolved. Changelings were healthier, more educated, and wealthier than the Trylle counterparts that stayed behind," Elora said. "Eventually, every child born became a changeling. Now we could easily match the benefits of the human population, but to what end? In order to maintain that level, we'd have to leave the solace of the compound and spend our lives doing menial jobs.

"We leave our children with the most sophisticated, wealthiest human families. The changelings live a childhood that is the best this world has to offer, and then return with an inheritance from their host families that infuses our society with cash. That, of course, isn't the only goal, but it is a large part of how we can live like this. The money you obtain from your host family will be how you will be able to live the rest of your life."

"Wait. I'm sorry. I know I'm not supposed to interrupt, but…" I licked my lips and shook my head. "I just had to clarify a few points."

"By all means," Elora said, but venom dripped from her voice.

"When I was a baby, you gave me to strangers to raise me so I could have a good education, a good childhood, and I would bring money back. Is that right?"

"Yes." Elora raised an eyebrow, daring me to question it.

I wanted to yell so badly I was shaking. But I was still afraid of her. She looked like she could snap me in half with her mind, so I just twisted my thumb ring and nodded confirmation with her. She

111

had dumped me off on a crazy woman that tried to murder me, just because Elora never wanted to work and needed cash.

"Shall I continue?" Elora asked, and she didn't even try to mask the condescending tone in her voice. I nodded meekly. "I don't even remember what I was saying." She waved her hand in irritation. "If you have any other questions, I suppose you can ask them now."

"What are the Vittra?" I asked, trying to distract myself from my anger with her. "I don't understand who they are or what they wanted with me."

"Förening is populated with Trylle." Elora gestured widely around, referencing the whole town. "The term Trylle is a distinction similar to a tribe. We are trolls, and over the years, the troll population has been dwindling. Our numbers used to be great, but there are less than a million of us on the entire planet.

"We are one of the largest tribes left, but we are not the only one," Elora continued. "The Vittra are a warring faction, and they are forever looking to pick off some of us. Either by turning us to their side, or simply by getting rid of us."

"So the Vittra want me to live with them?" I wrinkled my nose. "Why? What could I do for them?"

"I am the Queen." She paused letting me take it in. "You are the Princess. You are my only child, the last of my legacy."

"What?" I felt my jaw drop open.

"You are the Princess," Elora explained with a condescending smile. "You will one day be Queen, and being the leader of Trylle carries great weight."

"But if I'm not here, won't you just find another replacement? I mean, there's going to be a Queen here even if I'm not," I said, scrambling to make sense of this all.

"There is more to it than that. We are not all created equal," Elora went on. "We are far more gifted than the others. You have already tapped into persuasion, and you have the potential for much more. Vittra are lucky to have any abilities. Adding you to their ranks would greatly change their power to influence."

"You're saying I'm powerful?" I raised a sardonic eyebrow.

"You will be," Elora amended. "That is why you need to live here, to learn our ways so you can take your rightful place."

"Okay." I took a deep breath and ran my hand along my pajama pants.

None of this seemed real or made sense. The idea of myself as a Queen was completely absurd. I barely managed to pass for an awkward teenager.

"Finn will be staying to watch over you. Since they're looking for you, added protection would be prudent." Elora touched at something at her skirt, not looking at me. "I'm sure you have many more questions, but you'll get the answers over time. Why don't you go get yourself cleaned up?"

"Wait," I said, my voice feeling small and uncertain. She raised her head, looking at me with disdain. "Just… um… where's my father?"

"Oh." Elora looked away from me and stared out the window. "Dead. I'm sorry. It happened shortly after you were born."

Finn had promised me a different life where I belonged, but really, it seemed to be the exact same life with different trappings. My mother here seemed almost as cold as my fake mom, and in either life, my dad was dead.

"Also, I don't have any money." I shifted uneasily.

"Of course you don't," Elora thought I was being ridiculous. "You probably won't have access to your trust fund until you're twenty-one, but with persuasion, you can get it sooner. Finn tells me you're very advanced with that."

"What?" I shook my head. "No. I don't even know if I have a trust fund."

"I specifically chose the Everlys because of their wealth," Elora said matter-of-factly.

"Yeah, I know you chose them for their money, because it certainly wasn't for their mental health." I lowered my eyes, realizing I had been smart with her, but quickly plowed through it.

"My dad killed himself when I was five, so none of his insurance paid out. My mom never worked a day in her life, and she's been in a mental institution for the past eleven years, which has eaten a lot of her funds. Not only that, we've moved around a lot and wasted tons of money on houses and tuition. We're not poor by any means, but I don't think we're anywhere near the kind of rich you think we are."

"Stop saying 'we.' They're not part of you," Elora snapped and sat up. "What are you talking about? The Everlys were one of the wealthiest families in the country. You couldn't have bled them completely dry."

"I don't know how much money we – *they* – have, but we don't... er... I didn't live like they were that rich." I was almost shouting in frustration. "And you weren't listening, I had a *terrible* childhood! My fake mother tried to kill me!"

Elora had been more shaken about my confession that my family wasn't loaded than she had about Kim trying to kill me. She sat very still for a moment, then took a deep breath.

"Oh. So she was one of those."

"What do you mean by that?" I pressed, and by now, I was livid. The casual, callous air that she had about my attempted murder. "One of those?"

"Oh, well." Elora shook her head as if she hadn't meant to say that. "Every now and again, a mother knows. Sometimes they hurt the child or kill them."

"Whoa, whoa, whoa. You knew there was a chance that she might kill me?" I snapped and stood up. "You knew that I could die but you just left me? You didn't care what happened to me at all!"

"Don't be so melodramatic," Elora rolled her eyes. "This is the way we live. It's a very small risk, and it rarely happens. And you lived. No harm done."

"No harm done?" I pulled up my shirt, showing her the scar that stretched across my belly. "I was six-years-old, and I had sixty stitches. You call that no harm done?"

"You're being disgusting." Elora stood up and waved me off. "That's not at all how a Princess should behave."

I wanted to protest, but nothing came out of my mouth. Her reaction left me feeling dazed and strange. I let my shirt fall back down on my belly, and Elora glided over to the window. She clasped her hands in front of her and stared outside. She never said a single word, but a minute later, Finn appeared in the doorway.

"You need something, Elora?" Finn did a small bow to her back, but she probably had ways of seeing him even when she wasn't looking.

"Wendy is tired. Set her up in her room," Elora commanded diffidently. "See that she has everything she needs."

"Of course." Finn looked at me. His dark eyes felt comforting, and even though I knew this was just his job, I felt relieved knowing he was there.

He left hastily, and I hurried after him. I wrapped my arms tightly around myself, trying to steady my nerves. I was reeling from everything, and I couldn't make sense of how I really fit into it.

Elora was right, though. I probably did need to get cleaned up, and maybe if I slept on it, everything would seem better somehow. But I doubted it.

Finn led me up a winding staircase and down another elaborate hall. At the end, he opened a heavy wooden door, revealing what I assumed was my room. It was massive, with high-vaulted ceilings, and one entirely windowed wall that made it seem even larger.

A gigantic four post bed sat in the center, and everything was rather modernly furnished. A laptop, flat screen, gaming systems, iPod, and every other gadget I could possibly want. Finn opened the closet door, which was already stocked with clothing. He opened another door and flicked on the light, showing my own private bathroom that more closely resembled a spa.

"How do you know where everything is?" I asked. He seemed to know this house very well, and thinking about Finn helped calm me some.

"I stay here from time to time," Finn replied nonchalantly.

"What? Why?" I felt a terrible pang of jealousy, terrified that he was somehow involved with Elora in a perverse fashion. He did seem to revere here more than I thought he should.

"Protection. Your mother is a very powerful woman, but she's not all-powerful," Finn explained vaguely. "Since I'm a tracker, I can get tuned into her. I can sense danger and aid her if it's required."

"Is it required?" At that moment, I didn't particularly care if a band of raging marauders tried to do her in, but if there were frequent attacks on her "castle," I thought I should know.

"I'll help you get acclimated. Everybody knows this isn't a perfect system. Rhys's room is down the hall. My room, along with Elora's, is on the other wing." Finn ignored my question entirely.

I definitely felt better knowing he would be around. I didn't think I could handle it all if I was left alone in this house with that woman. While clearly stunning and powerful, there wasn't any warmth to her.

I hadn't realized that I even wanted that until now. After all the years of rejecting Maggie and even Matt's attempts at bonding, I hadn't known how much I craved it.

"So…did you do this?" I gestured to my high tech room.

"No. Rhys decorated it." Finn didn't look that interested in any of the expensive gear I had lying about, so that made sense. "The clothes were all Willa, I believe. You'll meet her later on."

"Rhys isn't my brother?" I asked again. I couldn't figure out how he fit into all of this. We had only met briefly, but he had seemed nice and normal.

"No. He's mänsklig," Finn answered, as if I would understand.

"What does that mean?" I furrowed my brow at him.

"It means he's not your brother," Finn replied glibly and made a step towards the door. "Is there anything you need before I go?"

His abrupt decision to go made me disappointed, especially when I felt so isolated and confused, but I had no reason to keep him. Still hugging myself tightly, I shook my head and sat back on the bed. Instead of leaving, Finn paused and looked back at me.

"Are you going to be alright with all of this?" Finn asked, looking at me very seriously.

"I don't know," I admitted. "This wasn't at all what I had expected." It was far grander and far worse than anything I had envisioned. "I just… I feel like I'm in the *Princess Diaries*, if Julie

Andrews had been a thief."

"Mmm," Finn murmured knowingly and walked back over towards me. He sat on the bed and crossed his arms over his chest. "I know this way of life is a hard concept for some."

"They're grifters, Finn." I swallowed hard. "That's all they are. I'm just a means to swindling money out of rich people. Joke's on her, though. My family's not that rich."

"I can assure you that you are much more than that to her, much more," Finn told me, looking at me intently. "Elora is a complicated woman, and showing emotion doesn't come easy for her. But she is a good woman. Regardless of whether you have money or not, you will have a place here."

"Do you know how much money they have?" I asked.

"Yes," Finn said almost hesitantly. "Elora had me checking your finances while I tracked you."

"How much?" I asked.

"Do you want to know your trust and what you stand to inherit, or your guardian and brother's total wealth?" Finn had gone expressionless. "Do you want net worth? Liquid assets? Are you including real estate, like the house they still own in the Hamptons? Dollar amount?"

"I don't really care," I shook my head. "I was just... Elora was convinced that we really did have a lot of money, and I was just curious."

"Yes. You really do have a lot of money," Finn said. "More than

119

even Elora had originally thought." I nodded and looked at my feet. "You lived well below your means."

"I think Maggie thought it would be better for me, and Matt and I never really cared that much about money." I kept staring at my feet, and then finally I looked up at Finn. "They would give me anything. They would give me all of it if I asked. But I'm never taking any money from them, not for myself and certainly not for Elora. Make sure you tell her that when you go back to her."

I had expected him to protest in some way, but Finn surprised me. His lips curled into the edge of a smile, and if anything, he looked almost proud of me. I was condemning their way of life, so I had thought he would defend it, but he approved of it.

"I will," he promised with small smile. "But right now, you should shower. You'll feel better after."

Finn helped me settle into my room. My closet was massive and over-stocked, but he knew exactly where my pajamas were. He taught me how to close the blinds for my windows, which were run by remote control, and how to turn on my overly complicated shower.

Once he left, I sat on the edge of the tub and tried not to let this all get to me. I was starting to think that Matt and Maggie might have been the only people that loved me for me, and now I was supposed to steal from them. Even if it wasn't really stealing. I knew they would freely give me anything I asked for, and that hurt worse.

9. Homesick

When I came out of my shower, wrapped in a fluffy bathrobe, I was surprised to find Rhys sitting on my bed. He had my iPod, the one that had come with the room, and he was scrolling through it. I cleared my throat loudly, since he apparently hadn't heard me exit the bathroom.

"Oh, hey!" Rhys set aside the iPod and got to his feet, grinning at me in a way that made his eyes sparkle. "Sorry. I didn't mean to interrupt you. I just wanted to see how you were doing, how you liked it here."

"I don't know." My hair had to be terrible mess, and I ran a finger through my wet tangles. "It's too soon to tell yet."

"You like the stuff?" Rhys asked, gesturing around the room. "I picked out everything that I liked, which I know sounds kind of vain. I asked for some input from Rhiannon, because she's a girl, but it's still so hard to pick out stuff for someone you've never met."

"No, it all looks really good. You did a good job." I rubbed my eyes and yawned.

"Oh sorry. You're probably exhausted." Rhys stood up. "Sorry. I just got done with school, and I didn't have a chance to talk to you earlier. But… yeah. I'll leave you be."

"Wait. You just got done with school?" I furrowed my brow, trying to understand. "Does that mean you're a tracker?"

"No." It was his turn to look confused. "I'm mänks." When he saw the perplexed look on my face, he corrected himself. "Sorry. It's just short for mänsklig."

"What the hell does that mean?" I demanded, growing exasperated.

"They'll explain it to you later," Rhys shrugged. "Anyway, I should let you wake up. If I'm not in my room, I'll be downstairs, getting some food."

"Are you happy here?" I blurted out before I could think about how rude that sounded. His eyes met mine, just for a second, revealing something more than that, but then he quickly dropped them.

"Why wouldn't I be happy?" Rhys asked wryly. He ran his fingers along my silk sheets, staring at the bedspread intently. "I have everything a kid could want. Video games, cars, toys, money, clothes, servants…" He trailed off, but then a slow smile returned to his face and he looked up at me. "And now I have a Princess living across the hall from me. I'm ecstatic."

"I'm not really a Princess," I shook my head and tucked my hair behind my ears. "Not in the real sense of the word. I mean… I just got here."

"You look like a Princess to me." The way he smiled at me made me want to blush, so I looked down, unsure of what else to do.

"So what about you?" I kept my head down, but I raised my eyes up to meet his. The smile playing on my lips felt oddly flirtatious, but

122

I didn't mind it. "Are you some kind of Prince?"

"Hardly," Rhys laughed. He ran a hand through his sandy hair, looking rather sheepish. "I should probably let you finish getting dressed. The chef is off tonight, so supper is on me."

Rhys turned and walked down the hall, whistling a song I didn't recognize. I shut my door, wishing I could understand this all better. I was a Trylle Princess to a grifter empire, and I had a mänsklig living across the hall from me, whatever the hell that meant.

I lived in this amazing stunning house with these cold, indifferent people, and the price of admission was stealing from the only people that cared about me. Sure, Finn was here, but he had made it perfectly clear that his only interest in me was business.

I went through my closet, looking for something to wear. Most of the clothes seemed too fancy for me. Not that I had grown up wearing rags or anything. In fact, if my mother... er, Kim hadn't gone crazy and left, these would be exactly the kind of clothes I'd be expected to wear now. All high class fashion pieces. Eventually, I managed to dig up a simple skirt and shirt that resembled something I'd actually wear.

I was starving, so I decided to take Rhys up on his offer and head to the kitchen. The floors were cold tile under my feet, and strangely, I had yet so see any rugs or carpet in the entire house.

I had never been fond of the feel of carpet on my feet, or really the feel of anything on them. When I thought back to my closet, as large and full as it had been, there hadn't been any shoes. It must be a

Trylle thing, and that thought was oddly comforting. I was part of something.

The bottom of the stairs led directly into the entryway, but to the left, below the wing where I lived, was the living room. A fire place filled the partial wall separating it from an elegant dining room. The furniture appeared to be hand crafted wood and upholstered with white. In here, the floors were all smooth golden wood, and the colors were in earth tones. Everything was aimed towards the glass wall, forcing you to admire the view.

"Nice digs, right?" Rhys said, and I whirled around to find him standing behind me, smiling.

"Yeah." I looked around the room appreciatively. "Elora definitely has good taste."

"Yeah," Rhys shrugged. "You gotta be hungry, though. Come on. I'll whip you up something in the kitchen." He started walking out of the room, and I followed him. "You'll probably hate what I make, though. You're into all that health food junk like everybody else, right?"

"I don't know." I had never thought of myself as a health nut, but the things I preferred tended to be organic and vegan. "I like natural things, I guess."

He nodded knowingly as he led me past the ornate dining room into a massive kitchen. There were two professional grade stoves, two massive stainless-steel fridges, a gigantic island in the center, and more cupboards than they could possibly use. Rhys went over to the fridge and pulled out a bottle of Mountain Dew and a bottle of water.

"Water, right?" Rhys held it out to me, and I took it from him. "I'm really not the best cook, but you'll have to settle for my cooking. The chef is off today."

"How often do you have a chef?" I asked. In a place like this, they definitely had some kind of staff.

"Part-time." Rhys took a drink from his Mountain Dew, then set it on the island and went to the other fridge to start rooting around. "Just weekends, but that's because it's usually when we entertain. I don't know what Elora eats during the week, but I'm on a fend-for-yourself basis."

I leaned on the island, drinking my water. This kitchen reminded me of the one in our house in the Hamptons, the one Kim had attempted filicide in, but that one had been smaller. If she hadn't left, this is probably how I would've been raised. In fact, I'm sure this is how she had been brought up.

Maggie easily could've lived like this. A beautiful house somewhere with a nanny raising Matt and me. She could've had the best cars, and paid off every school that tried to expel me. As it was, she had never really fought any of my punishments because she thought they were fair and I needed to learn something.

Instead, she had made the choice that taking care of me herself was more important than spending money. She had made a choice that my own mother never would have.

"So you like shitake mushrooms, right?" Rhys was saying. He

125

had been pulling things out of the fridge, but I had been too lost in thought to notice. His arms were overflowing with vegetables.

"Uh, yeah, I love mushrooms." I straightened up and tried see what all he had, but for the most part, it looked like things I enjoyed.

"Excellent." Rhys grinned at me and dropped his armload of food into the kitchen sink. "I'm going to make you the best stir fry you've ever tasted."

He went about chopping things up, and I offered to help him, but he insisted that he could handle it. The whole time, he talked amicably about his new motorcycle he'd gotten last week. I tried to keep up with it, but all I ever knew about motorcycles were that they went fast and I liked it.

"What are you making in here?" Finn came into the kitchen, sounding vaguely disgusted.

His hair was damp from a recent shower, and he smelled like the grass after a rain, only sweeter. He walked past me without even a glance in my direction and went over to where Rhys had thrown everything into a wok on the stove.

"Stir fry!" Rhys proclaimed.

"Really?" Finn leaned over his shoulder and peered down at the ingredients in the pan. Rhys moved to the side a little so Finn could reach in and grab something out of it. He sniffed it, then popped it into his mouth. "Well, it's not terrible."

"Stop my beating heart!" Rhys put his hand over his heart and feigned astonishment. "Has my food passed the test of the hardest food critic in the land?"

"No. I just said it wasn't terrible." Finn shook his head at Rhys's dramatics and went to the fridge to get a bottle of water. "And I'm certain that Elora is a much harsher food critic than I'll ever be."

"That's probably true, but she's never let me cook for her," Rhys admitted, shaking the wok to stir up the vegetables more.

"You really shouldn't let him cook for you," Finn advised, looking at me for the first time. "He gave me food poisoning once."

"You cannot get food poisoning from an orange!" Rhys protested and looked back at him. "It's just not possible! And even if you can, I *handed* you the orange. I didn't even have a chance to contaminate it!"

"I don't know." Finn shrugged. A smile was creeping up, and I could tell he was amused by how much Rhys was getting worked up.

"You didn't even eat the part I touched! You peeled it and threw the skin away!" Rhys sounded exasperated. He wasn't paying attention to the wok as he struggled to convince us of his innocence, and a flame licked up from the food.

"Food's on fire," Finn nodded to the stove.

"Dammit!" Rhys got a glass of water and splashed it in the stir fry, and I was starting to question how good this was going to taste when he was done with it.

"See?" Finn looked at me, and I smiled. "Are you doing okay?"

"Yeah, I'm doing great," I nodded.

"Good." He stood next to me, looking as if he wanted to say

something but thought better of it. He just nodded and walked out of the kitchen.

When Rhys finished cooking, his food was only moderately edible, but I picked at it anyway. He pulled stools up to the island, explaining that he only ate in the dining room when it was absolutely required.

He soaked his food in some kind of sauce, but it didn't smell at all appetizing. He downed his Mountain Dew with fervor, but I just sipped at my water.

"So what do you think?" Rhys nodded at the plate of food I was trying to eat.

"It's pretty good," I lied. He had obviously worked hard on it, and his blue eyes showed how proud he was of it, so I couldn't let him down. To prove my point, I took a bite and smiled.

"Good. You guys are hard to cook for." Rhys took a mouthful of his own food. "I don't know how you can eat this plain, though."

"I don't know how you can eat it with sauce." I wrinkled my nose at the smell of it.

"To each his own, I guess," Rhys laughed lightly. When he looked down at his plate, his sandy hair fell into his eyes, and he brushed it away.

"So… you know Finn pretty well?" I asked carefully, stabbing my fork into a mushroom.

Their banter earlier had left me curious. Finn seemed to genuinely enjoy Rhys, even if he didn't approve of his cooking, and I had never seen Finn enjoy anybody. Patrick, he had kinda liked, but I think that had been more of a means of getting closer to me. He openly looked down on Matt, and while he respected and obeyed Elora, I couldn't tell what his feelings were for her.

"I guess." Rhys shrugged like he hadn't really thought about it. "He's just around a lot."

"Like how often?" I pressed as casually as I could.

"I don't know." He took a bite and thought for a minute. "It's hard to say. Storks move around a lot."

"Storks?"

"Yeah, trackers," Rhys smiled sheepishly. "You know how you tell little kids that a stork brings the babies? Well, trackers bring the babies here. So we call them storks. Not to their faces, though."

"I see." I wondered what kind of nickname they had for people like me, but I didn't think that now was the best time to ask. "So they move around a lot?"

"Well, yeah. They're gone tracking a lot, and Finn is in pretty high demand because he's so good at it," Rhys explained. "And then when they come back, a lot of them stay with some of the more prestigious families. Finn's been here off and on for like the past five years or so. But when he's not here, somebody else usually is."

"So he's like a bodyguard?"

"Yeah, something like that," Rhys nodded.

"But what do they need bodyguards for?" I thought back to the rod iron gate and security guards that had allowed our entrance into

Förening in the first place.

When I had looked around the entryway, I remembered seeing a fancy alarm system by the front door. This all seemed like an awful lot of trouble to go to for a small community hidden in the bluffs. I wondered if this was all for the Vittra, but I didn't want to ask.

"She's the Queen. It's just standard procedure," Rhys answered evasively, and he purposely stared down at his plate. He tried to erase his anxiety before I noticed and forced a smile at me. "So how does it feel being a Princess?"

"Honestly? Not as awesome as I thought it would be," I said, and he laughed heartily at that.

Rhys kinda straightened up the kitchen after we finished eating, but he explained the maid would be in tomorrow to take care of the rest of it. He gave me a brief tour of the house, showing me all the ridiculous antiquities that had been passed down from generation to generation.

One room only held pictures of previous Kings and Queens. When I asked where a picture of my father was, Rhys just shook his head and said he didn't know anything about it.

Eventually, we parted ways. He cited some homework he had to get done, and he had to get to bed because he had school in the morning.

I wandered around the house a bit more, but I never saw either Finn or Elora. I played around with the stuff in my room, but I quickly tired of it. Feeling restless and bored, I tried to get some sleep, but I had slept too late in the afternoon.

I felt incredibly homesick. I longed for the familiar comfort of my regular sized house with all my ordinary things. If I were at home, Matt would be sitting in the living room, reading a book under the glow of the lamp light.

Right now, he was probably sitting in the kitchen, staring at the phone, or driving around. He had probably tracked down Patrick and threatened injury on him. Maggie was probably crying her eyes out, and I know Matt blamed himself for it.

My actual mother was somewhere in this house, or I assumed she was, anyway. She had abandoned me with a family that she knew nothing about except that they were rich, and she knew there was a risk that I could be killed. It happens sometimes. That's what she said. When I came back, after all these years away from me, she hadn't hugged me, or even been that happy to see me.

Everything felt way too big in this house. With all this vast space between everything, it felt like I was trapped on an island. I had thought that's what I had wanted. To be my very own island, but here I was, and I felt nothing but isolated and confused.

I was sure that people weren't telling me things. Every time I asked something, there were only half-answers and vague responses before they quickly changed the subject. For being set to inherit a kingdom of sorts, I was pretty low on the information rung.

10. Precognition

After sleeping fitfully, I got up and got ready for the day. I wandered around the house, but not intentionally. I had been trying to get to the kitchen, but I took a wrong turn somewhere and got lost. Rhys had given me some explanation of things the day before, but not enough apparently.

The palace was divided into two massive wings, separated by the grand entryway. All of the official business took place in the South wing, where there were meeting rooms, a ball room, a massive dining hall, offices, the throne room, as well as staff quarters and the Queen's bedroom.

The North wing had the more casual rooms in the house, like my room, guest bedrooms, a more casual living room, the kitchen, and the sitting parlor.

I stayed in the North wing, opening doors and investigating. As far as I could tell, this place had almost as many guest rooms as a Holiday Inn, and they were much fancier too. I eventually found Elora's drawing parlor, but she wasn't there, so it didn't help me any.

I moved on and tried to open the door across the hall from her, but it wouldn't budge. So far, this was the only door I'd found that had been locked, and I found it strange. Especially in this wing. I suppose in the North wing, locking up official business would make sense.

Fortunately, I knew a thing or two about lock-picking. In attempts to keep from being expelled, I had broken into school offices and stolen papers. I don't recommend it, and in the end, it was usually ineffective.

I pulled a bobby pin from my hair and looked around. I didn't see anyone, the same way I hadn't seen anyone all day, and I set about breaking in. After a few unsuccessful twists in the lock, I felt something give, and I turned the knob.

The door pushed open slowly, and I peeked in, half-expecting to find the Royal Bathroom or something. When nobody screamed at me to get away, I pushed the door open wider and stepped inside. Unlike the other rooms, this one was completely dark.

Feeling along the wall, I finally found the light switch and flicked it on. The room reminded me of a large storeroom. It had no windows, and the walls were a dark brown. With a simple light in the ceiling, it held none of the grandeur the rest of the house had, and it had no furniture.

But it was filled to the brim with paintings. Not hanging on the wall. Just stacked and piled around in every available space. At first I assumed they must be leftovers from the King and Queen room, but from what I could see, none of them were portraits.

I picked up the one nearest to me, and it was lovely picture of a newborn baby, wrapped in a blue blanket. I set it aside and picked up another, which appeared to be Elora, looking much younger and even more beautiful, dressed in a gorgeous white gown. Despite the beauty of the picture, her eyes looked sad and remorseful.

Holding the picture at arm's length so I could get a better look at it, I realized something. It had the same brush strokes, the same technique as the painting of the baby. I picked up another picture to compare, and it was the same too.

These were all painted by the same artist.

I thought back to the drawing room and the painting I had seen Elora working on. Something with dark smoke and chandeliers. I couldn't be certain, but I would say these were hers. She had a room overflowing with paintings, just shoved aside and locked away. It didn't make any sense.

I sifted through a few more of the paintings, growing even more bewildered, and then I saw one that stopped my heart cold. When I picked it up, I wasn't surprised to see my hands were shaking.

It showed me, looking about the same as I was now, except dressed nicer. I wore a beautiful, flowing white gown, but there was a tear in the side of the dress, revealing a thin line of red blood. My hair had been pulled back, but it was starting to come loose, letting wild strands fall free.

In the painting, I laid on my belly on a marble balcony. The ground around me was covered in pieces of glass that shimmered like diamonds, but I didn't seem to notice. My hand outstretched past the balcony, reaching into a dark oblivion.

But my face is what struck me the most. I looked absolutely horrified.

Once I got past that, I realized something more disturbing. This picture looked exactly like me. And I'd only been home for a day. There was no way Elora could've painted something this detailed within 24-hours of meeting me.

But how could she paint me with such accuracy if we'd never met?

"I should've known you'd be snooping," Finn said from behind me, startling me so much I dropped the painting.

"I-I got lost," I stammered and turned to look at him standing in the doorway.

"In a locked room?" He raised an eyebrow and crossed his arms over his chest.

"No, I-" I started to formulate some kind of lame excuse, but decided against it. I picked up the picture, the one of me reaching for nothing, and held it up for him to see. "What's this?"

"It appears to be a painting, and if you hadn't gathered by the locked door, it's also none of your business," Finn said, but he didn't sound that upset. At least not as upset as Elora would be if she found out I was in here, I'm sure.

"This is me." I tapped the picture.

"Maybe," he shook his head, as if he wasn't convinced.

"No, I wasn't asking. This is me," I insisted. "What am I doing?"

"I haven't the faintest idea," Finn sighed. "I didn't paint it."

"Did Elora?" I asked, and when he didn't say anything, I took that as my answer. "Why would she paint this? *How* did she paint this? We'd never met before yesterday."

"She gave birth to you. You'd met before," Finn replied dryly.

"Yeah, when I was a baby. That doesn't count." I waved him off, but I wouldn't be deterred. "Why would she paint this? Or any of these?"

"In all your myriad of questions about the manner of this room, do you stop to ask yourself *why* this room is locked?" Finn gave me a hard look. "That Elora might not want people looking at these?"

"Yeah, it did." I looked back down at the painting, ignoring him. "But this is me. I have a right to know."

"That's not how it works. You don't have the right to other people's thoughts just because they might include you," he said. "Just the same as I don't have the right to yours just because they're about me."

"You presume that I think of you." I fought the growing blush on my cheeks and shook my head, trying to chase his misdirection away. "Just tell me what's going on."

"Fine. But get out of there before Elora finds you." He moved back from the doorway, making room for me to step out.

I had to climb over all the paintings I had disturbed, but he didn't tell me to put them back, which is good because I didn't think I could. The room had no method, and paintings were placed haphazardly.

Once I made my escape, Finn shut the door, making certain it was locked properly.

"So?" I asked, looking at him expectantly. He had his back to me, testing the door again to be sure it wouldn't budge.

"So, that's Elora's private room." He turned to look at me and pointed at the door. "Do not go in there. Do not touch her private things."

"Sorry." I stared sheepishly at my feet, feeling guilt and shame for being scolded like a child. "I don't know what's so bad about them. Why does she paint them if she's gonna hide them away?"

"Her painting freaked you out, didn't it?" Finn asked pointedly.

"Well, yeah, but only cause-"

"Exactly." He started walking down the hall, so I went after him. "She paints them because she has to."

"What do you mean?" I crinkled my brow. "Like an artist's urge take's hold of her?" I thought about it more, and it made even less sense. "Elora doesn't seem like an artist type."

"She's not, really," Finn sighed. "She has precognition."

"What? Like she can see the future?" I asked dubiously.

"Kind of." He wagged his head, like that wasn't right. "She can't see it. She can only *paint* it."

"Wait." I stopped short, and he walked a few more steps before stopping to look back at me. "You're telling me all those paintings were of the future?"

"At the time they were painted, yes." Finn nodded. "Some of them are old, and they've already happened."

"But that means the picture of me, that's in the future!" I

pointed back at the room. "What does that mean? What am I doing?"

"I don't know," he shrugged, as if he hadn't thought of it. "Elora doesn't know."

"How can she not know?" I scoffed. "She painted it."

"Yes, and all she knows is what she painted," Finn explained slowly. "She doesn't see anything. She picks up the brush, and it just... comes out. Or at least that's my understanding of the process."

"But why would she just randomly paint me looking so scared?"

"It's just how it is," he said, sounding sad. Breathing deeply, he started walking away again. "And that's why the room is locked."

"What do you mean?" I chased after him.

"People want to know more about what she's painted, but she doesn't have the answers," Finn said. "Or they want her to paint a particular spot in the future, and she can't. She has no control over what she sees."

"What's the point of it then?" I asked, incredulous.

"She thinks it's a punishment."

"For what?" I asked.

"Everybody has something to be punished for," he shook his head vaguely.

"So... she has no idea what will happen to me? Or how to prevent it?" I asked.

"No."

"That's horrible," I said, more to myself than him. "That's even worse than not knowing anything."

"Precisely." Finn looked at me and slowed down, then stopped completely.

"Will I be able to do that? Have precognitive painting?" I asked.

"Maybe, maybe not." His eyes searched me, in that soft way they did sometimes, and if I hadn't been worrying about my impending doom, I would've felt my stomach flutter.

"Do you know what my abilities will be?" I asked.

"No. Only time will tell for sure." He looked away, staring off at nothing. "Based on your parentage, they'll be very strong."

"When will I know for sure?"

"Later. After your training starts, and maybe when you get a bit older," Finn smiled thinly at me. "You have much to look forward to."

"Like what?"

"Like everything," he smiled more genuinely, and turned to walk again. "Come on. I want to show you something."

11. Secret Garden

Finn led me through the house, past the kitchen down a hall I didn't even know existed. We went out the side door onto a narrow, gravel trail lined with tall hedges. It curved around the house, leading us down the bluffs before it opened into a beautiful garden. The house and balcony hung over part of it, leaving half of it in shadows, but the rest was bathed in the warm bright glow of the sun.

Brick walls covered in thick, flowered vines kept the garden blocked off from the rest of the world. Apple, pear, and plum trees blossomed all over the garden, making it more of an orchard than a garden. Flowers of pink and purple and blue sprung out in small beds, and mossy greens like creeping Charlie grew in patches along the ground.

It was on a hillside, the whole thing tilted down, and as we walked down the trail, I slipped a bit, and Finn took my hand to steady me. My skin flushed warmly, but the second I had caught my balance, he let go of my hand, but I refused to let it dampen my mood.

"How is this possible?" I asked as butterflies and birds flitted about the trees. "None of these things are in season. They shouldn't be flowering."

"They always flower, even in winter," Finn said, as if that made more sense.

141

"How?" I repeated.

"Magic," he smiled and walked ahead.

I looked up, at the house towering above us. From where I stood, I couldn't see any of the windows. The garden had been built in the perfect spot so it wasn't visible from the house, leaving it hidden amongst the trees. It was a secret garden.

Finn went ahead of me, and I hurried to catch up to him. The sounds of the wind in the trees and river flowing echoed through the bluffs, but over that I heard laughter. I walked around a hedge and saw a stream that inexplicably flowed into a small waterfall.

I found the source of the laughter on two curved stone benches poised around it.

Rhys lay on his back on one bench, laughing and looking up at the sky, and Finn stood next to him, admiring the sparkling pond. A girl looking a little bit older than me sat on the other bench, a Mountain Dew bottle in her hand. Her hair was a shiny red, her eyes sparkled green, and she had a nervous smile. When she saw me, she stood up and paled a little.

"You got here just in time, Wendy," Rhys smirked, sitting up. "We were having a show. Rhiannon was just about to burp the alphabet!"

"Oh my gosh, Rhys, I was not!" The girl protested, her cheeks flushing with embarrassment. "I just drank the Mountain Dew too fast and I said excuse me!" Rhys laughed again, and she looked apologetically at me. "I'm sorry. Rhys can be such an idiot

142

sometimes. I wanted to make a better first impression than this."

"You're doing okay so far." I wasn't used to the idea of anybody trying to impress me ever, and she definitely had a certain likable quality to her.

"Anyway, Wendy, this is Rhiannon, the girl next door," Rhys gestured between the two of us. "Rhiannon, this is Wendy, future ruler of everything around you."

"Hi, nice to meet you." She set down her pop and came over to me so she could shake my hand. "I've heard so much about you."

"Oh yeah? Like what?" I asked. Rhiannon floundered helplessly for a minute, looking to Rhys for help, but he just laughed. "It's okay. I was just kidding."

"Oh. Sorry." She flashed an embarrassed smile.

"Why don't you come have a seat, Rhiannon, and relax for a bit?" Rhys patted the seat next to him, trying to settle her discomfort. She felt awkward because of me, and I couldn't wrap my head around that concept.

"Is this new?" Finn asked Rhys and pointed to the pond.

"Uh, yeah," Rhys nodded. "I think Elora had it put in while you were gone. She's getting everything all fancied up, cause of everything that's coming up."

"Mmm," Finn said noncommittally.

I went over to inspect the pond and waterfall myself. The waterfall should've drained the pond, since it had no other water flowing into it. It sparkled brightly under the sun, but it shouldn't even be possible. But then again, none of this should be possible.

Rhys continued to tease Rhiannon about everything, and she kept blushing and making apologies for him. Their relationship resembled a normal healthy sibling relationship, and I had to push that thought away before I had a chance to think of Matt.

I sat down on the bench across from them, and Finn took a seat next to me. Rhys tended to dominate the conversation, with Rhiannon interjecting when he said things that were categorically untrue or apologizing when she thought he was being rude. He never was, though. He was funny and lively and kept things from ever feeling awkward.

Occasionally, Finn would look over at me and make quiet comments when Rhys and Rhiannon were otherwise engaged in some kind of debate. Every time he did, I felt his knee brush against mine.

At first, I assumed it was a simple accident because of our close proximity, but he had actually tilted himself towards me, leaning in closer. It was a subtle move, one that Rhys and Rhiannon probably wouldn't catch, but I definitely had.

"You are such a pest!" Rhiannon grumbled playfully after Rhys had flicked an unwanted flower at her. She twirled it in her hands, admiring the beauty of it. "You know you're not even supposed to pick these flowers. Elora will kill you if she finds out."

"So what do you think?" Finn asked me, his voice low. I leaned towards him so I could hear him better, and his dark eyes met mine.

"It's really lovely," I smiled, gesturing to the garden around us, but I couldn't look away from him.

"I wanted to show you that it's not all cold and intimidating," Finn explained. "I wanted you to see something warm and beautiful." A small smile played on his lips. "Although, when you're not around, it's not quite as nice here."

"You think so?" I asked, trying to make my voice sound sexier somehow, but I completely failed. Finn smiled wider, and my heart nearly hammered out of my chest.

"Sorry for interrupting your play time," Elora spoke from behind us. Her voice wasn't that loud, but somehow it seemed to echo through everything.

Rhys and Rhiannon immediately stopped their fighting, both of them sitting rigidly and staring down at the pond. Finn moved away from me, but he turned around to face Elora, making that look like it had been his intention. The way she looked at me made me feel guilty, even though I was pretty sure I hadn't done anything wrong.

"You weren't interrupting anything," Finn assured her, but I sensed nervousness below his calm words. "Were you planning to join us?"

"No, that'll be quite all right." Elora surveyed the garden with distaste. "I needed to speak with you."

"Would you like us to be excused?" Rhys offered, and Rhiannon already started standing up.

"That won't be necessary." Elora held up her hand, and

Rhiannon blushed as she sat back down. "We will be having guests for dinner tomorrow." Her eyes went back to Rhys and Rhiannon, and she seemed to cower under Elora's gaze. "I trust that you two will find a way to make yourselves useful."

"When they come over here, I'll go over to Rhiannon's," Rhys suggested cheerily. She nodded at him, showing that his response was sufficient.

"As for you, you will be joining us." Elora smiled at me, but it couldn't mask the unease behind it. "They are very good friends of our family, and I expect you to make a good impression with them." She gave Finn that intense look, staring at him so long I felt uncomfortable, and he nodded understanding. "Finn will be in charge of preparing you for the dinner."

"Okay," I nodded, figuring that I had better say something.

"That is all. Carry on." Elora turned and walked away, her skirt flowing behind her, but nobody said anything until she was long gone.

Finn sighed, and Rhiannon almost shivered with relief. She was even more terrified of Elora than I was, and I wondered what Elora had done to make her so deserving of that fear. Only Rhys seemed to shake it off as soon as she had left.

"I don't know how you can stand that creepy mind speak thing she does with you, Finn." Rhys shook his head. "I would freak out if she were in my head."

"Why? There's nothing in your head for her to get to," Finn

146

commented dryly as he stood up, and Rhiannon giggled nervously.

"What did she say to you, anyway?" Rhys pressed, looking up at him. Finn dusted of his pants, ridding them of some dirt and leaves from the bench, but he didn't respond. "Finn? What'd she say?"

"It's nothing to concern yourself with," Finn admonished him quietly, then turned to me. "Are you ready?"

"For what?" I asked dumbly.

"We have a lot to go over before tomorrow night." He glanced warily at the house, then back at me. "Come on. We better get started."

As we walked back to the house, I realized that whenever Elora left, I was able to breathe again. I didn't really feel it when I was with her, but it was as if she took all the oxygen from the room. Breathing deeply, I ran my hand up and down my arm to stifle the chill that ran over me.

"Are you holding up alright?" Finn asked, noticing my unease.

"Yeah, I'm great." I tucked some of my curls behind my ears, but mostly, I was just happy that I was still walking. "So... what's going on with you and Elora?"

"What do you mean?" Finn looked at me from the corner of his eye.

"I don't know." I shrugged, thinking of what Rhys had said after she left. "It just seems like she looks at you intently a lot, and like you understand exactly what she means." As soon as it came out of my mouth, it dawned on me. "That's one of her abilities, isn't it? Talking inside your head? Kind of like what I can do, but less manipulative. Cause she's just telling you what to do."

"Not even telling me what to do. She's just talking," Finn corrected me.

"Why doesn't she talk to me like that?" I asked.

"She wasn't sure if you'd be receptive. If you're not accustomed to it, hearing another person's voice in your head can be unsettling," Finn explained. "And she didn't really need to."

"But she needed to with you?" I slowed down, and he matched my pace. "She was talking to you privately about me, wasn't she?" Finn paused, and I could see that he was considering lying to me.

"Some of it, yes," Finn admitted.

"Can she read minds?" I felt slightly horrified at that thought.

"No. Very few can." When he looked over at me, he smiled crookedly. "Your secrets are safe, Wendy."

We went into the dining room, and Finn set about preparing me for dinner. As it turned out, I wasn't completely stunted socially and had a basic understanding of manners. What Finn said amounted to common sense things, like always say please and thank you, but he encouraged me to keep my mouth shut whenever possible.

I think his task had been less about preparing me for the dinner and more about keeping me in line. The secret things Elora had been telling him had just been warning him to baby-sit me, or else.

Dinner was at eight, and company was arriving at seven. About an hour or so before, Rhys had popped in to wish me good luck and let me know he was heading over to Rhiannon's, in case anybody cared. Finn came in shortly after I had gotten out of the shower, looking even sharper than usual.

He was clean shaven for the first time since he'd stopped going to school, and he wore a black button-up shirt with a narrow white tie and black pants with a black blazer over it. It should've been too much with all that black, but he managed to pull it off, all the while looking incredibly sexy.

I had on only my bathrobe, and I wondered why nobody thought it was inappropriate for boys to barge in when I wasn't dressed. At least I was doing something semi-sexy; sitting on the edge of my bed putting lotion on my legs. I did it every time I showered, but since Finn was in the room, I tried to play it off as being sensual when it really wasn't.

Not that Finn had even noticed. He knocked once, opened my bedroom door, and only gave me a fleeting glance as he headed straight to my closet. I sighed in frustration and hurriedly rubbed the lotion in while Finn busied himself. He flicked on the light and rummaged through my clothes.

"I don't think I have anything in your size!" I said and leaned farther on my bed, trying to see what he was doing in there.

"Funny," he muttered absently.

"What are you doing in there?" I asked, watching him, but he didn't even look at me.

"You are a Princess, and you need to dress like one." He leafed through my dresses and pulled out a long, white sleeveless gown. It was gorgeous and much too fancy for me, and when he came out of the closet, he handed it to me. "I think this might work. Try it on."

"Isn't everything in my closet suitable?" I tossed the dress on the bed next to me and turned to look at him.

"Yes, but different things are better for different occasions." He came over to the bed to smooth out the dress, making sure it didn't have any wrinkles or creases. "This is a very important dinner, Wendy."

"Why? What makes this one so important?" I asked.

"The Stroms are very good friends of your mother's and the Kroners are very important people. They affect the future." Finn finished smoothing the dress and turned to me. "Why don't you continue getting ready?"

"How do they affect the future? What does that mean?" I pressed.

"That's a conversation for another day." Finn nodded towards the bathroom. "You need to hurry if you're going to be ready in time for dinner."

"Fine," I sighed, getting up off the bed.

"Wear your hair down," Finn commanded. My hair was wet so it was lying nicely down, but I knew that as soon as it dried, it would turn into a wild thicket of curls.

"I can't. My hair is impossible." I ran my fingers through my dark hair.

"We all have difficult hair. Even Elora and I. It's the curse of being Trylle," Finn said. "It's something you must learn to manage."

"Your hair is nothing like mine," I said dourly. His hair was short and obviously had some product in it, but it looked smooth, straight, and obedient.

"It most certainly is," Finn replied.

I meant to prove him wrong, so instinctively, I reached out and touched his hair, running my fingers shallowly through the hair past his temples. Other than being stiff with product, it felt like my hair.

It wasn't until I had done it that I realized that there was something inherently intimate about running my fingers through another person's hair. I had been looking at his hair, but then I met his dark eyes and realized exactly how close I was to him.

Since I was short, I had stood on my tiptoes, leaning up to him as if I were about to kiss him. Somewhere in the back of my mind, I thought that would be a very good course of action right about now.

"Satisfied?" Finn asked, and I retracted my hand and took a step back. "There should be hair products in your bathroom. Experiment."

I nodded my compliance, still feeling too flustered to speak. Finn was unnaturally calm, and at times like that, I really hated it. I barely even remembered to breathe until I was in my bathroom.

Being that near to him made me forget everything but his dark eyes, the heat from his skin, his wonderful scent, the feel of his hair beneath my fingers, the smooth curve of his lips…

I shook my head, clearing it of any thoughts of him. That had to be the end of that.

I had a dinner tonight to worry about, and somehow, I had to do something with my hair. I tried to remember what Maggie had used in my hair before I went to the dance with Patrick, but that felt like a lifetime ago.

Thankfully, my hair had magically decided to behave itself tonight, making the whole process go easier. Finn seemed to think my hair looked better down, so I left the length of it hanging in the back and pulled the sides back with clips.

The dress turned out to be trickier than my hair. It had one of those stupid zippers that refused to move higher than my lower back, and I couldn't win. After struggling with it so long my fingers hurt, I had to get help.

Tentatively, I pushed open the bathroom door. Finn had been looking out the window, at the sun setting on the bluffs, and when he turned, his eyes rested on me for almost a minute.

"You look like a Princess," Finn smiled crookedly at me.

"I need help with the zipper," I said meekly, gesturing to the open slit down my back.

He walked over, and I almost felt relieved when I turned my back to him. The way he looked at me made my stomach swirl with nervous butterflies. One of his hands pressed warmly on my bare shoulder to steady the fabric as he zipped me up, and my skin shivered involuntarily.

When he had finished, I went over to the mirror to investigate for myself. Even I had to admit that I looked lovely. With the white dress and the diamond necklace, I almost looked too lavish. Maybe it was too much for just a dinner.

"I look like I'm getting married," I commented and glanced back at Finn. "Do you think I should change?"

"No, it's perfect." He looked pensively at me, and if I didn't know better, I'd say he looked almost sad. The doorbell chimed loudly, and Finn nodded. "The guests have arrived. We should greet them."

12. Introductions

We walked down the hall together, but at the top of the steps, Finn deliberately fell a few steps behind me. Elora and the Kroners were standing in the alcove as I descended the steps, and they all turned to look up at me. It was the first grand entrance I had ever made in my life, and there was something wonderful about it.

The Kroners consisted of a stunningly beautiful woman in a floor-length dark green dress, an attractive man in a dark suit, and an attractive boy about my age. Even Elora looked more extravagant than usual. Her dress had more detailing and her jewelry was more pronounced.

I could feel them appraising me as I walked towards them, so I was careful to keep my steps as smooth and elegant as possible.

"This is my daughter, the Princess." Elora smiled in a way that almost looked loving and held her hand out to me. "Princess, these are the Kroners. Aurora, Noah, and Tove."

I smiled politely and did a small curtsy. Immediately after, I realized that they were probably the ones that should be curtsying to me, but they all smiled pleasantly at me.

"It's such a pleasure to meet you," Aurora had a syrupy tone to her words that I wasn't sure if I trusted or not. A few perfectly placed curls fell from her dark hair wrapped up on her head. Her chestnut eyes were large and stunning.

155

Her husband, Noah, did a very small bow towards me, as did her son, Tove. Both Noah and Aurora looked appropriately respectful towards Elora and me, but Tove looked vaguely bored. His mossy green eyes met mine very briefly, then looked away, as if he were uncomfortable looking at me.

Elora ushered us into the sitting parlor to talk until supper. The conversation was overly polite and banal, but I suspected there were undercurrents that I wasn't really picking up. Elora and Aurora did most of the talking, with Noah adding very little. Tove said nothing at all, preferring to look anywhere but directly at anyone.

Finn was more in the background, speaking only when spoken to. He was very poised and polite, but from the way Aurora looked at him with disdain, I gathered she didn't approve of his presence.

The Stroms were fashionably late, as Finn had predicted they would be. He'd debriefed me extensively on both them and the Kroners earlier in the day, but he was much more familiar with the Stroms and talked of them in much affectionate tones.

Finn had been a tracker for Willa, so he knew her and her father, Garrett, quite well. Garret's wife (Willa's mother) had died some years earlier. Finn claimed that Garrett was easy-going, but that Willa was a tad high-strung. She was twenty-one, and prior to living in Förening, she'd been privileged to the point of excess.

When the doorbell rang, interrupting the irritatingly dull conversation between Aurora and my mother, Finn immediately excused himself to answer the door and returned with Garrett and

Willa in tow.

Garrett was a rather handsome man in his mid-forties. His hair was dark and disheveled, making me feel better about my own imperfect hair. When he shook my hand with a warm smile, he immediately put me at ease.

Willa, on the other hand, had that snobby look that was always simultaneously bored and pissed off. She was a waif of a girl with light-brown waves that fell neatly on her back, and she wore an anklet covered in diamonds. When she shook my hand, I could tell that her smile was an attempt at sincere, making me hate her a little less.

Once they arrived, we adjourned to the dining room for supper. Willa seemed to try to engage Tove in conversation as we walked into the other room, but he remained completely silent.

Finn pulled my chair out for me before I sat down, and I enjoyed it since I couldn't remember a single time that anyone had done that for me before. Garrett sat in the chair nearest to Elora, Willa took a seat next to him, and I sat at the other head of the table, with Finn and Tove flanking me on either side.

Finn waited until everyone was sitting to take a seat himself, and this would be the standard for the evening. As long as at least one person was standing, so would Finn. He was always the first to his feet, and even though the chef and a butler-type fellow were on staff tonight, Finn would offer to get anyone anything they needed.

The dinner dragged on much more sorely than I had imagined it could. Since I wore white, I barely ate out of fear of spilling anything on my dress. I had never felt so judged in my entire life. I could feel Aurora and Elora waiting for me to screw up so they could pounce, but I wasn't sure how either of them would benefit from my failure.

I could tell that on several occasions, Garrett tried to lighten the mood, but nobody allowed it. Aurora and Elora dominated the conversation, and everyone else rarely said anything.

Tove stirred his soup a lot, and I became mildly hypnotized by it. He'd let go of his spoon, but it kept swirling around the bowl, stirring the soup without any hand to guide it. I must have started to gape because I felt Finn gently kick me under the table, and I quickly dropped my eyes back to my own food.

"It is so nice to have you here," Garrett told me randomly, changing the entire topic of conversation. He smiled at me, and it seemed genuine. "How do you like the palace so far?"

"Oh, it is not a *palace*, Garrett," Elora laughed. It wasn't a real laugh, though. It was the kind of laugh rich people had whenever they talked about new money people. Aurora tittered right along with it, and that quieted Elora down somehow.

"You're right. It's better than a palace," Garrett said, and Elora smiled demurely.

"I like it. It's very nice." I tried to look happy, but I was afraid to elaborate more.

"Are you adjusting here alright?" Garrett asked.

"Yes, I think so," I said quietly. "I haven't been here that long,

158

though."

"It does take time." Garrett looked at Willa with affectionate concern. His easy smile returned quickly and he nodded at Finn. "But you've got Finn there to help you. He's an expert at helping the changelings acclimate."

"I'm not an expert at anything," Finn said quietly. "I just do my job the best I can."

"Have you had a designer to come over to make the dress yet?" Aurora asked Elora, taking a polite sip of her wine. It had been a minute since she'd last spoken, so it was time for her to take the conversation back over. "That dress the Princess has on is very lovely, but I can't imagine that was made specifically for her."

"No, it was not." Elora gave her a plastic smile and cast a very small but very distinct glare at my dress. Until just that second it had felt like the most beautiful thing I had ever worn. "The tailor is set to come over tomorrow."

"That is cutting it a bit short for Saturday, isn't it?" Aurora questioned, and I could see Elora bristling just below the surface of her perfect smile.

"Not at all," Elora explained with an overly soothing tone, almost as if she were talking to a small child or a Pomeranian. "I am using Fredrique Von Ellsin, the same one that designed Willa's gown. He works very quickly, and his gowns are always impeccable."

"My gown was divine," Willa interjected.

"Ah, yes," Aurora allowed herself to look impressed. "We have him on reserve for when our daughter comes home next spring. He's much harder to get then, since that is the busy season for when the children return."

There was something vaguely condescending in her voice, as if we had done something tacky by me arriving here when I did. Elora kept on smiling, letting Aurora to continue politely sticking barbs in everything she said.

"That is one major benefit at having the Princess come home in the fall," Aurora continued, her words only getting more patronizing as she spoke. "Everything will be so much easier to book. When Tove came home last season, it was so difficult to get everything just right. I suppose you'll have everything you want right on hand. That should make for a stunning ball."

Several things were setting off alarms in my head. First, they were talking about both me and Tove as if we weren't even there, although he didn't seem to notice or care about anything going on around him.

Secondly, they were talking about something going on Saturday that I apparently needed a specially designed dress for, and yet nobody had bothered to mention it to me. Then again, this shouldn't surprise me. Nobody told me anything.

"I haven't had the luxury of making plans a year in advance the way most people do, since the Princess came home most unexpectedly." Elora's sweet smile dripped with venom, and Aurora smiled back at her and pretended not to notice.

"I can certainly lend you a hand. I just did Tove's, and as I said, I'm already preparing for our daughter's," Aurora offered.

"That would be delightful." Elora took a long drink of her wine.

Dinner continued along that way. Elora and Aurora making conversation that tried to mask how much they detested each other. Noah didn't say much, but at least he managed not to look awkward or bored.

Willa and I ended up watching Tove quite a bit, but for entirely different reasons. She stared at him with unabashed lust, although I couldn't figure out what he'd done to deserve that, other than being attractive. I kept watching because I was certain he was moving things without touching them.

Unlike the Stroms, the Kroners didn't linger around after dinner. I assumed that was because Elora actually liked Garrett and Willa.

Elora, Finn, and I walked the Kroners to the door, with Finn coming along only to open the doors for them. When saying their goodbyes, Aurora and Noah bowed before us, making me feel quite ridiculous. There was absolutely no reason why anyone should bow to me.

To my astonishment, Tove gently took my hand in his, kissing it softly when he bowed. When he stood up, his eyes met mine, and very seriously he said, "I look forward to seeing you again, Princess."

"And I, you." I was so pleased that I had said something that sounded completely perfect for the moment that I smiled much too wide, I'm sure.

After they departed into the night, oxygen seemed to return to the house, and Elora let out an irritated sigh. Finn rested his forehead against the door for a moment before turning back around to face us. I felt much better knowing that everyone else had found the evening exhausting.

"Oh, that woman." Elora rubbed her temples and shook her head, then pointed at me. "*You*. You do not bow to anyone, ever. Especially not that woman. I know you thrilled her endlessly, and she's going to be telling everyone about the little dimwitted Princess who didn't know enough not to bow before a Marksinna." I looked at the floor, feeling any sense of pride vanish. "You don't even bow before me, is that clear?"

"Yes," I said.

"You are the Princess. *Nobody* is higher than you. Have you got that?" Elora snapped, and I nodded. "Then you need to start acting like it. You need to command the room! They came here to see you, to gauge your power, and you need to show them! They need to have confidence that you will be able to lead them all when I am gone!"

I kept my eyes locked on the floor, even though I knew that probably offended her, but I was afraid that I would cry if I looked at her yelling at me.

"You sit there like some beautiful, useless jewel, and that's exactly what she wants." She sighed disgustedly again. "Oh, and the way you gaped at that boy..."

After that, she abruptly stopped. She shook her head, as if she were too weary to continue, then turned and walked back to the sitting parlor. I swallowed back my feelings, and Finn gently touched my arm, smiling at me.

"You did just fine," he assured me quietly. "She's upset with Aurora Kroner, not you."

"It sure sounded like she was upset with me," I muttered under my breath.

"Don't let her get to you." He squeezed my arm, sending warming tingles through me, and I couldn't help but return his smile. "Come on. We need to get back to the guests."

In the sitting parlor, Garrett and Willa waited for us, but the entire atmosphere had changed to one of a more relaxed tone. Finn even loosened his tie. The outburst seemed to have calmed Elora completely, and she lounged on the chair next to Garrett. He seemed to capture a disproportionate amount of her attention, but I didn't mind.

A whole other side of Finn emerged. He sat next to me, his leg crossed over his knee, making charming small talk with them. He was still gracious and respectful, but he chatted easily. I bit my tongue, afraid to say the wrong thing, but he definitely entertained Garret and Willa, and even Elora looked pleased.

Garrett and Elora started talking politics, which I didn't really follow, and Finn became more engaged in the conversation. Elora had to appoint a new Chancellor in six months, but I didn't even know what that was, and I thought asking would only make me look foolish.

As the night progressed, Elora had to excuse herself because of a migraine. Garrett and Finn offered their condolences and help, but neither of them seemed that surprised or concerned. They continued with that whole Chancellor business again, and Willa had grown too bored. She said she needed fresh air and invited me to join her.

We went down to the far end of the hall to a small alcove of a room with nearly invisible glass doors. It led out to the balcony that ran from one corner of the house to the other, lined with a thick black railing up to my chest.

I froze, remembering the painting I had seen in Elora's room. It was this marble balcony I had been laying on, my hand outstretched at nothing, my face contorted in horror. I looked down at my dress, but it didn't feel right. This one was lovely, but the dress in the picture had shimmered. Broken glass had littered the ground also, and I didn't see any.

"Are you coming?" Willa glanced back at me.

"Uh, yeah," I nodded, and taking a deep breath, I followed her out.

Willa went over to the corner farthest away and leaned on the railing. Out here, the view was even more intimidating. The balcony literally hung over a hundred foot drop. Below us were only the tree tops of maples, oaks, and evergreens. The secret garden remained hidden out of sight.

Farther down, I could see the tops of houses, and way down at the bottom of the bluff, the turbulent river ran past us. A breeze blew over us, sending a cold chill down my bare arms, and Willa sighed.

"Oh knock it off!" Willa grumbled, and at first, I thought she was talking to me, confusing me.

She lifted her hand, waving her fingers lightly in the air, and almost instantly, her hair that had been blowing back in the breeze settled on her shoulders. The wind had died away.

"Did you do that?" I asked, trying not to sound as awed as I felt.

"Yeah. That's the only thing I can do. Lame, isn't it?" Willa complained and wrinkled her nose.

"No, actually, I think it's pretty cool," I admitted.

She controlled the wind! Wind was an unstoppable force, and she just wiggled her fingers, and it stopped. I thought it was magic.

"I kept hoping I'd get a *real* ability someday, but my mother only had command over the clouds, so at least I did better than that," Willa shrugged. "You'll see when your abilities start coming in. Everybody hopes for telekinesis or at least some persuasion, but most of us are stuck with basic use of the elements, if we're lucky. The abilities aren't what they used to be, I guess."

"Before you came here, did you know you were something?" I asked, looking back over my shoulder at her. She had her back on the railing, and she leaned back over it, letting her hair hang down towards the ground.

"Oh, yeah. I always knew I was better than everyone else." Her eyes fluttered close and she wagged her fingers again, stirring up a

165

light breeze to flow through her hair. "What about you?"

"Um… kind of." Different, yes. Better, not at all.

"You're younger than most of us are, though," Willa commented. "You're still in school, aren't you?"

"I was." Nobody had made any mention of school since I got here, and I had no idea what their intentions were for the remainder of my education.

"School sucks anyway." Willa stood up straight and looked at me solemnly. "So why did they get you early, anyway? Is it because of the Vittra?"

"What do you mean?" I asked nervously.

I knew what she meant, but I wanted to see what she knew of it. Nobody seemed that keen on talking about the Vittra, and Finn hadn't even mentioned their attack since I'd come here. Inside the compound, I assumed I was safe, but I didn't know if they still wanted me.

"I've just heard stories that the Vittra have been prowling around lately, trying to catch Trylle changelings," Willa said casually. "I figured you'd be a top priority cause you're the Princess, and that's kind of a big deal here."

She looked thoughtfully at her bare toes and mused, "I wonder if I'd be top priority. My dad's not a King or anything like that, but we are kind of royalty. What's lower than a Queen? Is that a Duchess or something?"

"I don't know," I shrugged. I knew nothing of monarchy and

titles, which was ironic considering that I was now integral to a monarchy.

"Yeah, I think I'm like that." Willa narrowed her eyes in concentration. "My official title is Marksinna, and my dad is a Markis. We're not the only ones, though. There are maybe six or seven other families in Förening alone with the same title. The Kroners were next in line for the crown if you didn't come back. They're real powerful, and that Tove is a real catch."

While he was attractive, nothing had impressed me about Tove other than his telekinesis. Still, it felt weird knowing that they were vying for my spot, and we had just eaten dinner with them.

"I don't have to worry that much about it, though." Willa yawned loudly. "Sorry. Boredom makes me sleepy. Maybe we should go inside."

It was getting cold, so I was happy to oblige. Willa lay on the couch as soon as we went back in and all but fell asleep, so Garrett excused himself shortly after. He went to say goodbye to Elora, and then helped Willa out to the car.

The butler had gone about cleaning everything else up, so Finn suggested that we head up to our respective rooms. The night had been surprisingly tiring, so I was eager to comply.

"What's going on?" I asked after the Stroms left. It was the first chance all evening I'd really been able to talk to him. "What is this ball or party or whatever that's happening on Saturday?"

"It's something like a debutante ball, except that boys go

through it too," Finn explained as we climbed the stairs.

Dully, I remembered how grand I had felt coming down the stairs a few hours earlier. For the first time, I had felt almost like a Princess, and now I felt like a child playing dress up. Aurora had seen through my fancy trappings (which she didn't even find that fancy) and realized that I wasn't special.

"I don't even know what a debutante ball is," I sighed. I knew nothing of high society.

"It's a coming out party, your presentation to the world," Finn elaborated. "Changelings aren't raised here. The community doesn't know them. So when they come back, they are given a small amount of time to acclimate, and then they are introduced to society. Every changeling has one, but most are very small. Since you are the Princess, you will have guests from all over the Trylle community. It is quite an ordeal."

"I am not ready for that at all," I groaned.

"You will be," Finn assured me.

We walked in silence the rest of the way to my bedroom as I fretted and worried about this upcoming party. It hadn't been that long ago that I had gone to my very first dance, and now I was expected to be the center of a formal ball.

I could never pull that off. Tonight had only been a semi-formal dinner, and I hadn't performed well at that.

"I trust you'll sleep well this evening," Finn said when I started to open the bedroom door.

"You need to come in with me," I reminded him, then pointed to my dress. "I can't unzip this thing on my own."

"Of course."

Finn followed me into the darkened room and flipped on the lights. The glass wall worked as a mirror thanks to the black night. In my reflection, I still thought I looked nice, and then I realized that's probably why I had to have other people pick out my clothes. My judgment was too flawed. I turned away from it, and waited for Finn to unzip me.

"I really botched things tonight, didn't I?" I asked sadly.

"No, of course not," Finn insisted.

His hand pressed warm on my back, and I felt the dress loosen around me as he pulled the zipper down. I wrapped my arms around me to keep it up, then turned back to look at him. Some part of me was distinctly aware that we were only a few inches from each other, my dress was barely on, and his dark eyes were fixed on me.

"You did exactly what I told you," Finn said. "If anyone ruined things, it was me. But the night wasn't ruined. Elora is just sensitive about the Kroners."

"Why? Why does she let them get to her so much?" I wondered. "She's the Queen."

"Monarchs have been overthrown before," Finn answered calmly. "If you seem unfit for the position, they can contest it, and they would be next in line to take the title."

All the color drained from my face. There was suddenly way too much pressure on me to perform. I felt sick, and I swallowed hard. The ball had scared me enough before I knew that if I failed, my mother could be overthrown.

"Don't worry. You'll be fine." His expression saddened again, and he added quietly, "Elora has a plan to appease them."

"What is it?" I asked.

Instead of answering, his eyes got far away and his expression blanked. His brow furrowed, and then he nodded.

"I am sorry," Finn said. "You're going to have to excuse me. Elora requires assistance in getting to her room."

"You're helping Elora?" I stumbled over the question, unable to hide my shock.

Somehow, it seemed vaguely inappropriate that Finn would be helping her to her room. Maybe it was because she had just asked him inside his head, and I couldn't get a read on what exactly was the nature of their relationship.

I might have been feeling a little jealous of my mother, and that added a nauseous feeling on top of everything else.

"Yes. Her migraine is quite severe." Finn took a step away from me.

"Alright, well, have fun with that," I muttered.

The door closed softly behind him, and I went into the bathroom to take off my jewelry and change into baggy pajamas. Sleep was very difficult for me that night. I was too anxious thinking about all the things I was expected to accomplish.

170

I knew nothing about this world or these people, and yet I was supposed to rule over them someday. That wouldn't have been so bad, except that I was supposed to master everything in less than a week so they would believe that I could rule.

If I didn't, everything my mother worked so hard for would be taken away. Even though I wasn't that fond of Elora most of the time, I was even less fond of Aurora, and I didn't like the idea of ruining my family's entire legacy.

13. Being Trylle

Lazy Sundays happened even in Förening, thankfully. I woke up late, and the chef was still on hand to make breakfast. I saw Finn briefly, passing him in the hall, but it was no more than a nod hello.

I flopped in my bed, thinking I would spend the day bored out of my mind. Rhys knocked on my door, interrupting my plans for moping, and invited me over to his room to watch movies with him and Rhiannon.

His room was a masculine version of mine, which made sense since he had helped decorate my room. A huge overstuffed couch sat in front of his TV, the one addition to his room. We ended up watching *The Lord of the Rings* trilogy because Rhys insisted it was much funnier once you'd spent time with actual trolls.

I sat on one end of the couch, and Rhiannon sat on the other, with Rhys between us. He started out directly in the middle, but somewhere around three or four hours into the marathon, I noticed him moving closer to me, not that I minded.

He talked and joked a lot with Rhiannon, and they had a way of making me feel comfortable. After spending the weekend failing to be the perfect little princess Elora wanted me to be, it felt good to just relax and laugh.

Rhiannon left right after the third movie started, saying she had to get up early in the morning. Even after she'd gone, Rhys didn't move away from me. He sat so close to me on the couch, his leg pressed up against mine.

I thought about moving away, but I didn't really have any reason to. The movie was fun, he was foxy, and I enjoyed being with him. It wasn't too long before his arm "casually" went around my shoulders, and I almost laughed.

He didn't make my heart race, not the way Finn did, but his arm felt nice. Rhys made me feel normal in a way that I never had before, and I couldn't help but like him for it. Eventually, I leaned into him and rested my head on his shoulder.

What I didn't realize is that watching all three extended edition versions of *Lord of the Rings* in one sitting ends up being over eleven hours of movie viewing. At one in the afternoon on a boring Sunday, that sounded genius, but by the time midnight rolled around, it became a war on sleep, and I eventually lost.

In the morning, while I slept soundly on the couch in Rhys's room, I had no idea of the commotion going on the house. I would've been happy to sleep through it, too, but Finn threw open the door in a panic, jolting me awake.

"Oh my gosh!" I shouted, jumping up off the couch. Finn scared the hell out of me, and my heart pounded manically in my chest. "What's going on? Is everything okay?"

Instead of answering, Finn just stood there, staring at me. Behind me, Rhys woke up much more slowly than me. Apparently, Finn hadn't terrified him the way he did me.

I glanced back at Rhys, dressed in a tee shirt and sweats that somehow managed to look good on him, and it dawned on me how this looked to Finn. I still wore my lazy day comfy clothes, but we had been curled up together. My mind scrambled to think of some kind of excuse, but suddenly, even the innocent truth escaped me.

"She's in here!" Finn said flatly.

Rhys groaned, so I knew things weren't good. He looked completely alert now, and he stood sheepishly next to me. I wanted to ask what was going, what Finn looked so pissed off about it, but Elora interrupted my thoughts.

She appeared in the door, her emerald robe flaring out from behind in her a dramatic billow. She stood behind Finn, but she somehow managed to eclipse everything else. Several times before I had thought she looked unhappy, but they had nothing on the severe expression she had now. She scowled so deep, it looked painful, and her hair still hung in a thick braid down her back.

"What do you think you're doing?" Elora's voice echoed painfully inside my head, and she had added some of her psychic voice to make it more intense.

"Sorry. We were just watching movies and fell asleep," I stumbled through an apology.

"It was my fault. I put the-" Rhys attempted to come to my aid, but Elora cut him off.

"I don't care what you were doing! Do you have any idea how inappropriate this behavior is?" Her eyes narrowed on Rhys, and he shrunk back even more. "Rhys, you know this was completely unacceptable." She rubbed her temples as if this was giving her a headache, and Finn looked at her with concern. "I don't even want to deal with you. Get ready for school, and get out of my sight!"

"Yes, ma'am," Rhys nodded. "Sorry."

"As for you-" Elora pointed a finger at me but couldn't find the words to finish. She just looked so disappointed and disgusted with me. "I don't care how you were raised before you came here, you still know what kind of behavior is ladylike and what isn't."

"I wasn't-" I started, but she held up her hand to silence me.

"But to be honest, Finn, you disappoint me the most." She had stopped yelling, and when she looked at Finn, she just sounded tired. He lowered his eyes in shame, and she shook her head. "I can't believe you allowed this to happen. You are supposed to be educating her in the ways of Trylle. You know you need to keep your eyes on her at all times."

"I know. I won't let it happen again." Finn bowed apologetically to her.

"I do not want to see any of you for the rest of the day." She held her hands up, like she was done with the lot of us, and then shook her head and turned out of her room.

"I am so sorry," Rhys apologized emphatically, his cheeks red with shame, and somehow, that only made him cuter.

Not that I was really paying attention to how he looked just then. My stomach had twisted in knots, and I was thankful that I hadn't started to cry. I didn't even fully understand what I'd done wrong, or why everyone came storming into Rhys's room so early in the morning.

"You need to get ready for school," Finn snapped, glaring at Rhys. Then he pointed to the hall and turned to me. "You. Out. *Now.*"

I had to sneak past him on my way out the door, and normally, I loved that but not today. My heart pounded erratically, but none of it was happy. Finn tried to keep his face expressionless, but tension and anger radiated from his body. I slunk across the hall to my room, and Finn barked something at Rhys about behaving himself.

"Where are you going?" Finn demanded when I opened my bedroom door. He had just emerged from Rhys's room and slammed the door behind him, making me jump.

"To my room?" I pointed at my room and looked confused.

"No. You need to come to my room with me," Finn said.

"What? Why?" I asked.

A very small part of me felt excited about the prospect of going to his room with him. That sounded like the start of a fantasy I might have, but the way he was looking at me now, I was afraid he might kill me once we were inside the privacy of his room.

"I need to get ready for the day, and I can't very well let you out of my sight." He wore pajama pants and a tee shirt, and his dark hair wasn't as sleek as it normally was. He had just woken up.

I nodded and hurried after him. He walked fast and pissed off, and I fell about a step or two behind. I didn't understand what had him so upset.

"I really am sorry, you know," I said, hoping to lessen his anger. "I didn't mean to fall asleep there. We were just watching movies, and it got late. If I had known it would be like this, I would've made sure to be in my room."

"You should've known, Wendy!" Finn exclaimed, exasperated. "You should know that your actions have consequences and the things you do matter!"

"I am sorry!" I repeated. "Yesterday was so boring and I just wanted to do *something*."

Finn whirled on me suddenly, startling me so I took a step backwards. My back hit the wall behind me, but he stepped closer to me. Putting one arm on the side of me, his face only a few inches from mine, and his dark eyes blazed. Somehow, his voice was calm and even.

"You know how it looks when a girl spends the night alone with a boy. I know you understand that. But it is *so* much worse when a *Princess* spends the night alone with a *mänsklig*. It could put everything in jeopardy."

"I-I don't know that means," I fumbled.

Finn stayed there, glaring at me for another painful minute, then sighed and took a step back. He rubbed his eyes and stood in the middle of the hallway. I swallowed back tears and caught my breath.

When he looked back at me, his eyes had softened a bit, but he didn't say anything. He just walked to his room, and uncertainly, I followed after him.

His room was smaller than mine, but a much more comfortable size. One of his walls was entirely glass, and he had the blinds shut. Dark blankets covered his bed, and books overflowed from his several bookshelves. In one corner, he had a small desk with a laptop on it.

Like me, he had an adjoined bathroom. When he went into the bathroom, he left the door open, and I heard the sound of him brushing his teeth. Tentatively, I sat on the edge of his bed and looked around.

"You must stay here a lot," I commented. I knew that he stayed here on and off, but to have a room this full of his stuff implied a more permanent living situation.

"I live here when I'm not tracking," Finn said.

"My mother is quite fond of you," I said dimly.

"Not right now she's not." Finn turned off the water and came out, leaning on the doorframe to his bathroom. Sighing, he lowered his eyes. "I'm sorry for yelling at you."

"It's okay," I shrugged. I still didn't understand why he'd been *that* mad, but he had a point. I'm a Princess now, and I had to start behaving like one.

"No, you didn't deserve it." He scratched his temple and shook his head. "My anger was misdirected. When you weren't in your room this morning, I panicked. With everything going on with the

Vittra…" He shook his head again.

"What's going on with the Vittra?" I asked, feeling my heart speed up nervously.

"It's nothing to concern yourself with," Finn brushed it off. "My point is that my emotions were high when I couldn't find you, and I snapped at you. I apologize."

"No, it's my fault. You guys were right." I said, but Finn just ran a hand through his hair and looked away from me, and then I realized something. "How did you even know I wasn't in my room?"

"I checked on you," Finn gave me a look like I was an idiot. "I check on you every morning."

"You check on me when I'm sleeping?" I gaped at him. "Every morning?" He nodded. "I didn't know that."

"Why would you know that? You're sleeping," Finn pointed out.

"Well… it just feels weird." I shook my head. Matt and Maggie used to check on me, but it felt strange knowing that Finn would come in and watch me sleep, even if it was only for a second.

"I have to make sure you're safe and sound. It's part of my job," Finn said.

"You sound like a broken record sometimes," I muttered wearily. "You're always just doing your job."

"What else do you want me to say?" Finn countered, looking at me evenly.

I just shook my head and looked away from him. My pants suddenly became very fascinating, and I picked lint off them. Finn kept looking at me, and I expected him to move on to finish getting ready. When he didn't, I decided that I had to fill the silence with talking.

"What is a mänsklig?" I looked over at Finn, and he exhaled.

"The literal translation for mänsklig is 'human.'" He tilted his head, resting it against the doorframe, and watched me. "Rhys is human."

"I don't understand. Why is he around?" I shook my head.

"Because of you," Finn said, and that only confused me more. "You're a changeling, Wendy. You were switched at birth. Meaning that when you took the place of another baby, that baby had to go somewhere else."

"You mean…" I trailed off, but it was incredibly obvious once Finn said it. "Rhys is Michael!"

Suddenly, my crush on him felt very weird. He wasn't my brother, but he was my brother's brother, even though Matt wasn't really my brother. It still felt… not right, somehow.

"Michael?" Finn looked perplexed.

"Yeah, that's what my mother – Kim, my fake mom – named him. She knew she had a son, and that's Rhys." My mind swirled. "But how… how did they do that? How did they switch us?"

"It's relatively simple," Finn explained, almost tiredly. "After Rhys was born, she induced labor with you, and using persuasion on the family and hospital staff, she switched you out for him."

"It can't be that simple. The persuasion didn't really work on

Kim," I pointed out.

"We normally do same-sex exchanges, a girl for a girl, a boy for a boy, but Elora had her mind set on the Everlys," Finn said. "It doesn't work as well when you do a boy to girl switch like that. Mothers are more likely to pick up on something being wrong, as was the case with your host mother."

"Wait, wait!" I held up my hands and looked at him. "She knew it was more dangerous, that Kim would be more likely to snap? But she did it anyway?"

"Elora believed that the Everlys would be the best for you," Finn maintained. "And she wasn't completely wrong. Even you freely admit that the aunt and the brother were good to you."

I had always kind of hated Kim. I thought she had been terrible and cruel, as had everyone else, but she had known that I wasn't her child. Kim had really been an insanely good mother. She had remembered her son, even when she shouldn't have been able to, and she refused to give up on him. It was tragic, when I thought about it.

"So that's why they don't want me with the mänsklig? Cause he's like a step-brother?" I wrinkled my nose at the thought.

"He's not your brother," Finn emphasized. "Trylle and mänsklig have absolutely no relation. The problem is that they're human."

"Are we like… physically incompatible?" I asked carefully.

"No. Many Trylle have left the compound to live with humans and have normal offspring," Finn said. "That's part of the reason our populations are going down."

"What happens to Rhys now that I'm back?" I asked, ignoring the clinical way Finn addressed everything. He was nothing if not professional.

"Nothing. He'll live here for as long as he wants. Leave if he decides to. Whatever he chooses," Finn shrugged. "Mänsklig aren't treated badly here. For example, Rhiannon is Willa's mänsklig."

"That makes sense," I nodded. Rhiannon seemed so skittish and nervous, but also rather normal, unlike everyone else. "So… what do they do with mänsklig?

"They aren't exactly raised as their children, but they are given everything to keep them happy and content," Finn said. "They receive an education at our schools. They even have a small trust fund set up for them. When they are eighteen, they are free to do as they please."

"But they're not equals," I realized. Elora tended to talk down to everyone, but she was worse with Rhys and Rhiannon. I couldn't imagine that Willa was much nicer either.

"This is a monarchy. There are no equals." For an instant, Finn looked almost sad, then he walked over and sat on the bed next to me. "That's part of what Elora is angry with me for not explaining sooner. There is a distinct hierarchy in how we live.

"In our community, there are classes. There is royalty, of which you are on the top," Finn gestured to me. "After Elora, of course. Below you, there are the Markis and Marksinna, but they can become Kings and Queens through marriage. Then there is your average

183

Trylle, the common folk if you will. Below that, there are trackers. And at the very bottom, there is mänsklig."

"What? Why are trackers so low?" I asked incredulously.

"We are Trylle, but we only track. My parents were trackers, and their parents before them, and so on," Finn explained. "We have no changeling population. Ever. That means that we have no income. We bring nothing into the community. We provide a service for other Trylle, and in return, we are provided a home and food."

"You're like an indentured servant?" I gasped.

"Not exactly," Finn tried to smile, but it looked forced. "Until we retire from tracking, we don't need to do anything else. Many trackers, such as myself, will work as a guard for some of the families in town. All of the service jobs, like the nannies, the teachers, the chefs, the maids, are almost entirely retired trackers, and they make an hourly wage. Some are also mänsklig, but they stick around less and less."

"That's why you always bow to Elora," I said thoughtfully.

"She is the Queen, Wendy. Everyone bows to her," Finn corrected me. "Except for you and Rhys, but he's rather impossible."

"It's nice to know that being the Princess has some perks, like not bowing," I smirked.

"Elora may seem cold and aloof, but she is a very powerful woman," Finn looked at me seriously. "*You* will be a very powerful woman. You will be given every opportunity the world has to offer you. I know you can't see it now, but you will have a very charmed life."

"You're right. I cannot see it," I admitted. "It probably didn't help that I just got in trouble this morning, and I don't feel very powerful."

"You're still very young," Finn said with a trace of a smile.

"I guess." I remembered how angry he had been this morning, and I turned to him. "I didn't do anything with Rhys. You know that, right? Nothing happened."

Finn stared thoughtfully at the ground. I studied him, trying to catch a glimpse of something, but his face was a mask. Eventually, he nodded. "Yes. I know that."

"You didn't this morning, though, did you?" I asked.

This time, Finn chose not to answer. He stood up and said he needed to shower. He gathered his clothes and went into the bathroom.

I thought this might be a good time to explore his room, but I suddenly felt very tired. He'd woken me early, and this morning had been draining. Lying back down, I rolled over and curled up in his blankets. They were soft and smelled like him, and I easily fell asleep.

14. Kingdom

Other than the garden out back, I'd seen little of the palace grounds. After breakfast, Finn took me outside to show me around. The sky was overcast and gloomy, and he stared up at it with a skeptical eye.

"Is it going to rain?" I asked.

"You never can tell around here." Finn sounded almost angry, then shook his head and walked ahead, apparently deciding to risk it.

We'd gone out the front door of the mansion this time, stepping out on the cobblestone driveway. Trees overshadowed the palace, arching high into the sky. Immediately at the edge of the driveway, lush ferns and plants filled in the gaps between the pines and maples.

Finn walked into the trees, pushing the plants aside gently to make a pathway. He'd insisted I wear shoes today, and as I followed behind him, I understood why. A rough trail had been made, but it was overgrown with moss and twigs and stones.

"Where are you going?" I asked, as the path climbed upwards.

"I'm showing you Förening."

"Haven't I already seen Förening?" I stopped and looked around. Through the trees, I couldn't see much of anything, but I suspected it all looked about the same as what I was seeing.

"You've barely seen anything yet." Finn glanced back at me, smiling. "Come on, Wendy."

Without waiting for my answer, he climbed on. The trail already had a steep incline, and it looked slick with mud and moss. Finn maneuvered it easily, grabbing onto the occasional branch or protruding root.

My climb wasn't anywhere near as graceful. I slipped and stumbled the whole way up, scraping my palm and knees on several sharp rocks. Finn didn't slow and rarely glanced back. He had more faith in my abilities than I did, but I suppose that was nothing new.

If I hadn't been mastering a slippery slope, I might've enjoyed the time. The air smelled green and wet from all the pine and leaves. The river below seemed to echo through everything, reminding me of when I put a conch shell to my ear. Over it, I heard birds chirping, singing a fevered song.

Finn waited for me next to a giant boulder, and when I reached him, he made no comment about my slow pace. I didn't have a chance to catch my breath before he grabbed onto a small handhold in the boulder and started pulling himself up.

"I'm pretty sure I can't climb up that," I said, eyeing up the slick surfaces of the rock.

"I'll help you." He had his feet in a crevice, and he reached back, holding his hand out to me.

Logically speaking, if I grabbed onto him, my body weight would pull him back off the boulder. But he didn't doubt his ability to pull us both up, so neither did I. Finn had this way of making me believe anything, and it scared me sometimes.

I took his hand, barely getting a chance to enjoy how strong and warm it felt before he started pulling me towards the rock. I squealed, which only made him laugh. He directed me to a crevice, and I found myself hanging to the boulder for dear life.

Finn climbed up, always keeping one hand out for me to grab if I slipped, but I did most of the actual climbing myself. I was surprised when my fingers didn't give and my shoes didn't slide, and I had to admit, when I pushed myself up to the top of the boulder, I couldn't help to feel a bit of pride.

When I stood up on the massive rock, wiping mud off my knees, I started to make some comment about my amazing agility, but then I caught sight of the view. On top of the boulder had to be the highest point, sitting high atop the bluffs. From here, I could see everything, and somehow, it was even more amazing than the view from the palace.

Chimneys dotted out amongst the trees, and I could see the plumes of smoke blowing away in the wind. Roads curved and winded through the town, and a few people walked along them. Elora's palace had been masked with vines and trees, but it still looked startlingly large hanging on the edge of the bluff.

With the wind whipping through my hair, it made it somehow exhilarating. Almost like I was flying, even though I was just standing there.

"This is Förening." Finn gestured to the hidden houses buried amongst the green foliage.

"It is breathtaking," I admitted, letting him see how in awe I felt.

"It's all yours," he said gravely, and I turned to look at him, certain I'd misunderstood.

"What are you talking about?"

"You'll be Queen, Wendy." His dark eyes met mine, emphasizing the severity of his words, and then he looked away, scanning the trees. "This is your kingdom."

"Yeah, but... it's not actually mine."

"Actually, it kind of is." He offered me a small smile.

I looked back at the bluff, and in the realm of kingdoms, I knew it was relatively small. It wasn't as if I'd inherited the Roman Empire or anything, but it felt strange to me that I might possess any amount of a kingdom.

"What's the point?" I asked softly. When Finn didn't answer, I thought my words might have been carried away by the wind, so I asked louder. "Why do I get this? What am I to do with it?"

"Rule over it." Finn had been standing behind me, but he stepped closer, moving next to me. "Make the decisions. Keep the peace. Declare the wars."

"Declare the wars?" I looked at him sharply. "That's really something we do?" He shrugged. "I don't understand."

"Most things will already be decided when you take the throne," Finn said, staring down at the houses instead of me. "The order is already in place. You just have to uphold it, enforce it. Mostly, you live in the palace, attend parties, trivial governmental meetings, and occasionally, decide on something substantial."

"Like what?" I asked, not liking the hard tone his voice had taken on.

"Banishments, for one." He looked thoughtful. "Your mother once banished a Marksinna. It hadn't been done in years, but its entrusted in her to make the decisions that best protect our people and our way of life."

"Why did she banish her?" I asked.

"She corrupted a bloodline." He didn't say anything for a minute, and I looked at him questioningly. "She had a child with a human."

I wanted to ask him more about that but I felt a drop of rain splash on my forehead. I looked up to the sky, to be certain I'd felt rain, and the clouds seemed to rip open, pouring water down before I had a chance to shield myself.

"Come on!" Finn grabbed my hand, pulling me.

We slid down the side of the rock, my back scraping against the rough surface of it, and fell heavily into a thicket of ferns. Rain soaked through my clothes already, chilling my skin, and still holding my hand, Finn led me to a shelter underneath a giant pine tree.

"That came on really suddenly," I said, peering out from around the branches. We weren't completely dry under the tree, but only a few fat drops of rain made their way through.

"The weather is so temperamental here. The locals blame it on the river, but the Trylle have more to do with it," Finn explained.

I thought back to Willa, and her complaint that she could only control the wind and her mother, the clouds. The garden behind the palace bloomed year round thanks to Trylle abilities, and it wouldn't be hard to fathom that they played a role in the rain.

The birds had fallen silent, and over the sound of the rainfall, I couldn't hear the river. The air smelled thick with pine, and even in the middle of the rainstorm, I felt oddly peaceful. I couldn't stop the growing chill inside me, and my teeth began to chatter.

"You're cold."

"I'm fine," I shook my head.

Without further prompting, Finn put his arm around me, pulling me closer to him. The abruptness of it made me forget to breathe, and even though he felt no warmer than I did, the strength of his arm wrapping around me made a warmth spread inside of me.

"I suppose I'm not much help," he said, his voice low and deep.

"I've stopped shivering," I pointed out quietly.

"We should get back inside, so you can change into dry clothes." He breathed deeply, looking at me a moment longer.

Just as abruptly as he grabbed me, he pulled away and started heading back down the bluff. The rain came down fast and cold, and without him to warm me, I had no urge to stay in it longer than I had to. I went down after him, half-running half-sliding to the bottom.

We ran inside the front doors, skidding on the marble floors, and water dripped off us into rapidly growing puddles. I only had a second to catch myself when I realized we weren't alone in the entryway.

Elora walked towards us, carrying herself with her usual regality. Her gown swam around, making her appear to float as she moved. Standing with her was an obese balding man, his jowls jiggling when he talked. He wore a white suit that I can't imagine looking good on anyone, but it made him look like a giant, sweaty snowball.

"How good of you to arrive now, as I'm showing the Chancellor out," Elora said icily, glaring at both Finn and me, and I'm not sure which of us she was more angry with.

"Your majesty, I can stay and talk," the Chancellor said, looking up at her with small, fevered eyes.

"Chancellor, I'm sorry we missed your visit," Finn said, doing his best to compose himself. Even dripping wet, he looked collected and obedient. On the other hand, I hugged my arms around myself and tried not to shiver.

"No, you've given me much to consider, and I don't want to waste your time further." Elora smiled thinly at the Chancellor, and her eyes burned with contempt.

"You will take it under advisement, then?" He looked up at her hopefully and stopped walking. She'd been trying to usher him to the door, and her smile strained with impatience when he stopped.

"Yes, of course," Elora sounded too sweet, and I assumed she was lying. "I take all of your concerns very seriously."

"My sources are very good," the Chancellor went on, and Elora had gotten him walking again, urging him closer to the door. "I have spies all over, even in the Vittra camps. That is how I got my

193

position."

"Yes, I remember your platform." Elora suppressed an eye roll, but his chest puffed up, as if she'd complimented him.

"If they say there's a plot, then there's a plot," the Chancellor said with conviction, and next to me, I saw Finn tense up, narrowing his eyes at the Chancellor.

"Yes, I'm sure there is." Elora nodded to Finn, who held the door open for the Chancellor. "I'd love to talk with you more, but you must hurry if you want to beat the worst of this storm. I don't want to keep you stranded."

"Oh yes, quite right." The Chancellor looked at the sheets of rain coming down, and his face paled slightly. He turned back toward Elora. Bowing, he took her hand and kissed it once. "My Queen. I'm at your service, always."

She smiled tightly at him, and Finn wished him a safe journey. The Chancellor barely even glanced in my direction before diving out into the rain. Finn shut the door behind him, and Elora let out a sigh of relief.

"What were you doing?" Elora looked disdainfully at me, but before I could answer, she waved me off. "I don't care. You're just lucky the Chancellor didn't realize you were the Princess."

I glanced down, at my dirty, soaking wet clothes, and I probably did look nothing like royalty. Somehow Finn still looked high class, and I had no idea how he managed that.

"What was the nature of the Chancellor's visit?" Finn asked.

"Oh, you know the Chancellor." Elora rolled her eyes and started walking away. "He always has some conspiracy brewing. I should really change the laws so the Chancellor is appointed instead of voted for. The people always fall for idiots like him."

"He mentioned something about a Vittra plot," Finn pressed. He followed her, staying a few steps behind, so I went after them.

"I'm sure it's nothing. We haven't had Vittra come into Förening in years," Elora said with an eerie confidence.

"Yes, but with the Princess-" Finn started, but she held up her hand, silencing him. She turned to him, and by the look on her face, I knew she was speaking in his mind. After a minute, he took a deep breath and spoke, "All I am proposing is that we take extra precautions, have extra guards on duty."

"That's why you're around, Finn." She smiled at him, something that almost looked genuine, but with a weird malicious edge to it. "It's not just for your pretty face."

"Your majesty, you put too much faith in me," Finn said, humbly disagreeing with her.

"Now that, I can believe." Elora sighed and started walking away. "Go change out of those clothes. You're dripping all over everything."

Finn watched her retreating figure for a minute, and I waited next to him, until I was certain she was out of earshot. If I thought about it, I wasn't sure that Elora was ever out of earshot. She probably heard everything.

"What was that about?" I whispered.

"Nothing," Finn shook his head. He glanced over at me, almost as if he'd forgotten I was there. "You need to change before you get sick."

"That wasn't nothing. Is there going to be an attack?" I demanded, but Finn turned and started walking towards the stairs. "What is with you people? You're always walking away from questions!"

"You're soaking wet, Wendy," Finn said matter-of-factly, and I jogged to catch up to him, knowing he wouldn't wait for me. "And you heard everything I heard. You know what I know."

"That's not true! I know she did that creepy mind-speak with you," I insisted.

"Yes, but she only told me to keep quiet." He climbed the stairs without looking back at me. "You'll be safe. You're the Princess, the most important asset to this kingdom right now, and Elora won't risk you. She just hates the Chancellor."

"Are you sure I'm safe?" I asked, and I couldn't help but think of that painting in Elora's hidden room. The one that showed me terrified and reaching for nothing.

"I would never do anything to put you at risk," Finn assured me when we reached the top of the stairs. He gestured down the hall to my room. "We still have much to go over. It'd be best if you forgot about this and changed into something warmer."

15. Education

After I had changed, Finn directed me to a sitting room on the second floor, down the hall from my room. The vaulted ceiling had a mural, all clouds and unicorns and angels. Despite that, the furniture looked modern and normal, unlike the expensive antiques that filled most of the house.

Finn explained that this had once been Rhys's playroom, but when he'd outgrown it, they had tried to turn it into an appropriate sitting room for him, but he rarely used it.

Lying on my back on the couch, I stared up at the ceiling. Finn sat on an overstuffed chair across from me with a book splayed open on his lap. Stacks of texts sat on the floor next to him, and he tried to give me a crash course on Trylle history.

Unfortunately, despite the fact that we were some type of mythical creatures, Trylle history wasn't any more exciting than human history had been.

"What are the roles of the Markis and Marksinna?" Finn quizzed me.

"I don't know. Nothing," I replied glibly.

"Wendy, you need to learn this," Finn sighed. "There will be conversations at the ball, and you need to appear knowledgeable. You can't just sit back without saying anything anymore."

"I'm a Princess. I should be able to do whatever I want," I

197

grumbled. My legs were hanging over the arm of the couch, and I swung my feet back in forth.

"What are the roles of the Markis and Marksinna?" Finn repeated.

"In other provinces, where the King and Queen don't live, the Markis and Marksinna are the leaders. They're like governors or something," I shrugged. "In times when the King or Queen can't fulfill their job duties, a Markis can step up and take their place. In places like Förening, they're mostly just a way of saying that they're better than everyone else, but they don't really have any power."

"That is true, but you can't say that last part," Finn said, then flipped a page in the book. "What is the role of the Chancellor?"

"The Chancellor is an elected official, much like the prime minister in England," I answered tiredly. "The monarchy has the final word and wields the most power, but the Chancellor serves as their advisors and helps give the Trylle a voice in the way the government is run.

"But I don't get it," I said, looking at him. "We live in America, and this isn't a separate country. Don't we have to follow their laws?"

"Theoretically yes, and for the most part, Trylle laws coincide with American laws, except that we have more of them," Finn said. "However, we live in separate pockets unto ourselves. Using our resources – namely cash and persuasion – we can get government officials to look the other way, and we conduct our business in private."

"Hmm." I twirled a hair on my finger and thought over what he was saying. "Do you know everything about Trylle society? When you were talking with Garrett and Elora, it was like there was nothing you didn't know."

I'm sure he would've easily won the Kroners over if he had tried. He had assumed it was his role to hide in the background with them, so he'd kept his mouth shut. But everything about him was more refined than me. Cool, collected, intelligent, charming, and handsome, he looked much more like a leader than I did.

"A foolish man thinks he knows everything. A wise man knows he doesn't," Finn replied absently, still looking down at the book.

"That's such a fortune cookie answer," I laughed, and even he smirked at me. "But seriously, Finn. This doesn't make any sense. You should be the Prince, not me. I don't know anything, but you're all set to go."

"I'm not a Prince," Finn shook his head. "And you are right for the job. You just haven't had the training that I've had."

'That's stupid," I grumbled. "It should be based on your abilities, not lineage."

"It *is* based on abilities," Finn insisted. "They just happen to come with lineage."

"What are you talking about?" I asked, and he shut the book on his lap.

"Your persuasion? That comes from your mother," Finn elaborated. "The Markis and Marksinna are what they are because of the abilities they have, and they are passed down through their children. Regular Trylle have some abilities, but they've faded with time. Your mother is one of the most powerful queens we've had in a very long time, and the hope is that you will help restore some of that power."

"But I can barely do anything!" I sat up. "I have mild persuasion, and you said it wouldn't even work on you!"

"Not yet, no, but it will," Finn corrected me. "Once you start your training, it will make more sense to you."

"Training? What training?"

"After the ball this weekend. Then you will begin working on your abilities," Finn said. "Right now, your only priority is preparing for the ball. So…" He flipped open the book again, but I wasn't ready to go back to studying.

"But *you* have abilities," I countered. "And Elora prefers you to me. I'm sure she'd like it better if you were Prince." I realized sadly that that was true, and I lay back down on the couch.

"I'm sure that isn't true."

"It is too," I said. "What is the deal with you and Elora? She definitely likes you better than me, and she seems to confide in you."

"Elora doesn't really confide in anyone." Finn fell silent for a moment, and then exhaled. "If I explain this to you, do you promise to get back to studying?"

"Yes!" I answered immediately and looked over at him.

"What I say to you cannot leave this room. Do you

understand?" Finn asked gravely, and I nodded, gulping painfully.

I had been growing more and more preoccupied with Finn and Elora's relationship. She was an attractive older woman, and he was definitely a foxy guy, and I could see her digging her cougar claws into him. That was what I was afraid of, anyway.

"About twelve or thirteen years ago, after your father was gone, *my* father came under the employ of your mother. He had retired from tracking, and Elora hired him to guard her and the estate," Finn explained.

"Elora was in love with my father," His eyes darkened and his lips tightened, and my heart raced. "No one knew, except for my mother, who is still married to my father. Eventually, my mother convinced my father to leave.

"However, Elora remained quite fond of him, and in turn, rather fond of me." He sighed and spoke casually, as if he were talking about the weather. "She has personally requested my services over the years, and because she pays well, I have accepted."

I stared at him, feeling nauseous and nervous. Since his father became involved with my mother after I was born, I could safely assume that we weren't siblings, so at least that was something.

Everything else made it feel rather disturbing, and I wondered if Finn secretly hated me. He had to hate Elora, and he was only here because of how much she paid him. Maybe he was some kind of glorified gigolo, and I had to fight to keep from vomiting.

"I am not sleeping with her, and she has never made any

advances of the sort," Finn clarified, looking at me evenly. "She is fond of me because of her feelings for my father. I don't blame her for what happened between them. It was a long time ago, and my father was the one that had a family to think of, not her."

"Huh." I looked up at the ceiling because it was easier than looking at him.

"I have distressed you. I'm sorry," Finn apologized sincerely. "This is why I was hesitant to say anything to you."

"No, no, I'm fine. Let's just go on," I insisted unconvincingly. "I have a lot to go over and all that."

Finn remained silent for a minute, letting me absorb what he had just told me, but I tried to push it from my mind as quickly as possible. Thinking about it made me feel dirty, and I still had too much on my mind.

Eventually, Finn continued on with the texts, and I tried harder to pay attention. If I was thinking about what exactly a Queen's job entailed, I wasn't thinking about my mother crushing on his father.

Frederique Von Ellsin, the dress designer, came over the next day. He was excitedly flamboyant, and I couldn't tell for sure whether or not he was Trylle. I wore only a slip as he took my measurements and sketched like mad in a notepad. Finally, he declared that he had the perfect gown in mind, and he dashed out of my room to get working on it.

All day long, there was an irritating succession of people. They were all staff of some kind, like caterers and party planners, so most of them ignored me. They just trailed after Elora as she listed an inconceivable amount of information about what she expected them to do, and they all scurried to write it down or punch it in their Blackberries.

Meanwhile, I had the pleasure of camping out in my sweats all day. Whenever Elora saw me, she glared at my apparel intensely, but she was always too busy making demands to somebody else to complain about me.

Everything that I managed to overhear only made my coming-out festivities sound even more terrifying. The most horrific thing I heard as she zipped by: "We'll need seating for at least 500." Five hundred people were going to be at a party where I would be the center of attention? Splendid.

The only upside of the day was that I got to spend the entire thing with Finn. That became less enjoyable because Finn refused to talk about anything that wasn't related to my performance at the party.

We spent two hours going over the names and pictures of the more prominent guests that would be attending. Two whole hours spent pouring over a yearbook-type thing trying to memorize the faces, names, and notable facts of about a hundred people.

Then there was the hour and a half spent at the dinner table. Apparently, I did not know how to eat properly. There were certain ways to hold the fork, tilt the bowl, lift the glass, and even place the napkin. Up until that time, I had never mastered any of those skills, and from what I gathered about the way Finn regarded me, I still hadn't.

Eventually, I gave up. Pushing my plate back, I laid my head down and pressed my cheek against the cold wood of the table.

"Oh my god, has he killed you?" Willa asked, sounding appalled.

I lifted my head to see her standing at the end of the dining room table, hands on her fashionable hips. She wore too much jewelry, her necklaces and bracelets overly adorned and jangly, but that was part of being a troll. They all seemed to have a fondness for trinkets, something I had somehow missed, other than my obsession with my thumb ring.

"He bored me to death, too," Willa smiled at me, and I couldn't believe I felt relieved to see her. No way would she try to bore me with the names of the past 300 monarchs.

"And yet, you look as alive as ever," Finn said dryly, leaning back in his chair across from me. "Perhaps I didn't try hard enough with you."

"Is that some kind of burn, *stork*?" Willa pulled back her lip in some kind of snide grimace, but she didn't completely pull it off.

"If you're feeling a burn, I suggest you defer to your former sexual partners," Finn gave her a small smile, and I gaped at him. I'd never heard him speak like that to anyone before.

"Funny," Willa tried to keep a straight face, but I was under the impression she was amused. "Anyway, I'm here to rescue the Princess."

"Really?" I asked a little too brightly. "Rescue me how?"

"Fun stuff." She shrugged in a cute way, and I looked to Finn to see if I could leave.

"Go." He waved vaguely at me. "You've worked hard and you need a break."

I didn't think I'd ever be happy to get away from Finn, but I nearly scampered after Willa. She looped her arm through mine, leading me away from the dining room and towards my room. I instantly felt bad about leaving Finn, but I couldn't take another lecture on silverware.

Willa chatted with me the whole way to my room, in one endless stream of commentary about how dreadful these first few weeks were. She'd been certain that Finn would stab her with a fork during dining service, or vice versa.

"This is the worst part," she said solemnly as we walked into my bedroom. "The whole boot camp before the ball." She wrinkled her nose. "It's *horrid*."

"Yeah, I'm not enjoying it," I admitted tiredly.

"But I made it through, so you'll definitely make it through." She walked into my bathroom, and when I didn't follow, she looked back at me. "Are you coming?"

"To the bathroom with you?"

"To practice hairstyles." She gave me a *duh* look, and reluctantly, I walked in after her. Out of the frying pan and into the fire.

"Hairstyles?" I asked, and Willa ushered me over to the stool in front of the vanity.

"Yeah, for the ball." She sifted through the hair products on the counter and stopped, meeting my eyes in the mirror. "Unless your mother is going to help you with it."

"Not that I know of," I shook my head.

"She's definitely not the nurturing type," Willa agreed, somewhat sadly. Picking a bottle of something and a brush, she turned to me. "Do you want your hair up or down?"

"I don't know." I thought back to when I'd first met Willa, and Finn had told me to wear it down. "Down. I guess."

"Good choice." She smiled and pulled out my hair tie, painfully taking my hair down. "So, did Frederique come today?"

"Uh, yeah, a few hours ago," I said between gritted teeth as she raked a comb through my hair.

"Excellent," Willa said. "When you have your fitting, you should take a picture and send it to me. I'd love to see what it looks like."

"Yeah, sure thing."

"I know how ridiculous and confusing everything is at first." Willa teased and primped at my hair, all the while chatting happily. "And Finn knows pretty much everything, but he can be a little... cold, at times. And I'm sure the Queen isn't much better."

"Not really," I admitted. But cold wouldn't be how I described Finn. Sometimes he was standoffish, but other times, when he looked at me just so, he was anything but cold.

"I'm just letting you know that I wanna help you." She stopped pulling at my hair long enough so she could meet my eyes in the mirror again. "And not like that backstabbing bitch Aurora Kroner, or because my father told me to, although he did. Or even like Finn because it's his job. I just know what it's like to be you. And if I can help, I want to."

She gave me a crooked smile, and I saw a sincerity in it that startled me. Underneath her vapid pretense, she was actually a kind person. So few people here had seemed to genuinely care about anything.

Immediately after that moment, Willa launched into a lengthy discussion about gowns. She could name every gown she'd seen since coming to Förening three years ago, and she only liked one or two of them.

So my training with Willa didn't turn out to be that much more interesting than with Finn. She had a lot more gossip, about who dated who and who was engaged and all that. But since I didn't know who any of the people were, it wasn't that interesting.

Willa was thus far single, and it didn't sit well with her. She kept saying that her father needed to arrange something, and mentioned a few guys she'd had her eyes on that slipped by. She spoke very fondly of Tove Kroner, but I didn't entirely understand why. Although, she did point out that by missing out on him, she'd also missed out on a monster of a mother-in-law.

Still, by the end of the day, I had a hairstyle picked out, a makeup "plan" in order, and I felt like I knew a little bit more about the Trylle royalty. She made it all sound a lot like high school, which would've been comforting, except I didn't do that well at high school.

16. Further Instruction

They had taken an interest in me, and I knew I should feel flattered, but I'd wished they just left me alone. Elora and Aurora Kroner stood on the opposite side of the table as me. A seating chart stretched across the giant oak table, and they both leaned over it, staring with intense scrutiny.

I had a feeling Elora had just dragged me with her because misery loves company. Aurora, I couldn't really see her interest in me, except that she hoped to understand me and cause my demise. That was the best I could figure from the too big way she smiled at me.

Finn had snuck into my room early in the morning, and my initial excitement faded when I saw how frantically he picked out my clothes. He instructed me to get ready with lightning speed and that I had to be on my best behavior, all day. I hated the way he treated me like I was five, and it was my first day of kindergarten.

But sitting here, watching them analyze every minute detail of a flippin' seating chart, I really felt like a five-year-old. One that had gotten in trouble and had to sit in a very agonizing timeout. I tried to look studious and interested in all of this, but I didn't know any of these people.

They had met in the War Room in the South wing of the house. The walls were plastered with maps. Red and green patches speckled all of them, revealing other tribes of trolls. I'd been trying to study them while Elora and Aurora talked, but Elora had snapped my attention back every time it wandered.

"If we put the Chancellor here, then Markis Laurent will have to move from this table entirely." Aurora tapped the paper.

"I don't see another way around it." Elora smiled as sweetly as she could manage, and Aurora matched it perfectly.

"He's travelling a great distance to be here for this," Aurora batted her eyes at Elora.

"He'll still be near enough where he can hear the christening," Elora said, and turned her attention to me. "Are you ready for the christening ceremony?"

"Um, yeah," I said. Finn had mentioned it to me, but I hadn't been paying that much attention. I couldn't say that to Elora, though, so I just smiled and tried to look confident.

"A Princess doesn't say 'um.'" Elora narrowed her eyes at me, and Aurora did a poor job of trying to mask a snicker.

"Sorry," I sighed.

Elora looked like she wanted to chastise me further, but Aurora watched us both like a hawk. Elora pursed her lips, biting her tongue so she wouldn't show any sign of weakness to Aurora.

I didn't understand what Aurora was doing here or what Elora had to fear from her. She was the Queen, and as far as I could tell, Aurora's only ability seemed to be making backhanded compliments and veiled threats.

She looked radiant, wearing a long burgundy gown that made me feel incredibly underdressed in a simple skirt. Aurora's beauty nearly overshadowed Elora's, and that was really saying something, but I don't think that kind of thing mattered to Elora. I couldn't figure out why she let Aurora get under her skin like that.

"Perhaps you should continue your training elsewhere," Elora suggested, glaring at me.

"Yes. Excellent idea." I jumped to my feet so quickly, I almost knocked the chair over behind me. Aurora's amused expression changed to downright disgust, and Elora rolled her eyes. "Sorry. I'm very excited about all of this."

"Contain yourself, Princess."

Using restraint, I left the room as calmly as I could. I wanted to rush out, feeling much like a kid on the last day of school. I wasn't sure that I knew my way back, and I had no idea where Finn was, but as soon as I thought it was safe, I picked up my pace, nearly jogging away.

I'd made it a little ways down the hall, past several closed doors, when somebody stopped me.

"Princess!" A voice said from one of the few open doors I'd come across.

I stopped, tentatively peering inside the room. It appeared to be more of a den, with a lush red rug in the center and leather chairs sat around. One wall was made of glass, but the shades had been pulled shut over most of it, leaving the room in shadows.

A heavy mahogany bar sat in the corner, and a man leaned in front of it, holding a highball in his hand. I squinted, trying to get a better look of him. His hair looked disheveled, and he dressed nice but casual.

"Don't you recognize me, Princess?" He had a smile in his voice, so I thought he might be teasing.

"It's just hard to see," I said, stepping more into the room.

"Garrett Strom. Willa's father," he told me, and I could see the grin widening on his face.

"Oh, right. It's good to see you." I smiled back, feeling more at ease. I'd only met him at dinner the other night, but I liked him. "Can I help you with something?"

"Nope. I'm just waiting for your mother, but I'm assuming it'll be a long day, so I got a jumpstart." Garrett motioned to the drink in his hand.

"Nice."

"Do you want something to drink?" Garrett offered. "I'm sure you need one with Elora putting you through your paces."

I chewed my lip, thinking. I'd never drank before, other than a glass of wine with dinner, but after the last few days, I definitely could use one. But Elora would kill me if she found out, and Finn would be more than disappointed in me.

"No, I'm good," I shook my head. "Thanks, though."

"Don't thank me. It's your liquor," he pointed out. "You do look worn out. Why don't you take a load off?"

212

"Alright." I shrugged and sat down in one of the chairs. The leather may have looked distressed, but the chair had the hard buoyancy of being brand new. I moved around, trying to get comfortable, before eventually giving up.

"What is she having you do?" Garrett asked, sitting down across from me.

"I don't know. She's making a seating chart." I leaned my head against the back of the chair. "I don't even know why she wanted me there, except to point out what I was doing wrong."

"She just wants you to feel included in all of this," Garrett said between sips of his drink.

"Well, I'd rather not be included," I muttered. "Between her and Aurora giving me icy glares and judging everything I say and do."

"Don't let her get to you," Garrett advised.

"Which one?"

"Both," he laughed. It was a warm sound, and I looked apologetically at him.

"Sorry. I don't mean to dump on you."

"Don't be sorry," he shook his head. "I know how hard this can be, and I'm sure Elora isn't making it any easier on you."

"She expects me to know everything and be perfect already, and I haven't been here that long."

"You're strong-willed. You get that from her, you know," Garrett smiled. "And as strange as it sounds, all this she's doing – it's to protect you."

It was the first time anyone had drawn any kind of comparison between Elora and me, and it warmed me in a weird way. I realized that he was one of very few people I'd met that called her "Elora" instead of "Queen," and I wondered exactly how well he knew her.

"Thanks," I said, unsure of what else to say.

"I heard Willa visited you last night." His eyes settled on me. My vision had adjusted to the darkness of the room, and I could see the soft way he looked at me.

"Yeah, she did. She's been very helpful," I smiled.

"Good. I'm glad to hear it." Garrett looked relieved at that, and I wondered what he'd been expecting me to say. "I know at times she can be a little-" He wagged his head, searching for the right word. "-*Willa* at times, but she means well."

"I can tell," I nodded. My first impression had been that she was just a spoiled rich kid, and while that still seemed true, I felt like she had more underneath that, a sincere kindness.

"She's rude to Finn, but that's not personal." He cleared his throat and shifted in his chair. "Well, actually it *is* personal. He was a tracker, and a good one, so he kept her in line. Willa *hates* that. She resents him for it, but she respects him too."

"Finn seems like he can handle her." I wanted to defend Finn, but based on his interactions with her, she didn't really seem to bother him. In fact, in a weird way, I think Finn liked her too.

"That he can," he nodded. "I've been working on her to lighten up on the mänks. Rhiannon in particular. But it's a work in progress."

"Why is she so hard on her?" I hadn't seen Willa talk to Rhiannon much, but what little she did had been filled with jabs and snide remarks, even worse than Aurora's.

"Rhiannon got to live with me nineteen years before Willa did," Garrett explained. "Willa's always been secretly afraid that I preferred Rhiannon over her, but the fact is, while I love Rhiannon, I only have one daughter."

I had never thought about him loving Rhiannon, or anyone loving the mänsklig left behind. I looked in the direction of the War Room, as if I could see Elora through the wall. I couldn't imagine her loving anyone.

But the only babies in Trylle society were mänsklig, and at some point, paternal instincts had to take over. Certainly not with everyone, but with some, like Garrett, they had to feel as if the child they raised was their own.

"Do you think Elora loves Rhys?" I asked.

"I think Elora is an incredibly hard woman to get close to," Garrett allowed carefully, then he smiled at me. "I know she loves you, though."

"Yeah, I can tell," I said dryly, unwilling to even think about what he said, let alone believe it. I'd been burned enough by crazy moms already.

"She speaks very fondly of you. When you're not around, of course," he gave a small chuckle. Something about the way he said that, I felt a sense of intimacy in it.

I had a flash of an image. Elora sitting at her vanity, wearing a robe, and putting on jewelry. Garrett was behind her, still lying in her bed with the sheets covering him. She made some offhand comment about me being prettier than she expected, and before he could agree, she told him he needed to hurry and get dressed.

I shook my head, clearing it of the thought.

"Are you dating Elora?" I asked directly, even though I already knew the answer.

"I definitely wouldn't call it dating," he scoffed and took a long drink. "Let me put it this way: I'm about as close to her as anyone can get. Well, at least anyone can get *now*."

"Now?" I furrowed my brow. "What do you mean by that?"

"Elora wasn't always the cool, collected Queen you know and fear." When he talked, his words came out bitterly, and I wondered how long he'd been seeing her. Had it been while she was married to my father? Or when she was in love with Finn's father?

"What made her change?" I asked.

"The same thing that makes everyone change: experience." He turned his glass in his hands, admiring what little liquor he had left.

"What happened to my father?"

"You're really digging deep, aren't you?" Garrett cocked an eye at me. "I do not have enough alcohol for this conversation." He knocked back the rest of it one swallow.

"Why? What happened?" I pressed, leaning forward in my chair.

"It was a very long time ago." He took a deep breath, still

looking down. "And Elora was devastated."

"She really loved him then?" I still found it weird to believe that she'd loved anyone. She didn't seem capable of any emotion deeper than anger.

"I honestly don't know. I didn't know her that well back then." Garrett abruptly got up from his chair and walked over to the bar. "My wife was still alive, and we only had a casual acquaintance with the Queen." He poured himself another drink, keeping his back to me. "If you want to know more about all of this, you'll have to talk to Elora."

"She won't tell me anything." I sighed and leaned back in the chair.

"Some things are better forgotten," Garrett mused. He took a long drink, still keeping his back to me, and I realized belatedly I'd upset him.

"Sorry." I stood up. I didn't know how to correct the situation, so I thought leaving might be the best way to fix it.

"No need to be sorry," he shook his head.

"I should get back, anyway." I edged back towards the door. "Finn is probably looking for me by now."

"Probably," Garrett nodded. I'd made it almost out the door when he stopped me. "Princess?" He turned his head to the side, so shadows darkened his profile. "Elora's hard on you because she's afraid to care about you. But she'll fight to the death for you."

"Thanks," I mumbled.

The light in the hallway felt too bright after the dimness of the den. I didn't know what I'd said that had upset Garrett so much. Maybe bringing up memories of his dead wife. Or maybe reminding him that while Elora couldn't openly care for him now, she had once, with another man.

I shook my head, clearing it of the confused way Garrett had made me feel. I'm not sure if I could trust the things he said about Elora. I didn't think he was a liar, but he'd wanted to make me feel better. Convincing me that I had a mother that actually loved me probably would help, but I had long since stopped holding out for that dream.

I found Finn in the front hall, directing several of Elora's aides with the planning for the ball. He had his back to me, so he didn't notice me right away. I stood for a moment, just watching him direct and take control. He knew exactly what do with everything, and I couldn't help but admire him for it.

"Princess." Finn caught sight of me when he glanced over his shoulder, and he turned fully to me, smiling at me. An aide asked him something, and he gestured vaguely to the dining hall before walking over to me. "How did this morning go?"

"It could've been worse," I shrugged.

"That doesn't sound promising," he raised an eyebrow. "But I suppose you've earned a bit of a reprieve."

"A reprieve?" It was my turn to look skeptical.

"Yeah, I thought we'd do something fun for awhile," Finn

smiled.

"Fun?" I remembered yesterday, and his attempts at trying to convincing me his mind-numbing training had been fun. "Do you mean fun fun? Or do you mean looking at pictures for two hours fun? Or Using a Fork 101 fun?"

"Something that at least resembles actual fun," Finn answered. "Come on."

17. Jealousy

As Finn led me down a hall to the South wing of the house, I realized that I'd never seen any of this before. When Garrett had teased Elora about this being a palace, he wasn't kidding. There were so many places I had yet to see. It was astounding.

Finn gestured to a few rooms, pointing out the library, meeting halls where they conducted business, the opulent dining hall where we would hold the dinner on Saturday, and then finally, the ball room.

Pushing open the doors, which seemed to be two stories high, Finn led me into the grandest room I had ever seen. Massive and exquisite, the ceiling seemed to stretch on forever, thanks in part to the fact it was entirely skylight. Gold beams ran across it, holding up glittering diamond chandeliers. The floors were marble, the walls were off-white with gold detailing, and it looked every bit like the ballroom for Disney fairytales.

The decorators had started bringing things in, and stacked chairs and tables leaned up against one of the walls. Table cloths, candlesticks, and all sorts of decorations were piled around them. The only other thing in the room was a white grand piano sitting in the opposite corner. Otherwise, the room was empty, except for Finn and me.

I hated how taken I was with the splendor. I hated it even more

221

that the room was so magnificent, and I looked like I did. My hair was in a messy bun, and my skirt looked too plain. Finn wasn't exactly dressed to the nines either, but his standard buttoned shirt and dark washed jeans looked much more fitting.

"So what's the fun part?" I asked, and my voice echoed off the walls.

"Dancing," Finn's lip twitched with a smile, and I groaned. "I've danced with you before, and I know that it needs some improvement."

"The slow circles don't cut it?" I grimaced.

"Unfortunately, no. A proper waltz should be enough, though. If you can master that, you'll be set for the ball on Saturday," Finn said.

"Oh no." My stomach dropped as I just realized something. "I'm going to have to dance with these people, aren't I? Like strangers and old men and weird handsy boys?" Finn laughed at that, but I wanted to curl up in a ball and die.

"I could lie to you, but to be honest, those are probably the only people that will ask you to dance," Finn admitted with a wry smirk.

"You are enjoying this more than I've ever seen you enjoy anything!" I said, and that only deepened his smile. "Well, I'm glad you find this funny. Me being felt up by complete strangers and tripping all over them. What a great time."

"It won't be so bad." He motioned for me to come over. "Come on. If you learn the basic steps, at least you won't be tripping over them."

I sighed loudly and walked over to him. Most of my trepidation about dancing with strangers melted away the instant Finn took my hand in his. It suddenly occurred to me that before I had to dance with them, I got to dance with *him*.

After a few directions from him and a rough start by me, we were dancing. His arm was around me, strong and reassuring. He instructed me to keep my eyes locked on his so I wouldn't get in the habit of watching my feet while I danced, but I wouldn't have looked anywhere else anyway. His dark eyes always mesmerized me.

We were supposed to keep a certain distance between our bodies, but I found it impossible. His body nearly pressed against mine, and I was certain we weren't going as fast as we should, but I didn't care. I was back in that moment with him, that wonderful one that seemed too impossibly perfect to be real.

"Right, okay." Finn suddenly stopped and took a step away from me. Disappointed, I let my hands fall to the side. "You've got that down pretty well, but there's going to be music. So you should see how you do with that."

"Okay?" I said unsurely.

"Why don't I play the piano, and you count out the steps yourself?" Finn had already started backing away to the piano, and I wondered what I had done wrong that made him stop so suddenly. "That might be a better way for you to learn."

"Um, okay," I shrugged uncertainly. "I thought I was doing fine before."

"We weren't going fast enough. The music will help you keep time," Finn said.

I frowned at him, wishing he would just come back and dance with me. Before he had told me I was a terrible dance partner, and maybe that was the problem.

He sat down at the piano and started playing a beautiful, elaborate waltz. Of course, he could. He could do anything. I just stood there, staring at him, until he directed me to start dancing.

I whirled around on the dance floor, but it definitely wasn't as fun as it had been with him. In fact, it wasn't really that fun at all. It might have been if I weren't trying to figure out what I did wrong that always made Finn back away from me.

It was hard to concentrate on that, though, when Finn kept barking out corrections at me. Funny, he hadn't noticed any when we had been dancing together.

"Nope, that's it," I panted after what felt like an eternity.

My feet and legs were getting sore, and a sheen of sweat covered my body. I had had my fill of dancing for the day, and I sat down heavily on the floor, then leaned back, sprawling out on the cool marble.

"Wendy, it hasn't even been that long," Finn insisted.

"Don't care. I'm out!" I breathed deeply and wiped the sweat from forehead.

"Haven't you ever worked at anything?" Finn complained. He got up from the piano bench and walked over to me, so he could lecture me up close. "This is important."

"I'm aware. You tell me every second of every day," I grumbled.

"I do not." Finn crossed his arms over his chest and looked down at me.

"This is the hardest I've ever worked at anything," I said, staring back up at him. "Everything else I've quit before this, or I never even tried. So don't tell me I'm not putting effort into this."

"You've never tried harder than this? On anything?" Finn asked incredulously, and I shook my head. "That brother you had never made you do anything?"

"Not really," I admitted thoughtfully. "He made me go to school I guess. But that's about it." Matt and Maggie encouraged me to do many things, but there was very little they actually made me do.

"They spoiled you more than I thought." Finn looked surprised at that.

"They didn't spoil me," I sighed, then quickly amended, "They didn't spoil me rotten. Not the way Willa was spoiled, and I'm sure a lot of the other changelings were. They just wanted me to be happy."

"Happiness is something you work for," Finn pointed out.

"Oh, stop with that fortune cookie crap," I scoffed. "We worked for it just like anybody else. They were just really careful with me, probably because my mom tried to kill me. It set them up to treat me more gently than they would've otherwise."

"How did your mother try to kill you?" Finn asked, startling me. I hadn't told him much about it, but he very rarely wanted to talk

225

about my past.

"It was my birthday, and I was being my usual bratty self. I was angry because she'd gotten me a chocolate cake, and I hated it," I said. "We were in the kitchen, and she snapped. She started chasing after me with this giant knife. She called me a monster, and then she tried to stab me but she just managed to cut my stomach pretty badly. Then my brother Matt rushed in and tackled her, saving my life."

"She cut open your stomach?" Finn furrowed his brow with concern.

"Yeah." I pulled up my shirt, revealing the scar that stretched across it.

Immediately after I'd done it, I regretted it. Lying on the floor and flashing Finn the fattest part of my body did not sound like a good idea.

Finn crouched on the ground next to me, and tentatively, his fingertips traced along the mark etched on my belly. My skin quivered underneath his touch, and this nervous warmth spread through me. He just stared intently at it, then laid his hand flat on my belly, covering the scar. His skin felt hot and smooth, and inside, my stomach trembled with butterflies.

He blinked, and seeming to realize what he was doing, he pulled his hand back and got to his feet. Quickly, I pulled my shirt back down, and I didn't even feel that comfortable lying down anymore. I sat up and fixed my bun.

"Matt saved your life?" Finn asked, filling that semi-awkward silence that had shrouded us. He still had a contemplative look on his face, and I wished I knew what he was thinking.

"Yeah," I nodded, and I got to my feet. "Matt always protected me, ever since I could remember."

"Hmm." Finn looked thoughtfully at me. "You bonded so much more with your host family than the changelings normally do."

"'Host family?'" I grimaced. "You make me sound like a parasite."

Then I realized that I probably was. They had dropped me off with them so I would use their resources, their money, their opportunities, and then come back here with them. That's exactly what a parasite did.

"You're not a parasite," Finn said. "They loved you, and you genuinely loved them in return. It is unusual, but that is not a bad thing. In fact, it's a very good thing. Maybe it's given you a compassion that the Trylle leaders have been lacking for a very long time."

"I don't think I'm very compassionate," I shook my head.

"I see how it bothers you the way Elora talks to people. Elora thinks the only way to command respect is to command fear, but I have a feeling that you will have an entirely different way of ruling."

"And how will I rule?" I arched my eyebrow at him.

"That is for you to decide," Finn said simply.

He finished our lesson after that, saying I needed to rest up for tomorrow. The day had exhausted me, and I was eager to curl up in my blankets and sleep until Sunday, straight through the ball and all the angst that accompanied it.

Sleep didn't come easy, though. I found myself tossing and turning, thinking about the way it felt dancing with Finn, and his hand resting warmly on my stomach.

But I would always end up thinking of Matt and how much I still missed him. I had expected it to lessen the longer I was here, but it only seemed to get worse. After all this, I really needed to know that someone had my back and cared about me unconditionally.

I woke up early that morning. Actually, I'd been waking up all night long, and at six, I finally just gave into it. I got up with the intention of sneaking downstairs to grab a bite to eat, but when I hit the top of the stairs, Rhys came barreling up them to meet me, chomping on a bagel.

"Hey, what are you doing up?" Rhys grinned, swallowing down his bite.

"Couldn't sleep," I shrugged. "You?"

"Same. I have to get up for school soon anyway." He pushed his sandy hair out of his eyes and leaned back against the stair railing. "Are you worrying about this Saturday?"

"Kind of," I admitted.

"It is pretty intense," Rhys said, his eyes wide. I nodded noncommittally. "Is something else bothering you? You look pretty… upset, I guess."

"No." I shook my head and sighed, then sat down on the top

step. I didn't feel much like standing anymore, and I wanted to cry. "I was just thinking about my brother."

"Your brother?" Something flashed across Rhys's face, and slowly, he sat down next to me. He seemed almost breathless, and at first, I didn't understand, then it dawned on me.

This must be so weird for Rhys. His whole life he had known that this wasn't his real family, and it wasn't even the same as being adopted. His family hadn't wanted to give him up. He had been stolen, and not even by a family that had wanted him. They had just wanted me to have his life.

"Yeah. I mean... *your* brother actually," I corrected myself, and it felt painful saying that. Matt would always be my brother, no matter what our genetics claimed.

"What's his name?" Rhys asked quietly.

"Matt. He's pretty much the nicest guy in the whole world," I said,

"Matt?" Rhys repeated, in an awed tone.

"Yeah," I nodded. "He's the bravest guy ever. He would do anything to protect the people he cares about, and he's completely selfless. He always puts everybody first. And he's really, really strong. He's..." I swallowed and decided that I couldn't talk about him anymore. I shook my head and looked away.

"What about my mom and dad?" Rhys pressed, and I didn't know how to answer that.

"Dad died when I was five," I said carefully. "My mother took it pretty hard, and um... she's been in the hospital ever since. For psychiatric problems. Matt and my dad's sister, Maggie, they raised me."

"Oh." His face contorted with concern.

I suddenly hated Kim even more. I knew that she had done everything because she loved Rhys, but this is what I was left with telling him. And she'd never be able to have a life with him because she'd always be locked up. All she had done was hurt him and me and Matt and everyone.

"I'm sorry." I placed my hand gently on his, to comfort him. "It's hard to explain how I know it, but your mom really loved you. She really wanted you. And I think she always hated me because she knew I wasn't you."

"Really?" There was something hopeful and sad in his eyes when he looked at me.

"Yeah. It kind of sucked for me, actually," I smiled wanly at him, and he laughed.

"Sorry about that," Rhys smiled back at me. "I guess I'm too hard to forget."

"Yeah, I guess you are," I agreed. Rhys moved his hand so it was actually holding mine, and even though his mood seemed to brighten, I didn't take it from him.

"So what about this Maggie? What's she like?" Rhys asked.

"She's pretty cool. A little overly attentive sometimes, but cool," I said. "She put up with a lot of crap from me. They both did, really."

I thought about how strange this all was, that they weren't my family anymore. "This is so weird. They're your brother and your aunt."

"No, I understand. They're your family, too," Rhys said. "They loved you and raised you. That's what family is, right?"

I had needed someone to say that to me for so long, and I squeezed his hand gratefully. I still loved them and always would, and I just wanted that to be okay.

"Wendy!" Finn had just woken up, and he was on his way to check on me when he spotted me sitting on the steps. Instinctively, I pulled my hand back, and Rhys stood up. "What are you doing?"

"I just woke up. We were just talking." I looked up at Rhys, who nodded in agreement, but Finn glared at us both. I felt like we'd been caught robbing a bank by the way Finn looked at us.

"I suggest you get ready for school," Finn said icily.

"Yeah, that's what I was doing anyway," Rhys said somewhat defensively, then smiled down at me. "I'll see you later, Wendy."

"Yeah, okay," I smiled back at him.

"What are you doing?" Finn hissed, glowering down at me.

"I already told you," I insisted and stood up. He was still intimidating, but we were closer to the same height now, so I felt a bit better. "We were just talking!"

"About what?" Finn asked.

"My family," I shrugged. "What does it matter?"

"You cannot talk to him about your host family," Finn said firmly. "Mänsklig cannot know where they come from. If they did,

231

they would be tempted to track down their families, and that would completely ruin our entire society. Do you understand that?"

"I didn't really tell him anything!" I said, but I felt stupid that that hadn't occurred to me. "I missed Matt, and I just said stuff about how neat he was. I didn't tell Rhys where he lived or anything like that."

"You have to be more careful, Wendy," Finn said.

"Sorry. I didn't know." I didn't like the way he was glaring at me, so I turned and started walking down the hall toward my room.

"Wait." Finn grabbed my arm gently so I would stop and look at him.

He took a step closer to me so he was right in front of me, but I was trying to be mad at him, so I refused to look at him. I could still feel his eyes on me and the heat from his body, and it did little to help me maintain my anger.

"What?" I asked.

"I saw you holding his hand," Finn lowered his voice.

"So?" I said. "Is that a crime?"

"No, but... you *can't* do that," Finn explained emphatically. "You cannot get involved with a mänsklig."

"Whatever." I pulled my arm from his grip, irritated that the only thing he ever thought about was the job. "You're just jealous."

"I am not jealous," Finn said defensively and took a step back from me. "I am watching out for your well-being. You don't understand how dangerous it would be to get involved with him."

232

"Yeah, yeah," I muttered and started walking back to my room. "I don't understand anything."

"That's not what I said," Finn followed me.

"But it's true, isn't it?" I countered. "I don't know anything."

"Wendy!" Finn snapped, and grudgingly, I turned back to look at him. "If you don't understand things, it's because I didn't explain them well enough."

He swallowed hard and looked down at the ground, his dark eyelashes falling on his cheeks. There was something more that he wanted to say to me, so I crossed my arms, waiting.

"But you were right." He struggled with what he was saying, and I watched him carefully. "I was jealous."

"What?" My jaw literally fell open, and my eyes widened with surprise.

"That does not affect the job I have to do, nor does it change the fact that you absolutely cannot become involved with a mänsklig," Finn said firmly, still looking at the ground instead of at me. "Now go get ready. We have another long day ahead of us." He turned around and started to walk away.

"Wait, Finn!" I called after him, and he paused, half looking back at me.

"The matter is not open for discussion," Finn replied coolly. "I promised I would never lie to you, so I didn't."

I stood in front of my bedroom door, reeling from his confession. For the first time, he had really admitted that at least some of his feelings for me had nothing to do with the job at hand. Yet somehow, I was supposed to forget all that and go about as if everything were normal.

18. Intimidation

I spent a long time getting ready, still making sense of what Finn had told me. It thrilled me that he cared enough to feel jealous, but I also realized how pointless it was. He'd never do anything to jeopardize his sense of honor and duty.

Even with me taking so much time, Finn never came down to get me. Eventually, I went down to the spiraling staircase to wait for him. I thought about going down to his room, but I didn't really feel comfortable with it. Besides, he'd probably send me away.

From the top of the stairs, I could see the front door, and I was surprised when Tove Kroner pushed it open a few minutes later. He hadn't knocked or anything, and he ran a hand through his messy hair, looking around.

"Can I help you?" I called down. As Princess, I felt like I ought to be hospitable, even if I felt flustered and confused as hell.

"Uh, yeah. I'm looking for you." He shoved his hands in his pockets and walked to the bottom of the steps but didn't go any further.

"What for?" I wrinkled my nose, then realizing it sounded rude, shook my head. "I mean, I beg your pardon?"

"Just to help," Tove shrugged.

I walked slowly down the stairs, watching his eyes search the room. He never seemed comfortable looking at me. His dark hair had soft, natural highlights coursing through it, and it was longer and unruly, hitting just above his shoulders.

His tanned skin had a mossy undertone, the green complexion that Finn had told me about. Nobody else had skin like that, except maybe his mother, but hers was even fainter than Tove's already subtle coloring

"Help me with what?" I asked.

"What?" He'd taken to chewing on his thumbnail, and he glanced back at me, still biting it.

"What are you here to help me with?" I spoke carefully and slowly, almost condescending, but I don't think he noticed.

"Oh." He dropped his hand and stared off, as if he'd forgotten why he came. "I'm psychic."

"What? You can read minds?" I tensed up, trying to block him reading any of my thoughts.

"No, no, of course not." He brushed me off and walked away, admiring the chandelier hanging from the ceiling. "I can sense things. And I can move things with my mind. I can't read your thoughts, though. And I can see auras. Yours is a bit brown today."

"What does that mean?" I asked, crossing my arms over my chest, as if I could hide my aura. I didn't even really know what an aura was.

"You're unhappy." Tove sounded distracted, and he glanced back at me. "Normally it's orange."

"I don't know that means, either," I shook my head. "I don't know how any of that is supposed to help me."

"It's not really." He stopped moving and looked over at me. "Has Finn talked to you about training?"

"You mean the Princess training I'm doing now?"

"No." He shook his head, chewing the inside of his cheek. "For your abilities. It won't start until after the christening. They think if you had any handle on them *before* you were indoctrinated you'd run wild." He sighed. "They want you calm and docile."

"This is you calm?" I raised a skeptical eyebrow.

"No." Tove stared off at nothing again, then turned back to me, his green eyes meeting mine. "You intimidate me."

"*I* intimidate you?" I laughed, unable to stop myself, but he wasn't offended. "I'm the least intimidating person ever."

"Mmm." His face hardened in concentration. "Maybe to some people. But they don't see what I see or know what I know."

"What do you know?" I asked gently, startled by his confessions.

"Have they told you?" Tove eyed me up again.

"Told me what?"

"Well, if they haven't told you, I'm certainly not going to." He scratched at his arm and put his back to me as he walked away, looking around the room.

"Whatever it is you're doing, it's not helping," I said, growing frazzled. "You're only confusing me more."

"My apologies, Princess." Tove stopped moving and bowed at me. "Finn wanted me to talk to you about your abilities. He knows you can't start your real training until after the ball, but he wants you to be prepared."

"Finn asked you to come over?" My heart thumped in my chest.

"Yes." His brow creased with confusion. "Does this upset you?"

"No, not at all," I lied. Finn had probably sent Tove over so he wouldn't have to deal with me. He was avoiding me.

"Do you have questions?" Tove asked, stepping closer to me.

"Tons," I sighed. He cocked his head at me. "You'll have to be more specific."

"You have nothing to be afraid of, you know." Tove watched me closely, and I think I might've preferred it when he was scared to look at me.

"I'm not afraid." I squirmed away from his gaze.

"I can tell when you lie," he said, still watching me. "Not because I'm psychic, but because you're so obvious about it. You should probably work on that. Elora is very good at lying."

"I'll practice," I muttered.

"That's probably for the best." Tove spoke with an intense sincerity that I found disarming. His scattered insanity had its own charm to it. Running a hand through his thick hair, he looked down at the floor, his expression turning sad. "I rather like you this way. Honest and flustered. But it'd never work for a Queen."

"No, I don't suppose it would," I agreed, feeling a bit of melancholy myself.

"I'm a bit scattered myself, if you hadn't noticed." He gave me a small, crooked smile, but his green eyes stayed sad. With that, he crouched down, picking up a small, oval stone off the floor. He flipped it around his hand, staring down. "I find it hard to stay focused, but I'm working on it."

"So... not to sound mean or anything, but why did Finn want *you* to help?" I rubbed my arms, hoping I didn't upset him.

"Because I'm strong." Tove tossed the stone aside, apparently tiring of it. "And he trusts me." He looked back at me. "So let's see what you can do."

"With what?" I asked, confused by the abrupt change of subjects.

"Anything." He spread his arms wide. "Can you move stuff?"

"With my hands, yeah."

"Obviously," he rolled his eyes. "You're not a paraplegic so I assumed you were physically capable."

"I can't do much. Just some persuasion and I haven't used it since I've been here."

"Try." Tove pointed to the chandelier dangling above us. "Move that."

"I don't want to move that," I said, alarmed.

An image flashed in my mind. The painting I had seen in Elora's room, all dark smoke and red fires around broken chandeliers. Except the image seemed much more vivid, as if I could smell the smoke and the fire seemed to move, casting new shadows in the painting. The sound of glass shattering echoed in my ear.

I swallowed hard and shook my head, taking several steps back from the chandelier. I hadn't been underneath it exactly, but I wanted to get further away.

"What was that?" Tove asked, cocking his head at me.

"What?"

"Something happened." He studied me, trying to decipher my reaction, but I just shook my head. It felt like too much to explain, and I wasn't sure that I didn't imagine it. "Interesting."

"Thanks," I mumbled.

"I hate do this since you look so frightened, but I need to get you out of my head." He looked up at the chandelier, and my eyes followed his.

My heart raced in my chest, and my throat felt dry. The shards of glass twinkled and chimed and started to shimmer. I took several steps back, wanting to yell at him to stop, but I didn't even know if he'd listen. Then the whole chandelier started to sway, and I couldn't hold back.

"Stop!" I shouted, my voice echoing through the front hall. "Why are you doing that?"

"I am sorry." He exhaled deeply, and looked back down at me. I kept my eyes locked on the chandelier until I was certain it'd stopped moving. "I had to do something, and there was nothing else in the room I could move, except for you yourself, and I didn't think you'd like that either."

"Why did you have to move anything?" I snapped. My panic had started to fade, replaced by a pulsating anger, and I clenched my fists at my sides.

"When you get frightened like that, you project it so intensely." He held up his hands, pushing them out to demonstrate. "Most people can't hear it or feel anymore, but I'm particularly sensitive to that. And when I move things, it helps focus me. It kinda shuts off the noise for a while. You were too strong. I had to silence it." He shrugged. "I'm sorry."

"You didn't need to freak me out like that." I calmed a bit, but my words still came out hard.

"It's such a shame." Tove watched me, looking both bemused and rueful. "They won't even be able to see what you really are. They've all gotten so weak that they won't be able to tell how powerful you are."

"What are you talking about?" I momentarily forgot my anger.

"Your mother is so powerful," Tove sounded almost awed by it. "Probably not as much as you, and maybe not as much as me, but it's in her blood, crackling like electricity. I feel her walking through a room, and she's almost magnetized. But the rest of them..." He shook his head.

"You mean the other Trylle?" I clarified, since Tove insisted on being so cryptic.

"We used to move the earth." He sounded wistful, and his whole demeanor had changed. He hadn't been pacing or looking around, and I realized that the moving the chandelier really had done something to him.

"Are you speaking literally or metaphorically?" I asked.

"Literally. We could make mountains, stop rivers." He moved his arms dramatically, as if he could move them now. "We created everything around us! We were magic!"

"Aren't we still magic?" I asked, surprised by the passion in his voice.

"Not the way we were before. Once the humans created their own magic with technology, the dependence switched. They had all the power and the money, and we started to depend on them to raise our children," he scoffed. "Changelings stopped coming back, when they realized we didn't have that much to offer them anymore."

"We came back," I pointed out emptily.

"Your gardener, who makes the flowers bloom, she's a Marksinna!" Tove pointed to the back of the house, where the garden lay. "A *gardener*! I'm not one for class, but when one of the most powerful members of your population is the gardener, you know it's a problem."

"Well… why is she a gardener then?" I asked.

"Because. Nobody else can do it." He looked at me, his green eyes burning with something. "Nobody can do anything anymore."

"You can. I can," I said, hoping to alleviate whatever distressed him.

"I know." He sighed and lowered his eyes. "Everyone's just gotten too fixated on the human system of monarchy. With designer dresses and expensive jewels." His lip curled back with disgust. "Our obsession with riches has always been our downfall."

"Yeah," I nodded. "But your mother seems to be the worst with it."

"I know." Tove raised his eyebrows with a knowing weariness. Something softened, and he looked almost apologetically at me. "I'm not against humans. It sounds like I am, doesn't it?"

"I don't know. It sounds like you're passionate," I said.

When I'd first met him, I'd mistaken his inattention as boredom and arrogance. But I was starting to think his abilities had something to do with that, giving him kind of an unfocused ADD, and behind that, he had a fearless honesty that few Trylle seemed to possess.

"Maybe." He smiled and lowered his eyes, looking slightly embarrassed.

"How old are you?" I asked.

"Nineteen. Why?"

"How do you know so much about the past? You talked about the way things were like you were there, like you saw it happen. Or like you're a major history buff or something."

"My mother is keen on me studying, in case I ever get a chance for the throne," Tove said, but the idea seemed to tire him. I doubted he was any more excited about the prospect of ruling than I was. Aurora's scheming for the crown was entirely her idea.

"So you just study a lot?" I asked.

"What'd you see when you looked at the chandelier?" Tove

asked me directly.

"I don't know." I shook my head. I wanted to answer honestly, but I didn't know how to. "I saw... a painting."

"Some people see the future." He stared up at the chandelier, the lights twinkling above us. "And some people see the past." He paused, thinking. "In the end, they're not all that different. You can't prevent either of them."

"How profound," I said, and he laughed.

"I haven't helped you at all, have I?"

"I don't know," I admitted.

"You're too much for one afternoon, I'm afraid," Tove said. I didn't know what he meant by that, but if I asked, he'd only answer with something that confused me more.

"Sorry?"

"I know you have a lot to go over, and you don't need me wasting your time." He walked towards the door, and I had a suspicion that Tove was a rather abrupt person.

"Hey, wait," I said, and he stopped. "You said that Finn wanted you to help prepare me. For what?"

"Finn's a protector. It's his job to worry," Tove explained, and my heart twisted. I hated it when people pointed out that I was just part of Finn's job. "He needs to know that in any event, you'll be taken care of. Whether he's there or not."

"Why wouldn't he be there?" I asked, feeling fear ripple through me.

"I don't know," Tove shrugged. "But when something really matters to you, you make sure it's safe."

With that, Tove turned and walked of the house. I thanked him for his help, but I wasn't even sure what he'd done. Other than confuse me more. And I felt a new sense of dread settling over me.

I had no idea what was going on with Finn, and my thoughts insisted on going back to the other painting I'd seen in Elora's secret room. I had been reaching off the balcony, looking horrified. Tove's words echoed through my mind, sending a chill down my spine.

You can't prevent the future.

I looked up at the chandelier. I'd been too terrified to even try to move it, thinking it would collapse, and I'd bring Elora's other painting into life. But I hadn't.

Had I changed the future? Or was I simply wrong about what the pictures were interpreting? Was the worst still to come?

19. Christening

With the party only twenty-four hours away, Elora felt the need to check on my progress, not that I blamed her. Her plan was a dress rehearsal through dinner, testing my ability to converse and eat, apparently.

She didn't want a massive audience to witness my possible failure, so she just invited Garrett, Willa, and Rhiannon over to join her, Finn, Rhys, and me. It was the biggest group she could assemble without risk of embarrassment. Since I had already met with these people, I didn't feel all that nervous, even though Elora informed me beforehand that I needed to act the same way I would tomorrow night.

Everyone had been instructed similarly, and they all appeared far more regal than normal. Even Rhys had dressed in a blazer, and he looked rather handsome. As usual, Finn was unnecessarily attractive.

Thanks to Finn's random confession of jealousy, I wasn't entirely sure how to act around him. He had come into my room before dinner to make sure that I was getting ready, but I couldn't help but feel that he was purposefully avoiding looking at me.

When I reached the dining hall, Elora instructed us where to sit, with her at one end of the table, and me at the other. Rhys and Finn flanked me, and Rhiannon and Willa filled in the empty places.

"Who will I be sitting by tomorrow?" I asked between careful sips of wine.

"Between Tove Kroner and I." Elora narrowed her eyes at the way I was drinking my wine. "Hold the glass by the stem."

"Sorry." I thought I had been, but I moved my fingers, hoping I was holding it more correctly.

"A Princess never apologizes," Elora corrected me.

"Sorry," I mumbled, then realized what I did and shook my head. "That was an accident. It won't happen again."

"Don't shake your head; it's not ladylike," Elora chastised me. "A Princess doesn't make promises, either. She might not be able to keep them, and she doesn't want them held against her."

"I wasn't really making a promise," I pointed out, and Elora narrowed her eyes more severely.

"A Princess is never contrary," Elora said coolly.

"I've only been a Princess for like two weeks. Can't you give me a little break?" I asked as kindly as I could.

I'd grown frustrated by all the Princess talk. Nearly every sentence she'd said to me in the past two days had started with "a Princess" and it was followed by things that a Princess never or always did.

"You've been a Princess your entire life. It's in your blood," Elora said firmly, sitting up even straighter in her chair, trying to loom over me. "You should know how to behave."

"I am working on it," I grumbled.

"Speak up. Use a clear strong voice no matter what it is you're saying," Elora snapped. "And you don't have time to work on it. Your party is tomorrow. You must be ready *now*."

I wanted to snap something back at her, but both Rhys and Finn were giving me warning stares to keep my mouth shut. Rhiannon stared nervously at her plate, and Garrett just went about munching his food politely.

"I understand," I exhaled deeply and took another drink of my wine. I'm not sure if I held the glass right this time, but Elora didn't say anything.

"So, I got your picture of the dress," Willa smiled at me. "It was really stunning. I'm a little jealous, actually. You only get to be the belle of the ball once, and you definitely will be tomorrow. You're going to look amazing."

She was coming to my aid, changing the subject from things I was doing wrong to something I was doing right. Even if she was a bitch to Finn and Rhiannon, I just couldn't bring myself to hate her.

"Thank you," I smiled gratefully back at her.

My final fitting had been earlier in the day, and since Willa had requested it the other night at dinner, I had sent her a picture. It had actually been Finn's idea, and he had used his camera phone.

I felt very awkward and not at all pretty posing for it, and he never reassured me that I looked good in the dress. It felt too fancy for me, and I would've liked a little boost just then. But Finn had just snapped the picture, and that had been the end of that.

"Have you seen the dress?" Willa turned to Elora, who nibbled primly at a piece of broccoli.

"No. I trust Frederique's designs, and Finn has final approval," Elora answered absently.

"I'm going to insist on being involved in the process when my daughter gets her gown," Willa offered thoughtfully. Elora bristled imperceptibly at that, but Willa didn't notice. "But I've always loved dresses and fashion. I could spend my whole life at a ball." She looked wistful for a moment, then smiled at me again. "That's why it's so great that you're here. You're going to have such a monumental ball."

"Thank you," I repeated, unsure of how else to respond.

"You had a lovely party yourself," Garrett interjected, feeling slightly defensive about the party he had thrown for his daughter. "Your gown was fantastic."

"I know," Willa smiled immodestly. "It was pretty great." Finn made a noise in his throat, and both Elora and Willa glared at him, but neither of them said anything.

"My apologies. Something caught in my throat," Finn explained, taking a sip of his wine.

"Hmm," Elora murmured disapprovingly, then cast her stare back at me. "Oh, that reminds me. I have been too busy this week to ask you. What were your plans for your name?"

"My name?" I asked, raising any eyebrow.

"Yes. At the christening ceremony." She looked at me for a moment, then looked sternly at Finn. "I thought Finn told you about it."

"Yes, but isn't that name already decided?" I was definitely confused. "I mean, Dahl is the family name, isn't it?"

"Not the surname," Elora clarified, annoyed. "I meant your first name."

"I don't understand." I furrowed my brow and tried to read her stony expression. "My name is Wendy."

"That isn't a proper name for a Princess," Elora scoffed. "Everyone changes their names. Willa used to be called something different. What was it, dear?"

"Nikki," Willa said. "I took the name Willa, after my mother."

Garrett smiled at that, and Elora tensed up slightly, but quickly tried to erase it. Her plan seemed to push all her tension in my direction.

"So what is it? What name would you like?" Elora pressed.

"I... I don't know," I stumbled.

Irrationally, my heart had started pounding my chest. I didn't want to change my name, not at all. When Finn had told me that about the christening ceremony, I had assumed it would only be my last name, and while I wasn't that thrilled about that, I didn't care that much. Eventually, I would probably get married and change my name anyway.

But Wendy, that was *my* name. I turned to Finn for help, but Elora noticed and snapped my attention back to her.

"If you need ideas, I have some." Elora had a clipped tone to her voice, and she was cutting her food with an irritated fervor. "Ella, after my mother. I had a sister, Sybilla. Those names are both lovely. One of our longest running queens was Lovisa, and I've always thought highly of that name."

"It's not that I don't like any of those," I explained carefully. Although, really, I thought Sybilla was quite terrible. "I like my name. I don't know why I have to change it."

"Wendy is a ridiculous name," Elora waved off the idea. "It's entirely improper for a Princess."

"Why?" I persisted, and Elora glared up at me.

I flat out refused to change my name, no matter what Elora said. It's not that I thought Wendy was a particularly fabulous name, but Matt had given it to me. He was the only one that had ever wanted me, and I wasn't going to get rid of the one thing that I had left of him.

"It is the name of a mänsklig," Elora said through gritted teeth. "And I have had enough of this. You will find a name to suit a Princess, or I will choose one for you. Is that clear?"

"If I am a Princess, then why can't I decide what is proper?" I forced my voice to stay even and clear, trying not to let it shake with anger and frustration. "Isn't that part of the glory of being a Princess, of ruling a kingdom? Having some say in the rules? And if I want my name to be Wendy, why is that so wrong?"

"No Princess has ever kept her human name, and no one ever will." Her dark eyes glared severely at me, but I matched it firmly.

"My daughter, the Princess, will not carry the name of a *mänks*."

There was a bitter edge dripping from the word "mänks," and I saw Rhys' jaw tense. I knew what it was like to grow up with a mother that hated me, but I had never been required to sit quietly why she openly made derogatory remarks about me. My heart went out to him, and I had to struggle even harder to keep from shouting at Elora.

"I will not change my name," I insisted. Everyone had taken to looking down at their plates while Elora and I stared down each other. This dinner had to be considered an epic failure.

"This is not the proper place to have this discussion," Elora said icily. She rubbed her temple, then sighed. "It's no matter. There isn't a discussion to be had. Your name will be changed, and clearly, I will be picking for you."

"That's not fair!" Tears welled up in my eyes, and I had started to whine. "I am the Princess and it's what I want! You said I didn't have to answer to anybody!"

"Anybody but me," Elora clarified calmly.

"With all due respect," Finn interrupted our argument, startling everyone into looking at him, but he kept his voice emotionless. "If it is as the Princess wishes, then perhaps it's as it should be. Her wishes are going to be the highest order of the land, and this is such a simple one that I can't imagine anyone would find offense with it."

"Perhaps," Elora forced a thin smile at him, giving him a hard look, but he stared back at her, his eyes meeting hers unabashedly.

"But right now, my wishes are still the highest order, and until that has changed, my word will remain final."

Her smile deepened, growing even more menacing, as she continued. "With all due respect, *tracker*, perhaps you care too much for her wishes and too little for her duties." His expression faltered momentarily, but he quickly met her eyes again. "Was it not your duty to inform her of the specifics of the christening and have her completely ready for tomorrow?"

"It was," Finn replied without any trace of shame.

"It seems you have failed, as well," Elora surmised. "I'm beginning to question how exactly you've been filling your time with the Princess. Has any of it been spent on training?"

Suddenly, Rhys knocked over a glass of wine. The glass shattered and liquid splattered everywhere. Everyone had been too busy staring at Elora and Finn, but out of the corner of my eye, I saw him do it on purpose.

Rhys started apologizing and rushing about to clean it up, but Elora had stopped glaring at Finn, and he no longer had to defend himself. Rhys had come to his rescue, and I couldn't be more relieved.

After the mess was cleaned up, Willa, who had never been that fond of Rhys, suddenly began chatting incessantly with him, and he eagerly reciprocated. They talked just so that Elora and Finn couldn't.

Elora still managed to squeeze in a few biting comments towards me, such as "really, Princess, you must know how to use a fork." But as soon as she had finished her sentence, Willa would pipe up with a funny story about this girl she knew or this movie she saw or this place she went. It was endless, and in general, we were all grateful.

When dinner was over, Elora claimed she had a migraine brewing and a million things to do for tomorrow. She apologized that dessert would not be served tonight, but she didn't leave her seat at the head of the table. Unsure of what else to do, everybody started to excuse themselves. Garrett suggested that they should be heading out, and she nodded noncommittally.

"I will see you tomorrow evening," Elora replied hollowly. She stared into space instead of looking at him, and he tried not to look troubled by this.

"Take care of yourself," Garrett said, touching her shoulder gently.

Finn, Rhys, and I rose to see Garrett, Willa, and Rhiannon to the door, but Elora's voice stopped me cold. I think it stopped everyone else, too, but they did a better job of playing it off.

"Finn?" Elora said flatly, still staring off at nothing. "Would you escort me to my drawing room? I'd like to have a word with you."

"Yes, of course," Finn replied, giving her a small bow.

I froze and looked to him, but he refused to look at me. He just stood stoically, hands crossed behind his back, and waited for Elora to ask for further assistance.

I might've stood there until Elora commanded me to go, but Willa looped her arm through mine and started to drag me away. I wanted to hate her for it, but I knew she was just saving me from another of Elora's tirades.

Rhys and Rhiannon were just ahead of us, whispering quietly to each other. Garrett stole one last glance at Elora and walked on to the front door.

"So, I'll come over about ten tomorrow morning," Willa said, purposely keeping her tone light and cheery.

"What for?" I asked, feeling somewhat dazed.

"To help you get ready. There is *so* much to do!" Willa said, and then shot a look in the direction of the dining room. "And your mother doesn't seem to be the helpful type."

"Willa, don't talk bad about the Queen," Garrett said without conviction.

"Well, anyway, I'll be over to help you with everything. You'll be fabulous." She gave me a reassuring smile and squeezed my arm.

"Thanks." I wanted to smile at her, but I couldn't make it work.

I was genuinely relieved to have her helping me, but a sick feeling grew inside of me. Whatever Elora was saying to Finn, it couldn't be good. Garrett flashed me an unconvincing smile, then they disappeared out the door, leaving Rhys and I standing in the entryway.

"You okay?" Rhys asked.

"Yeah, I'm fine," I lied.

I felt oddly shaky and ill, and I was pretty sure that I didn't want to be a Princess anymore. There weren't many more dinners like this

I could handle. I took a step away, preparing to tell Elora just that, but I felt Rhys's hand warm on my arm, stopping me.

"If you go in there, you'll just make it worse," Rhys insisted gently. "Come on."

He put his hand on the small of my back and ushered me over to the stairs. When we reached them, I expected him to try to push me up the stairs to my room, but he didn't. He knew that I had to wait for Finn and find out what happened.

I peered over the railing, hoping to catch a glimpse of something. I'm not sure what that would help, but I thought if I could just *see* what was happening, I could somehow make it okay.

"That was a rough dinner," Rhys said with a joyless laugh and sat down on the steps. I couldn't see anything, so I gave up. Pulling my skirt underneath me, I sat on the stairs next to him.

"I'm sorry," I said.

"Don't be sorry. It wasn't your fault," Rhys assured me with his lopsided grin. "You just made this house a whole lot more interesting."

Elora had purposely made that spectacle public. Otherwise, she would've said it privately, inside Finn's head. For some reason, she had wanted me to witness that. I didn't understand what exactly he had done wrong, except disagree with her. But he had been respectful and hadn't said anything that wasn't true.

"What do you think she's saying?" I asked.

"I don't know," Rhys said. "She's never really yelled at me."

"You've got to be kidding," I stared at him skeptically. Rhys behaved like a kid that had gotten in trouble a lot in his life, and Elora was about as strict as they came.

"No, seriously," Rhys laughed at my shock. "She's snapped at me to knock stuff off when she's around me, but do you know how often she's even around? I was raised by nannies. Elora made it perfectly clear from day one that she wasn't my mother, and she never wanted to be."

"Did she ever want to be a mother at all?" What little I knew of her seemed to be lacking even the slightest bit of maternal instinct.

"Honestly?" Rhys debated whether or not to tell me, before sadly replying, "No. I don't think she did. But she had a lineage to carry on. A duty."

"I'm just part of her job," I muttered bitterly. "For once, I just wish that somebody actually wanted me around."

"Oh, come on, Wendy," Rhys admonished me softly and leaned in closer to me. "Lots of people want you around." His blue eyes searched over me, so I swallowed hard and looked down at the floor. "You can't take it personally that Elora's a bitch." Rhys looked away, and I felt an odd combination of relief and disappointment

"It's a little hard not to." I fidgeted with my dress. "She's my mother."

"Elora is a strong, complicated woman that you and I can't even begin to understand," Rhys explained tiredly. "She is a Queen above all else, and that makes her cold and distant and cruel."

"What was it like growing up with that?" I glanced over at him.

"I don't know." He shrugged. "Probably like growing up in a boarding school with a strict headmistress. She was always lurking in the background, and I knew that she had the final say on everything. But her interaction with me was at an absolute minimum." He looked at me again, this time uncertainly.

"What?"

"She's not quite as secretive as she thinks, though. This is a big house, but I was a sneaky little kid." He bit his lip and fiddled with a button on his blazer. "You know she used to sleep with Finn's dad?"

"I did," I said quietly.

"I thought he would tell you." Rhys fell silent for a minute, chewing his lip. "Elora was in love with him. She's strange when she's in love. Her face is different, softer and more radiant." Rhys shook his head, lost in a memory. "It was almost worse seeing her like that, knowing that she's capable of kindness and generosity. It made me feel gypped that all I ever got were icy glares from across the room."

"I'm sorry." I put my hand gently on his arm. I couldn't imagine how horrible it had been for him to grow up like that. He forced a smile, then shook his head, clearing it of the memory.

"Anyway. He left Elora, for his wife, which was just as well." Rhys looked thoughtful for a moment. "Although, I bet she would've thrown it all away to be with him, if he had really loved her. But that's not the point."

"What is the point?" I asked shakily.

"Rumor has it she keeps Finn around because she stills loves his old man, even though he never loved her. Nothing's ever happened between Finn and Elora, I'm sure." Rhys let out a heavy sigh. "But…"

"What?" I asked when he didn't say anything.

"Finn's dad never looked at her the way Finn looks at you." He let it hang in the air for a second as I tried to figure out what he meant by that. "So you've got that strike against you too. She never wanted to be a mother, and you're getting the one thing she never had."

"What are you talking about?" I demanded nervously.

"Wendy." Rhys looked at me with a sad smile. "I know that I wear my heart on my sleeve, but you're just as bad."

"I don't know what you're talking about," I stuttered and looked away from him.

"Alright," Rhys laughed hollowly. "Whatever you say."

To lighten the moment, Rhys made some joke that I didn't really catch. My mind raced and my heart pounded. Rhys must be imagining things. And even if he wasn't, surely Elora wouldn't punish Finn for that. Would she?

20. Resignation

Finn reached the stairs, and I scrambled to my feet. He had probably only been with Elora for fifteen minutes, but in my mind, it seemed like forever. Rhys sat next to me, but he got up much slower than I had. Finn looked over us with some disdain, then turned and started walking up the stairs without a word towards me.

"Finn!" I jogged after him, but Rhys rather smartly made his escape to the kitchen. "Wait! Finn! What happened?"

"A conversation," Finn replied glibly. I scurried to keep up with him, but he made no effort to slow down, so I grabbed his arm, stopping him halfway up the stairs. He glanced back over his shoulder, looking for Rhys, but refused to look at me. "I thought I told you to stay away from the mänsklig."

"Rhys was just sitting with me while I waited for you," I said. "Get over it."

"It's very dangerous for you to be around him." Finn faced the top of the stairs but looked at me from the corner of his eye. "It's dangerous for you to be around me." I didn't appreciate the way he wouldn't look at me anymore. He was always looking everywhere but at me, and I missed his dark eyes.

"What's that supposed to be mean?" I demanded.

"Let go of my arm," Finn said.

"Just tell me what's going on, and I'll leave you alone," I said,

261

refusing to let go. He was much stronger than me, and I didn't hold on that tightly, but he didn't even try to free himself.

"I have been relieved of my duties," Finn answered carefully. "Elora no longer perceives a threat, and I have been insubordinate. I am to pack my things and leave the premises as soon as possible."

The air completely went out of my lungs. It was my worst fear. Finn was going to leave, and it was my fault. He had been defending me when I should've been defending myself. Or I should've just kept my mouth shut.

"What?" I gaped at him when I could finally speak. "That's not right. You can't... You've been here for so long, and Elora trusts you. She can't... It's my fault! I'm the one that refused to listen!"

"No, it's not your fault," Finn insisted firmly. "You didn't do anything wrong."

"Well, you can't just leave! I have the ball tomorrow, and I don't know anything!" I continued desperately. "I'm not a Princess at all! You have so much left to help me with!"

"I wouldn't be helping you after the ball anyway," Finn shook his head. "A tutor will be coming in to help you learn everything you need to know from here on out. You're ready for the ball, no matter what Elora says. You'll do wonderfully tomorrow."

"But you won't be here?" I looked at him, unbelieving, and he turned away from me.

"You don't need me," Finn said quietly.

"This is my fault!" I repeated. "I'm gonna talk to Elora. You can't leave. She has to see that."

"Wendy, no, you can't-" Finn tried to stop me, but I had already started down the stairs.

There was this unbearable panic settling over me. Finn had forced me to leave the only people who had ever made me feel loved, and I had done it because I trusted him. But now he was going to leave me alone with Elora and a monarchy I didn't want.

Rhys would still be here, but I knew that it was only a matter of time before she sent him off as well. I was going to be more alone and isolated than I ever had been before, and I couldn't handle it.

Even as I was running down to Elora's drawing room, I knew it was more than that. I couldn't stand to lose Finn, and it didn't matter how Elora or anyone else treated me. A life without him just didn't seem possible anymore. I hadn't even realized how important he had become to me until Elora threatened to take him away.

"Elora!" I threw open the drawing room door without knocking, and I knew it would piss her off, but I didn't care. Maybe if I was insubordinate enough, she would send me away too.

Elora stood in front of the windows, staring out at the black night, and she wasn't startled at all by the door slamming open. Without turning to look at me, she calmly said, "That's completely unnecessary, and it goes without saying that that is not at all how a Princess behaves."

"You're always going on about how a Princess should behave, but what about how a Queen should act?" I countered icily. "Are you

263

such an insecure ruler that you can't handle the slightest bit of dissention? If we don't bow instantly to your opinion, you ship us off?"

"I assume this is about Finn," Elora sighed.

"You had no right to fire him!" I shouted. "He did nothing wrong!"

"It doesn't matter if he did anything wrong, I can 'fire' anyone for any reason. I am the Queen." Slowly, she turned to me, her face stunningly emotionless. "It is not the act of disagreeing that I had a problem with; it was why."

"This is about my stupid name?" I spouted incredulously.

"There is much you still have to learn. Please, sit." Elora gestured to one of the couches, and she laid back on the chaise lounge. "There's no need to get huffy with me, Princess. We need to talk."

"I don't want to change my name," I said, but I sat down on the couch across from her. "I don't know why it's such a big deal to you. Names can't be that important."

"It's not about the name," Elora waved it off. Her hair flowed out like silk around her, and she ran her fingers through it absently. "I know that you think I'm cruel and heartless, but I'm not. I care very deeply for Finn, more than a Queen should care for a servant, and I am sorry that I have been so negligent in the examples that I have set for you. It pains me to see Finn go, but I can assure you that I did it for you."

"You did not!" I yelled. "You did it because you were jealous!"

"My emotions played no part in this decision. Not even the way I feel about you factored into this." Her lips tightened, and she stared emptily at me. "I did what I had to do because it was best for the kingdom."

"How is getting rid of him best for anybody?" I asked.

"You refuse to understand that you are a Princess!" Elora sounded mildly irritated but quickly pushed it away. "It doesn't matter if you understand the gravity of the situation. Everyone else does, including Finn, which is why he is leaving. He knows this is best for you, too."

"I don't understand." I furrowed my brow with confusion and frustration. It would be so much easier if she would just spit things out.

"I know you think this is all about money, but it's about something more powerful than that. Our bloodline is rich with tremendous abilities, far exceeding the general Trylle population," Elora explained. "Unfortunately, Trylle have become less interested in our way of life, and the abilities have begun to weaken. It is essential to our people that the bloodline is kept pure, that the abilities are allowed to flourish.

"The titles and positions seem arbitrary," Elora continued. "But we are in power because we have the most power. For centuries, our abilities outshined every other family, but the Kroners are rapidly overtaking us. You are the last chance for hanging onto the throne and restoring power to our people."

"What does this have to do with Finn?" I demanded, growing tired of political talk.

"Everything," Elora answered with a thin smile. "In order to keep the bloodlines as pure and powerful as possible, certain rules were put into effect. Not just for royalty, but for everyone. It's not meant just as a repercussion for behaving outside of societal norms, but also so their half-breed spawn won't weaken our bloodlines." Something about the way she said "spawn" sent a chill down my spine.

"Consequences vary in severity," Elora continued. "When a Trylle becomes involved with a mänsklig, they are asked to leave the community.

"There's nothing going on between Rhys and me," I interjected, but Elora nodded skeptically.

"While trackers are Trylle, they don't possess abilities in the conventional sense," Elora went on, and I started to realize what she was getting at. "Trackers are meant to be with trackers. If Trylle are involved with them, they are looked down upon, but it is allowed.

"Unless you are royalty," she looked severely at me. "A tracker can never have the crown. Any Marksinna or Princess caught with a tracker is immediately stripped of her title. If the offense is bad enough, such as a Princess destroying an essential bloodline, then they would both be banished."

I swallowed hard. If anything happened between Finn and me, I wouldn't be able to be a Princess, and I wouldn't even be able to live in Förening anymore. That was shocking at first, until I realized that I didn't even want to be a Princess or live here. What did I care?

"So?" I said, and Elora looked momentarily surprised.

"I know that right now all of this means nothing to you." Elora gestured widely to the room around us. "I know you hate this, and I understand. But this is your destiny, and even if you don't see it, Finn does. He knows how important you are, and he would never let you ruin your future. That is why he offered up his resignation."

"He *quit?*" I didn't believe her.

Finn wouldn't quit. He wouldn't leave me here, not when he knew how much I needed him. And he had to know. That's why he stood up for me with Elora. He knew that I would be lost without him, and he couldn't do that to me. It would go against everything he believed in.

"I blame myself because the signs were so obvious," Elora sighed. "And I blame Finn, because he knows better than to get involved, better than anyone. But I commend him for realizing what the right thing was for you. He is leaving to protect you."

"There's nothing I need protection from!" I got to my feet. "He has no reason to leave! Nothing's going on! I'm not involved with anyone."

"I would find that much more believable if you hadn't raced down here with tears in your eyes to plead for his job," Elora replied coolly. "Or if he had promised me he could keep things purely business from here on, I would've kept him." She looked down at the chaise, playing with a loose thread in the fabric. "But he couldn't even do that. He didn't even try."

I wanted to argue with her, but I started to realize exactly what she was saying. Finn cared about me, and he'd admitted it to Elora, knowing how she would react. He cared about me so much, he had been unable to continue his job. He couldn't keep things separate anymore, and he was upstairs packing to leave right now.

I would've liked to yell at Elora more, blame her for everything horrible in my life and tell her that I was giving up the crown, but I didn't have time to waste. I had to catch him before he left, because I had no idea where he would go.

By the time I made it to his room, my breath was ragged. My hands were trembling, and that familiar butterfly feeling Finn gave me spread out through me. I was in love with him, and I wasn't going to give him up. Not for anything in this world or the next.

When I opened his bedroom door, he stood over his bed, folding clothes and putting them in a suitcase. He looked back at me, surprised by my appearance, and he let his dark eyes rest on me again.

Dark stubble covered his cheeks, and there was something so ruggedly handsome about him, he was almost unbearable to look at. The top few buttons of his dress shirt were undone, revealing a hint of chest that I found strangely provocative.

"Are you alright?" Finn stopped what he was doing and took a step to me.

"Yeah," I nodded, swallowing hard. "I'm going with you."

"Wendy..." His expression softened, and he shook his head. "You can't go with me. You need to be here."

"No, I don't care about here!" I insisted. "I don't want to be a stupid Princess! And they don't need me!"

"They do need you. You have no idea how badly they need you." Finn turned away from me. "Without you, it will completely fall apart."

"That doesn't make any sense! I'm just one stupid girl who can't even figure out which fork to eat with! I have no abilities! I'm awkward and silly and inappropriate! That Kroner kid is much better suited for this!" I yelled. "I don't need to be here, and I'm not going to stay if you're not here!"

"There is much you have yet to learn," Finn said tiredly, almost to himself. He had started folding his clothes again, so I walked over to him and grabbed his arm.

"I want to be with you, and... I think you want to be with me." I felt sick to my stomach saying it aloud. I expected him to laugh at me or tell me that I was insane, but instead, he slowly looked over at me.

In a rare moment of vulnerability, his dark eyes betrayed everything they had been trying to hide from me; affection and warmth, and something even deeper than that. His arm felt strong under my hand, and my heart pounded in my chest. Gently, he placed his hand on my cheek, letting his fingers press warmly on my skin, and I stared hopefully at him

"I am not worth it, Wendy," Finn whispered hoarsely. "You are going to be so much more than this, and I cannot hold you back. I refuse to."

"But Finn, I-" I wanted to tell him more, but he pulled his hand away.

"You have to go." He turned his back to me completely, busying himself with anything so he wouldn't have to look at me.

"Why?" I demanded, tears stinging at my eyes.

"Because." Finn picked up some of his books off a shelf, and I followed right behind him, unwilling to relent in my pursuit of him.

"That's not even a reason!"

"I've already explained it to you."

"No, you haven't! You've just made vague comments about the future!" I insisted.

"I don't want you!" Finn snapped.

I felt like I had been slapped. For a moment, I stood in a stunned silence, just listening to the sound of my heartbeat echo in my ears.

"You're lying!" A tear slipped down my cheek. "You promised you would never lie to me!"

"Wendy! I need you to leave!" Finn growled.

He breathed heavily, with his back to me, but he had stopped moving around. He leaned against the bookshelf, his shoulders hunched forward.

This was my last chance to convince him, and I knew it. I

touched his back, and he tried to pull away from me, but I wouldn't move my hand. He whirled on me, grabbing my wrist. He pushed me until my back was against the wall, pinning me there.

His body pressed tightly against mine, the strong contours of his muscles against the soft curves of mine, and I could feel his heart hammering against my chest. He still gripped my wrist, restraining one of my hands against the wall.

I'm not sure what he intended to do, but he looked down at me, his dark eyes smoldering. Then suddenly, I felt his lips pressed roughly against mine.

He kissed me desperately, like he couldn't breathe without me. I felt his stubble scraping against my cheeks, my lips, my neck, everywhere he dared press his mouth against me. He let go of my wrist, allowing me to wrap my arms around him and pull him even closer to me.

Seconds ago, I had been crying, and I could taste the salt from my tears on his lips. Tangling my fingers in his hair, I pushed his mouth more eagerly against mine. My heart beat so fast, it hurt, and an intense heat spread through me.

Somehow, he managed to pull his mouth from mine. His hands gripped my shoulders, holding me to the wall, and he took a step back. Breathing hard, he looked at the ground instead of at me, and his dark lashes lay on his cheeks.

"This is why I have to go, Wendy. I can't do this to you."

"To me? You're not doing anything to me." I tried to reach out

271

for him, but he held me back. "Just let me go with you."

"Wendy…" He put his hand back on my cheek, using his thumb to brush away a fresh tear, and looked at me intently. "You trust me, don't you?" I nodded hesitantly. "Then you have to trust me on this. You *need* to stay here, and I need to go. Okay?"

"Finn!"

"I'm sorry." Finn let go of me and grabbed his half-packed suitcase off his bed. "I stayed too long." He started walking to the door, and I ran after him. "Wendy! Enough!"

"But you can't just leave…" I pleaded.

He hesitated at the doorway and shook his head. Finn opened the door and left.

I could've followed him, but I didn't have any more arguments. His kiss had left me feeling dazed and disarmed, and I wondered dimly if that had been his plan all along. He knew his kiss would leave me too weak to chase after him and too confused to argue with him.

After he had gone, I just sat down on the bed that still smelled like him, and I started to sob.

21. The Ball

I'm not sure I had slept at all when Willa burst in my room the next morning to wake me for the ball. My eyes were red and swollen, but she made very little comment about it. She just started in on getting me ready and talking excitedly about how much fun it was all going to be. I didn't really believe her, but she didn't notice.

Almost everything I did required verbal and physical prompts. She even had to remind me to rinse the shampoo from my hair, and I was just lucky that modesty had never been her strong suit.

It was impossible to combine fresh heartbreak with the fervor of a ball. Willa kept trying to get me excited or at least nervous about something, but it was completely futile. The only way I managed to function was by being completely numb.

I didn't even understand how this had happened. When I had first met Finn, he had seemed creepy, and then he was just irritating. Repeatedly, I had rejected him and told him that I didn't need him or want to be around him.

How had it turned into this? I had lived my whole stupid life without him, and now I could barely make it through the hour.

I sat on a stool, wrapped in my robe, while Willa did something to my hair. She had offered to do it in front of a mirror so I could see her progress, but I didn't care. Holding a bottle of spray in her hand, she stopped what she was doing and just looked at me.

"Wendy," Willa sighed. "I know Finn's gone, and you're obviously taking it pretty hard. But he's just a stork, and you are a *Princess.*"

"You don't know what you're talking about," I mumbled.

I had thought about defending him, but in all honesty, I was kind of pissed that he had left without me. There was no way that I could've left him after that kiss. As it was, it had been torture to stay behind. I just lowered my eyes and tried to close the subject.

"Fine. I don't." Willa rolled her eyes and went back to spraying my hair. "But you're still a Princess, and this is your night." I didn't say anything as she yanked and teased. "You're still young. You don't understand how many fish there really are in the sea, especially your sea. The most eligible, attractive men are gonna be all over you, and you're not even gonna remember that stupid stork that brought you here."

"I don't like fishing," I muttered dryly, but she ignored me.

"You know who is a catch? Tove Kroner." Willa made a pleased sound "I wish my dad would set me up with him." She sighed wistfully and jerked on a strand of my hair.

"He's really foxy, really rich," Willa went on, as if I had asked her to tell me more. "He's like the highest Markis in the world, which is so weird. The Marksinna are usually the ones with all the abilities. Guys can do some things, but they pale in comparison to what women can do, but Tove has more ability than anybody else. I wouldn't be surprised if he could read minds."

"I thought nobody could do that," I said, amazed that I was even following her.

"No. Only very, very few can. So few it's almost the stuff of legends these days." She gently fluffed at my hair. "But Tove is the stuff of legends, so that makes sense. And if you play your cards right, you'll be pretty damn legendary yourself." She whipped me around so she was facing me again and smiled at her handiwork. "Now we just need to get you into your gown."

Somehow, while getting me ready, Willa had managed to ready herself. She had on a floor length light blue gown that swept around her, and she looked so beautiful, I had no hope of topping her.

After she had finally gotten me into my own dress, she forced me in front of the mirror, insisting that I looked too amazing to ignore.

"Oh wow." Saying that to my reflection felt egotistical, but I couldn't help it. I had never looked better in my life, and I doubted that I would ever look this good again.

The gown was a shimmery silver and white that flowed around me. It was strapless in an elegant way, and the diamond necklace Willa had chosen set it off. My dark curls fell perfectly behind me, and Willa had added subtle touches of diamond clips in my hair.

"You're gonna rock it tonight, Princess," Willa promised with a sly smile.

That was the last calm moment of the night. As soon as we stepped out of my bedroom, we were swept off by aides and staff that I didn't even know Elora had. They were giving me a rundown of the times that everything was set to happen and where I had to be and who I had to meet and what I had to do.

It was already more than I could comprehend, and at least momentarily, I was pushed out of the dull heartache that I got from thinking of Finn. I looked helplessly for Willa, and later on, I knew I would have to try to make this up to her. Without her, it would've been completely impossible for me to make it through.

First, there was some kind of meet and greet in the ball room. Elora stood on one side, and thankfully, Willa stayed on my other side, explaining herself as some kind of assistant to me. The three of us stood at one end of the ballroom, flanked by security. A long line of people waited to meet me.

Willa filled in the names and titles as they approached. Most of them were famous in the Trylle world, but Elora explained that anybody could come meet me today, so the line was absolutely endless. My face hurt from smiling, and there were only so many different ways I could say "pleased to meet you" and "thank you."

After that, we went to the dining hall, and that was a more exclusive function. The table only seated a hundred (that's right – *only* a hundred), and with Willa sitting five places down from me, I felt lost.

Whenever I felt insecure, my eyes instinctively searched for Finn, only to remember that he wasn't there. I tried to concentrate on eating my food properly, which wasn't that easy considering how nauseous I felt and how badly my jaw hurt from the forced smiles.

My mother sat to my right at the head of the table, and Tove Kroner sat next to me on my left. Throughout the dinner, he said hardly a thing, and Elora went about making polite conversation with the current Chancellor.

The Chancellor didn't seem to remember me from the other day when I'd come in drenched from the rain, and I was glad for it. The way he looked at me creeped me out, and I found it impossible to smile at him out of fear I might vomit.

"Drink more wine," Tove suggested quietly. Holding a wine glass in his hand, he leaned in a bit towards me to be heard over the din. His mossy eyes rested on mine briefly before averting and staring at an empty space across from us. "It relaxes the muscles."

"I beg your pardon?"

"From smiling." He gestured to his own mouth and forced a smile before quickly dropping it. "It's starting to hurt, right?"

"Yeah." I smiled lightly at him, feeling a growing soreness in the corners of my mouth.

"The wine helps. Trust me." Tove took a long drink from his wine, much larger than was polite, and I saw Elora eying him up as she chatted with the Chancellor.

"Thanks." I took his suggestion, but I drank much more slowly than he did, afraid of inciting the wrath of Elora. I didn't think she'd do anything publicly, but I didn't really think she'd let me get away with anything either.

As the dinner wore on, Tove grew restless. He leaned back in his seat, leaving his hand lying on the table. His wine glass would suddenly slowly slide over to his hand, then it would slowly slide away, without him ever touching it. It was a trick that I had seen him pull before, but I couldn't help but stare.

"You pretty on edge tonight? Tove asked, glancing at me. I'm not sure if he caught me watching his trick or not, but I looked down at my plate anyway.

"Mmm, a little," I nodded.

"Yeah, I can tell." He leaned forward, resting his elbows on the table, and I imagined Elora was livid.

"I'm trying to stay calm," I stabbed absently at some kind of vegetable I had no intention of eating. "I think I've been handling this very well, considering everything."

"No, you're acting fine. I can sense it." He tapped the side of his head. "I can't explain it but… I know how tense you are." He chewed his lip. "Your persuasion is immensely powerful."

"Maybe," I allowed. His gaze was unnerving, and I didn't want to disagree with him.

"Here's a tip: use it tonight," Tove was barely audible over the chatter. "You're trying to please so many people and it's exhausting. You can't be everything to everyone, so I try not to be anything to anyone. My mother hates me for it but…" He shrugged. "Just use it a little bit, and you'll charm everyone. Without really trying."

"It takes effort to use persuasion," I whispered. I could feel

Elora listening to us, and I didn't think she'd approve of what we were saying. "It would be just as exhausting."

"Hmm," Tove mused, then leaned back in his seat.

"Tove, the Chancellor was just telling me that you had discussed working for him this spring," Elora interjected brightly. I barely glanced up at her, but in that second, she managed to glower at me before returning to her overly cheery expression.

"My mother discussed it," Tove corrected her. "I've never said a word to the Chancellor, and I have no interest in the position."

I was increasingly becoming a fan of Tove, even if he weirded me out and I didn't understand what he meant most of the time. He just said whatever he wanted without fear of repercussion, and I admired it.

"I see." Elora raised an eyebrow, and the Chancellor started saying something about the wine they were drinking.

Tove managed to look bored and irritated the rest of the dinner, chewing his nails and looking at everything except me. There was something very strange and unstable about him. He belonged in this world even less than I did, but I imagined that there really wasn't any place that he fit in.

Moving on to the ballroom for dancing was by far the worst experience of the evening. Meeting people had been rough, but this was forced one-on-one interaction that went on for several minutes.

The ballroom looked positively magical when it was all done up, and I couldn't help but think of the brief dance I had shared with

279

Finn a few days before. That, of course, reminded me of the passionate kiss we had shared last night, making me feel weak and sick. I couldn't even force a smile when I thought of Finn.

Garrett managed to steal a dance with me, and that was a relief. I had been dancing nonstop for an hour because everyone kept cutting in. He complimented me, but not in the creepy perv way everyone else seemed to be going for.

Every now and then, I would catch Elora spinning around on the floor, or Willa would sneak me a smile as she twirled around with some foxy young guy. It was unfair that she got to pick who she danced with, but I was stuck with every stranger that asked.

"You're probably the most ravishing Princess we've ever had," the Chancellor told me after he cut in a dance.

His pudgy cheeks were red from exertion, and I wanted to suggest that he sit down and take a break, but I thought Elora would disapprove. He held me much closer than was necessary, but his hand was like a massive ham on my back, pressing me to him. I couldn't pull away without making a scene, so I just tried to force a smile.

"I'm sure that's not true," I demurred. He sweated so badly, it had to be bleeding onto my dress. The beautiful white fabric would be stained yellow after this.

"No, you really are." His eyes were wide with some kind of weird pleasure, and I wished someone would hurry up and cut in. We had just started dancing, but I couldn't take much more of this. "In fact, I've never seen anyone more ravishing than you."

"Now that, I'm certain, cannot be true." I glanced around, hoping to spot Willa somewhere so I could try to pawn him off on her.

"I know that you'll be expected to start courting soon, and I'd just like you to know that I have a lot of things going for me," the Chancellor went on. "I'm very wealthy, very secure, and my bloodline is immaculate. Your mother would approve of this arrangement."

"I haven't made any arrangements yet..." I trailed off.

I craned my neck around, knowing that if Elora saw me, she would accuse me of being rude. But I didn't know how else to react. This blubbery man grabbed my ass during some kind of marriage proposal. I had to get out of there.

"I've been told I'm an excellent lover, as well," the Chancellor lowered his voice. "I'm sure that you don't have any experience but I could definitely teach you."

He actually had a hungry look, and his eyes had dropped lower than my face. It was taking all my restraint not to push him off me, and in my head, I screamed to get away from him.

"May I cut in?" Tove appeared at my side. The Chancellor looked disappointed at the sight of him, but before he could say anything, Tove had put his hand on his shoulder and taken my hand, pulling me away from him

"Thank you," I breathed gratefully as we waltzed away from a very confused looking Chancellor.

"I heard you calling for help," Tove smiled at me. "You seem to be using your persuasion more than you think." In my mind, I had been begging for a way out, but I hadn't uttered an actual word.

"You heard me?" I gasped, feeling pale. "How many other people heard me?"

"Probably just me. Don't worry. Hardly anybody can sense anything anymore," Tove said. "The Chancellor might've noticed if he hadn't been too busy staring at your chest, or if you were more skilled at it. You'll get the hang of it."

"I don't really care if I get the hang of it. I just wanted to get rid of him," I muttered. "I'm sorry if I'm wet. I'm probably covered in his sweat."

"No, you're fine," Tove assured me.

We danced the appropriate width apart, so he probably couldn't feel my dress to tell if it was soaked or not, but there was something relaxing about being with him. I didn't have to say anything or worry about being felt up or ogled. He barely looked at me and said nothing else at all.

Elora finally interrupted the festivities. The christening ceremony would be happening in twenty minutes, and she noted that I needed a break from all the dancing. The dance floor emptied and everyone took seats at the tables on the sides, or milled around the refreshments table.

I knew that I should sit down while I had the chance, but I was desperate to have a moment to breathe, so I went to a corner hidden behind extra chairs and leaned against the wall.

"Who are you hiding from?" Rhys teased, finding me in the corner. Dressed in a flashy tux, he looked dashing as he sauntered over to me, grinning.

"Everyone," I smiled at him. "You look really good."

"Funny, I was just gonna tell you the same thing." Rhys stood next me, putting his hands in his pockets and smiling even wider at me. "Although, 'good' doesn't even begin to do you justice. You look... otherworldly. Like nothing else here can even compare to you."

"It's the dress." I looked down, hoping to keep my cheeks from blushing. "That Frederique is amazing."

"The dress is nice, but trust me, *you* make the dress."

I felt his blue eyes searching over me again, and gently, he reached over and fixed a strand of my hair back that had fallen out of place. He let his hand linger there a minute, looking me in the eyes, then dropped his hand.

"So, having fun yet?" Rhys asked.

"A blast," I smirked. "What about you?"

"I can't dance with the Princess, so I'm a little bitter," he said with a sad smile.

"Why can't you dance with me?" I would've loved to dance with him. It would've been a blessed reprieve after everything I'd been through tonight.

"Mänks," he pointed his thumbs at himself. "I'm lucky I'm even allowed in."

"Oh." I looked down at the floor, thinking about what he'd just said. "Not to sound rude or anything, because I'm glad you're here but... why are you here? Why aren't you banned or something equally ridiculous?"

"Didn't you know?" Rhys asked with a cocky grin. "I am the highest mänks in the land."

"And why is that?" I couldn't tell if he was teasing me or not, so I tilted my head, watching him as his expression got more serious.

"Because I'm yours," he replied softly.

He was invited because he was my mänsklig, my opposite, but when he answered, that's not what he meant at all. Something in his eyes made me blush for real this time, and I smiled sadly at him.

One of Elora's aides burst into the corner, ruining what was left of the moment, and demanded that I take my seat at the head table with the Queen. The christening ceremony was about to start, and a knot formed in my stomach. I hadn't heard what my name was to be, and I was depressed about the idea of changing it.

"Duty calls," I smiled apologetically at Rhys and started to walk past him.

"Hey." Rhys grabbed my hand to stop me, and I turned to look at him. "You're gonna be great. Everyone's raving about you."

"Thanks." I squeezed his hand gratefully.

A cracking echoed through the room, followed by a tinkling that I didn't understand. The sound was coming from everywhere so it was hard to place right away. But then it looked like the ceiling was raining glitter, and the skylights crashed to the ground.

22. Falling

Rhys realized what was happening before I did, and still holding my hand, he yanked me behind him. We were in the corner, out of the way of most of the glass, but from the painful screams, I gathered that everyone else wasn't so lucky.

People fell through the broken skylights, landing on the ground with surprising grace. Blood and broken glass layered the floor. Before I recognized them, I remembered the uniform. Matching long black trench coats, like a crime fighting team.

The word seemed to well through the room without anybody saying anything: *Vittra*.

About fifteen Vittra had broken in, crashing through the ceiling, and Trylle guards circled them. In the very center, I saw Jen, the tracker that had been so fond of hitting me, and his eyes scanned the room.

"You are not invited. Please leave." Elora's voice boomed above everything else.

"You know what we want, and we're not leaving until we get it." Kyra stepped forward, Jen's accomplice from before. She walked on glass in bare feet but didn't seem to notice. "She's got to be here. Where are you hiding her?"

Jen turned towards me, and his black eyes met mine over Rhys's shoulder. When he grinned wickedly, Rhys realized we were in trouble. He tried to push me towards the door, but I didn't want to go. They were after me, and I didn't want people getting hurt over me.

Before I could protest, Jen bolted towards us, and everyone burst into life. The Vittra scrambled, going after the guards and other Trylle.

Elora glared at Kyra, who collapsed on the ground, writhing in pain. Nobody touched her, and based on the look on Elora's eyes, I figured that Kyra's agony had something to do with Elora's abilities.

I saw Tove bound over the table he sat at, using his powers to send Vittra flying without even touching them. People screamed, and I felt a strong wind blow through the room, something I attributed to Willa's attempts at helping.

Then Jen was in front of us, blocking out the chaos of the ballroom. Rhys stood his ground in front of me. He moved to defend me in some way, but Jen lunged forward and punched him, throwing him back to the ground.

"Rhys!" I reached out for Rhys, but he didn't move. I wanted to make sure he wasn't dead, but Jen grabbed me around my waist, restraining me.

"That's what you have protecting you now?" Jen laughed. "Did we scare off Finn?"

"Let go of me!" I kicked at him and tried to pry his arm off me.

With his arm still gripped around me, we both abruptly went flying backwards, as if someone had pushed him. He slammed into the wall, and his arm loosened enough where I could scramble away from him.

Dazed, I got to my feet and tried to figure out what happened. Tove stood on the other side of the table across from us, holding his hand palm out at Jen. He had used his powers to kinetically throw Jen into the wall, and Jen just happened to take me with him.

I smiled appreciatively at him, but it disappeared as soon as I got a look at the room. Somehow, the Vittra had the upper hand in the room. Kyra tried to get to my mother, and someone on the other side of the room had started using fire.

Other than Tove, Willa, and Elora, none of the Trylle really seemed to have abilities, or at least they weren't using them. The room was total pandemonium, and it was about to get worse. Even more Vittra streamed in through the ceiling. There was no way we could beat them.

"This is why you need to work on your persuasion." Tove looked at me evenly, and another Vittra charged at his back.

"Watch out!" I yelled.

Tove turned, throwing his hand back and tossing the Vittra across the room. I looked around to grab a weapon when I felt Jen's arms around my waist again. I yelled and fought as hard as I could, but his arms felt like granite around me.

Tove turned his attention back to me, but two other Vittra chased after him, so he only had a moment to send Jen flying back into the wall again. We hit even harder this time, and it jostled me painfully, but Jen let go.

My head throbbed from hitting the wall, and I blinked to clear it. A hand took mine, helping me to my feet, and I wasn't sure if I should accept it, but I did anyway.

"You've got to be more careful, Tove," he said.

"I was just trying to get her free!" Tove snapped, and another Vittra yelled as he sent them flying into a table across the room. "And I'm busy here!"

I turned back to see who had helped me, and all the air went out of my lungs. Wearing a black hoodie under a black jacket, Finn surveyed the mess around me. He stood right next to me, holding my hand, and I couldn't think or move.

"Finn!" I gasped, and he finally looked at me, his dark eyes a mixture of relief and panic.

"This is Bedlam!" Tove growled.

A table had been flipped on its side, and it separated Tove from Finn and me. Using his abilities, Tove sent it sailing into a Vittra attacking the Chancellor, and then Tove walked over to us. All the Vittra seemed to be busy, so he had a moment to catch his breath.

"It's worse than I thought," Finn pursed his lips.

"We've gotta protect the Princess," Tove said.

I squeezed Finn's hand and watched the two of them. Jen started to get up, so Tove slammed him back into the wall.

"I'll get her out of here," Finn nodded. "Can you handle it down here?"

"I don't have a choice." Tove barely had time to answer when Willa started screaming across the room. I couldn't see her, and that scared me even more.

"Willa!" I tried to run to see what was happening, but Finn wrapped his arms around me, pulling me back.

"Get her out of here!" Tove commanded as he took a step in the direction of Willa screaming.

Finn started dragging me out of the ballroom while I strained to see what was going on. Tove had disappeared, and I couldn't see Elora or Willa. As Finn pulled me, my feet hit Rhys' leg, and I remembered that he was laying unconscious, bleeding on the ground. I struggled against Finn's arms, trying to reach Rhys.

"He's fine! They won't touch him!" Finn tried to reassure me. He still had one arm around my waist, and he was much stronger than me. "You've got to get out of here!"

"But Rhys!" I pleaded.

"He'd want you to be safe!" Finn insisted and finally managed to get me to the ballroom doors.

I looked up from Rhys to see the chaos of the room. All the chandeliers suddenly crashed to the ground, and the only light was coming from someone who controlled a fire ability and the things that were in flames. People were screaming and yelling, and it was echoing off everything.

"The painting," I murmured, and my mind flashed on the picture I'd seen in Elora's room. This was it. This was the exact scene.

I hadn't averted danger when I'd been with Tove. I'd been hoping I had prevented the future, but he was right. I couldn't prevent it. I couldn't even understand it until it was too late.

"Wendy!" Finn shouted, trying to move me into action.

He let go of my waist and took my hand, yanking me out of the room. Using my free hand, I pulled up my dress to keep from tripping on it as we raced down the hallway. I could still hear the carnage from the ballroom, and I had no idea where he planned to take me.

I didn't have time to question him, or even really to feel thankful that I was with him again. My only consolation was that if I died tonight, I at least spent the last few minutes of my life with Finn.

We rounded the corner towards the entryway, but Finn stopped sharply. Three Vittra were coming in the front doors of the palace, but they hadn't seen us yet. Finn changed direction, darting across the hall into one of the sitting rooms, pulling me by the hand with him.

He closed the door quietly behind us, leaving us in the darkness of the room. Moonlight spilled in through the glass, and he ran to a corner between a bookcase and the wall. He pulled me tightly to him, shielding me with his body.

We could hear the Vittra outside. I held my breath, pressing my face into Finn's chest and praying they didn't come in the room.

When they finally walked past, Finn still didn't loosen his grip on me, but I could hear his heartbeat slow. Somewhere beneath all my panic and fear, I became aware of the fact that Finn held me tightly in his arms. I looked up at him, barely able to make out his features in the light from the windows next to us.

"I saw that before," I whispered, looking up at him. "What happened in the ballroom. Elora painted it! She knew that was going to happen!"

"Sh," Finn shushed me gently.

"Sorry," I lowered my voice. "But why didn't she stop it?"

"She didn't know when it would happen or how," Finn explained. "She just knew, and the only thing she could do to prevent it was to add more protection."

"So then why did you leave?" I asked softly.

"Wendy…" He pushed back stray curls from my face, and his hand lingered on my cheek as he looked down at me. "I never really left. I was just down the hill, and I never stopped tracking you. I knew what was happening as soon as you did, and I raced back here."

"Are we gonna be okay?" I asked

"I won't let anything happen to you," Finn promised.

I looked up at him, searching his eyes in the dim light, and I wanted nothing more than to stay in his arms forever.

The door creaked open, and Finn tensed up instantly. He pushed me back harder against the wall, wrapping his arms around me to hide me. I held my breath and tried to stop my heartbeat. We heard nothing for a second, and then the light flicked on.

"Well, well, if the prodigal stork hasn't returned," Jen smirked.

"You won't get her," Finn said firmly.

He pulled away from me just enough so he could face Jen. I peered around him, watching Jen walk in a slow semi-circle towards us. He walked in an oddly familiar way, like something I had seen on Animal Planet. Jen was stalking his prey.

"Maybe I won't," Jen allowed. "But getting you out of my way would probably make it easier, if not for me, then for somebody else. Because they won't stop coming for her."

"We won't stop protecting her."

"You're willing to die to protect her?" Jen raised an eyebrow.

"You're willing to die to get her?" Finn challenged evenly.

In the ballroom, Tove insisted they had to protect me, and I hadn't thought that Tove had cared for me all that much. Was it just that I was a Princess? Had Elora endured similar things when she first came home?

I clenched my fingers onto the back of Finn's jacket, and I watched the two of them stare each other down. I didn't understand what was so damn important about me that so many Vittra were willing to kill, and according to Finn, so many Trylle were willing to die.

"Neither one of you have to die," I said. I tried to slip around Finn's arm, but he pushed me back. "I'll go, okay? I don't want anybody else to get hurt over this!"

"Why don't you listen to the girl?" Jen suggested, wagging his eyebrows.

"Not this time."

"Suit yourself." Jen had apparently tired of talking and dove at Finn.

Finn was wrenched from my fingertips, and I screamed his name. They both went flying through the glass out onto the balcony, sending shards flying everywhere. I was barefoot, but I ran forward without regard.

Jen managed to land a few good blows on Finn, but Finn was much quicker and seemed to be stronger. When Finn hit him, he staggered back several feet.

"You've been working out." Jen wiped fresh blood from his chin.

"You could give up now, and I wouldn't think any less of you," Finn said.

"Nice try." Jen lunged forward, kicking Finn in the stomach, but Finn held his own.

I grabbed a giant shard of glass from off the balcony, and moved around them, trying to find an opening to attack. I managed to slice open a finger, but I barely noticed. Jen knocked Finn to the ground. He pounced on top of him and started hitting him in the face. Using all my might, I stabbed the glass into his back.

"Ow!" Jen shouted, but he sounded more irritated than wounded.

I stood right behind him, panting. That was not the reaction I had expected and I didn't know what to do.

Jen turned quickly, smacking me so hard across the face that I went flying to the edge of the balcony. I only had a moment to notice the dizzying drop below as my head hung over the edge, and then I was scrambling to my feet and gripping onto the railing.

Finn had already jumped up and knocked Jen back down. Kicking him as hard as he could, Finn growled through gritted teeth, "Don't. Ever. Touch. Her. Again."

When Finn went to kick him again, Jen grabbed his foot and yanked him back to the ground. I heard the sound of Finn's head cracking against the heavy concrete of the balcony. It didn't really hurt Finn, but it stunned him long enough where Jen could bend over and wrap his hand around Finn's throat. He lifted him off the ground by his neck.

I jumped on Jen's back, which wasn't as smart as it sounded because Jen had a giant shard of glass sticking out of his back. I cut through my dress and my side without actually impaling myself on it. It was enough to bleed and hurt, but not enough to kill.

"Get off!" Jen growled, then jerked his arm back, elbowing me hard in the stomach and knocking me off his back.

I landed on my feet but Jen already had Finn pressed back over the railing. The top half of his body dangled over the edge, and if Jen let go, Finn would plummet to his death hundreds of feet below.

For a moment, I couldn't breathe or move. All I could see was the painting of me. The broken shards of glass glinting in the moonlight. My beautiful white dress with the slit of blood in the side. The vast darkness that went on beyond the balcony, and the horrified look on my face as I reached for it.

"Stop!" I pleaded, tears streaming down my face. "I'll go with you! Please! Just let go of him! *Please!*"

"I hate to break it to you, Princess, but you're going with me either way!" Jen laughed.

"Not if I can help…" Finn barely managed to speak through Jen's hand clamped on his throat.

Finn kicked his leg up, planting it squarely between Jen's legs, and Jen groaned, but didn't loosen his grip on Finn. Keeping his leg there, Finn started tilting backwards. Jen realized what he was doing, but Finn had reached forward and grabbed onto Jen's jacket.

He had changed the weight ratio, and in a moment that felt oddly slow motion, Finn went backwards over the railing, pulling Jen with him.

"*No!*" I screamed and lunged towards them, grabbing at empty air.

23. Aftermath

As soon as I reached the railing, Finn floated up to the top, coughing hoarsely. I gaped at him, too shocked to believe he was real. He came over the top of the railing, then dropped heavily onto the balcony.

Lying on his back, he coughed again, and I rushed to his side, kneeling next to him. I touched his face, checking to make sure he was real, and his skin felt soft and warm under my hands.

"That was quite the gamble," Tove remarked from behind me, and I turned to look at him.

Tove had lost his blazer, and his white shirt looked slightly burned and bloody. Other than that, he didn't look that bad as he took a step towards us. When Finn had gone over the balcony, Tove had used his power to catch him and lift him back up, setting him down safely.

"Nah, you always come through," Finn said.

I went back to staring down at him, unable to completely believe that he was alive and here with me again. My hand was on his chest, above his heart, so I could feel it pounding. He placed his hand over mine, holding it gently, but he looked past me at Tove.

"What's going on in there?" Finn asked Tove and nodded to the house.

"They're retreating." Tove stood over us. "A lot of people were hurt, but Aurora is working on them. For the most part, I think everyone will be okay."

"Good." Finn sighed in relief and looked back over at me. "What happened? Are you alright?" His hand went to my side, where I bled all over my dress. I winced under his touch but shook my head.

"It's nothing. I'm fine."

"Have my mother look at it. She'll patch you both up," Tove said. When I gave him a confused look, he went on, "Aurora's a healer. She can touch you and fix you. That's her ability."

"Come on," Finn forced a smile at me and slowly sat up.

He tried to seem like he was perfectly fine, but he had taken quite a beating and there was a hesitation in his movements. Tove helped him to his feet, then took my hand and pulled me up.

I wrapped my arm around his waist, and Finn put his arm around my shoulders, reluctantly putting some of his weight on me. We walked carefully through the broken glass back into the house, and Tove gave more details about the attack.

Other than the trackers that had been guarding, most of the Trylle had played defenseless, myself included. The Vittra might not have as many abilities, but they mastered physical combat much better than the Trylle. Eventually, though, Tove, Elora, and a few others had managed to defeat them.

The ballroom looked even worse than we left it. Someone had lit lanterns around the edge of the room so we could at least see better than before.

Willa ran over to me when she saw me and threw her arms around me. I hugged her back, feeling tremendous relief that she was alive. Despite a few scrapes and bruises, she looked okay.

She then launched into an excited tale about how she had blown a Vittra out of the ceiling, and I told her I was proud. I wanted to listen to her talk, but the destruction was too overwhelming.

When Elora saw us, she pulled Aurora from where she helped a bleeding man. I noted with some dark happiness that the Chancellor had a nasty cut on his forehead, and I hoped that Aurora couldn't make time to fix him.

Elora didn't look any worse for the wear at all. If I hadn't known, I would've never thought she'd been here when the fight was going on. Aurora, on the other hand, looked beautiful and regal, but she showed signs of the battle. Her dress was torn, her hair was a mess, and there was blood all over her hands and arms, but I doubted most of it was hers.

"Princess," Elora looked genuinely relieved when she walked over to us, delicately stepping over broken tables and a Vittra corpse. "I'm glad to see you're alright. I was very worried about you."

"Yeah, I'm fine."

She reached out and touched my cheek, but there was nothing affectionate about it. It was the way I would touch a strange animal that they assured me was safe, but I didn't really believe it.

"I don't know what I would've done if something happened to you." She smiled wanly at me, then dropped her hand and looked at

Finn. "I'm sure a thank you is in order for saving my daughter."

"No need," Finn replied rather curtly, and Elora gazed at him intently for a moment, saying something in his mind. Then she turned and walked away, going to deal with something far more pressing than her daughter.

Aurora squeezed Tove's arms and looked at him warmly, making me feel a horrible pang at my own mother's reaction. Aurora had seemed like an ice queen, too, but she could at least show signs of genuine happiness that her son hadn't died.

The moment passed quickly, and she moved on to me. She tore open the hole in my dress wider so she could put her hand on my wound, and I gritted my teeth at the pain. Finn tightened his arm around my shoulders, a warm tingling sensation passed over my side, and moments later, the pain stopped.

"Good as new," Aurora smiled tiredly at me.

She seemed to have aged since before she'd touched me, and I wondered how much all that healing took out of her. She started taking a step away, going back to help other people, and Finn leaned on me, clearly in pain.

"What about Finn?" I asked, and she looked back at me, startled. Apparently, I had asked something wrong, and she didn't know how to react.

"No, no, I'm fine," Finn waved her off.

"Nonsense," Tove clapped him on the back. He nodded at his mother. "Finn saved the day. He deserves a little help. Aurora, wanna take care of him?" She looked uncertainly at her son, then nodded and walked over to Finn.

"Of course," Aurora said.

She looked over him for his wounds, trying to find out specifically what he needed fixing. I glanced away from them, and I saw Rhys sitting on the edge of a table. He held a bloody cloth to his forehead and stared down at the ground.

"Rhys!" I shouted, and when he looked up and saw me, he smiled.

"Go see him," Finn suggested. Aurora poked at something painful in his side and he winced. "She's taking care of me."

"I got him." Tove took Finn's arm, so he would be leaning on Tove instead of me.

I looked back at Finn, but he nodded at me for me to go and tried not to let on how much pain Aurora was causing him.

I didn't really want to leave Finn, but I felt like I should at least say hi to somebody that tried to save my life. Especially since Rhys had been the only person that had told me I looked beautiful all night without sounding really creepy about it.

"You're alive!" Rhys grinned. He tried to stand up, but I gestured for him to sit back down. "I wasn't really sure what happened to you." He looked past me at Finn, and his expression faltered. "I didn't know Finn was back. If I had, I wouldn't have worried."

"I was worried about you." I reached out and carefully touched his forehead. "You took quite the punch there."

"Yeah, but I couldn't get one in," Rhys grumbled, looking down at the floor. "And I couldn't stop him from taking you."

"Yes, you did!" I insisted. "If you hadn't been there, they would've hauled me off before anybody had a chance to do anything about it. You kind of saved the day."

"Yeah?" His blue eyes were hopeful when he looked at me.

"Definitely," I smiled back at him.

"You know, back in the day, when a guy saved a Princess's life, she would reward him with a kiss," Rhys commented.

His smile was light, but his eyes were serious. If Finn hadn't been standing a few feet behind me, watching, I probably would've kissed him. But I didn't want to do anything to spoil having Finn back, so I just shook my head and smiled.

"Maybe when I slay the dragon. Then I'll get a kiss?"

"I promise," I agreed. "Would you settle for a hug?"

"A hug from you is never settling."

I leaned over and hugged him tightly. A woman sitting next to us on the table looked aghast at the new Princess openly hugging a mänsklig. Things were really going to have to change when I was Queen.

After Aurora healed up Finn, she suggested we both get rest. The room was still a disaster, but Tove insisted that he and his mother were taking care of everything. I wanted to protest and help more, but I was exhausted. Tove said that we were safe and demanded that I go to my room.

Using his abilities during the fight had focused Tove. His entire personality shone through, and he took control of the situation with ease. I had a feeling that for the first time, I was seeing the real Tove, and not the kid trapped behind the noise of his powers.

In a way, we worked in opposite ways. I projected intensely, which was why my persuasion was strong, whereas Tove received everything. He could pick up on my emotions and thoughts whether he wanted to or not. But I imagined that he sensed other people too, and his mind had to be a fog of everyone's emotions.

Finn went with me to my room, just in case it wasn't completely safe. Before we even reached the stairs, Finn had taken my hand in his. Most of the way, I was silent, but when we got close to my door, I felt like I had to say something.

"So… are you and Tove like pals or something?" I was teasing, but I was curious. I had never really seen them even speak before, but there seemed to be a kind of familiarity between them.

"I'm a tracker," Finn answered. "I tracked Tove. He's a good kid." He looked over at me, smiling a little. "I told him to keep an eye on you."

"If you were so worried about me, why didn't you stay in the palace?" I asked more sharply than I meant to.

"Let's not talk about that now," Finn shook his head. We had stopped in front of my bedroom door, and there was something playful in his dark eyes.

"What should we talk about then?" I looked up at him.

"How beautiful you look in that dress." Finn looked me over appreciatively, and he put his hands on my sides.

I laughed, and then he was pushing me against the door. His body was so tight against me, I could barely breathe, and his mouth searched mine. He kissed me in the same frantic way he had before, and I loved it.

I wrapped my arms around him and pushed myself against him eagerly. He reached around me, opening the door, and we tumbled into my room. He caught me before I actually fell, then lifted me easily into his arms and carried me.

Gently, he tossed me onto the bed, and then lowered himself on top of me. His stubble tickled my neck and shoulders as he covered me in kisses.

Sitting back, he peeled off his jacket and hoodie, and I expected him to take off his tee shirt, but he stopped, looking down at me. His black hair was slightly disheveled, but his expression was completely foreign to me. He just stared at me, making my skin redden with shame.

"What?"

"You're just so perfect," Finn said, but he sounded distressed about it.

"Oh, I am not," I blushed and laughed. "You know I'm not."

"You can't see what I see." He leaned over me again, his face right above mine but not kissing me. After a minute's hesitation, he kissed my forehead and my cheeks, and then very tenderly, kissed my lips. "I just don't want to disturb you."

"How are you going to disturb me?"

"Mmm." A smile played on his lips and then he sat up, climbing off me. "You should go change into pajamas. That dress can't be comfortable."

"What do I need pajamas for?" I sat up. I tried to sound flirty, but I knew there was a panicked edge to it. As soon as we'd come in here, I thought things were going to go much farther than pajamas would allow.

"I'll stay with you tonight," Finn tried to reassure me. "But nothing more can happen except for sleep."

"Why?"

"I'm here," Finn looked at me intently. "Isn't that enough?"

I nodded and carefully climbed out of the bed. I stood in front of him so he could unzip my dress, and I felt his hands linger on my skin. I didn't understand what was going on, but I would be happy for anything I could have with him.

After I changed into my pajamas, I climbed back into bed with him. He stayed sitting on the edge for a minute, then almost reluctantly, he came over to me. I curled up in his arms, burying my head in his chest, and he held me tightly to him.

Nothing had ever felt better than being with him like that, and I tried to stay up so I could relish every minute, but eventually, my body gave in and passed out.

In the morning, I woke up to Elora coming in my room for the first time ever. She was wearing pants, something I had never seen her in. I was still curled up in Finn's arms, and she didn't seem surprised or that offended by it. I thought I was finally making progress when I moved a little bit away from him to look at her.

"I trust you slept well." Elora looked around the room, but not in a nervous way. She had just never been here before. "And I trust that Finn was a gentleman."

"He always is," I yawned.

He had started pulling away from me and getting out of the bed. I furrowed my brow but didn't say anything. It wasn't that shocking that she'd be upset that we were together, so I didn't think that much of it when Finn started to gather up his jacket and sweatshirt.

"Thank you for protecting my daughter," Elora said without looking at him.

Finn paused at the doorway, and he looked back at me, his dark eyes looking conflicted. He nodded, then turned and walked out of my room, shutting the door behind him.

"Well, you took that much better than I thought you would," I admitted, sitting up.

"He's not coming back," Elora turned to look at me.

"What?" I stared at the door in dismay.

"He saved your life, so I gave him last night to say goodbye to you," Elora explained. "I will be transferring him out of here as soon as possible."

"You mean he knew?" I gaped at her.

"Yes. I made the agreement with him last night," Elora said. He had known and hadn't let me in on it, and hadn't tried to steal me away.

"But... he saved my life!" I insisted, feeling a terrifying lump grow in my chest. The one that said I couldn't possibly survive without Finn. "He should be here to protect me!"

"He is emotionally compromised and unsuitable for the job," Elora explained flatly. "Not only that, if he stayed around, you would be banished from Förening. He doesn't want that, and neither do I." She sighed.

"I shouldn't even have given him last night, but... I don't want to know what you did with him. Don't tell me. Don't tell anyone. Is that clear?"

"Nothing happened," I shook my head. "But I want him back. He'll protect me better than anyone!"

"Let me put it to you this way: he will do anything to keep you alive, Princess," Elora looked at me evenly. "That means he would die to save you, without hesitation. Do you really want that? Do you really want him to die because of you?"

"No..." I trailed off, looking dazedly at my blankets. I knew she was right. Last night he had almost died to save me. If Tove hadn't come out, he would be dead.

"Very well. It's in his best interest that he's not around you, either," Elora said. "Now, you need to get up and get ready. We have much to go over."

24. Goodbye

The next few days were an endless stream of defense meetings. There hadn't been an attack this severe on Förening ever. Elora and Aurora led all the meetings, while Tove and I sat quietly in the back. He was the most powerful and should've had more of a say, but he didn't seem that interested.

The twenty or so other people that always seemed to be in attendance offered advice that was completely pointless. Tove just told me that my best defense was to get my abilities under control. Willa took his advice to heart and busied herself with self-defense classes and getting a better control of her wind ability. Elora barely spoke to me, and never uttered a kind word.

The one positive was that I'd been spared the christening ceremony, and Elora decided to allow me to keep my own name.

I wandered around in a daze. I didn't care whether I lived or died. If they attacked again, I would deal with whatever happened.

"You're gonna have to snap out of this one day," Rhys said.

I lay in my bed, staring at the ceiling, and he leaned against the doorway, looking at me. He still had a nasty cut above his eyebrow, since Aurora wouldn't resort to healing a mänks. It was healing okay, but it pained me to see it. It was just a reminder that he had gotten hurt for me.

"Maybe." I didn't feel like I ever would, and I hoped I didn't.

"Oh come on," Rhys sighed and came over to sit on the bed next to me. "I know that everything that's happened has really taken its toll on you, but it's not the end of the world."

"I never said it was," I muttered. "I just hate this house. I hate my mother. I hate being a Princess. I hate everything about being here!"

"Even me?" Rhys asked honestly.

"No, of course not you," I shook my head. "You're about the only thing I like anymore."

"I feel privileged," he smiled at me, but when I didn't smile back, his quickly faded. "Look, I hate it here too. It's a hard place to live, especially this house, with Elora. But... what else are we gonna do? Where else can we go?"

That's when it occurred to me. I absolutely did not want this life, and this life truly didn't want Rhys. He had grown up in a cold indifference even worse than my own childhood, and he deserved so much more. Since I had been here, Rhys had been about the only one to show me genuine kindness, and he deserved that in return.

I didn't particularly care whether I lived or died, so I didn't need protection, should anyone decide to come after me again, but I wasn't so sure they would anymore. Tove had explained that the Vittra numbers had been damaged, and another attack any time soon would be highly unlikely.

But somewhere out there, I knew that my brother Matt was sitting, worried sick about me. He and Maggie would welcome me back with open arms, and they would be delighted to have Rhys. I didn't know how I would explain him to them, but I'd figure something out.

I was not a Princess, and I didn't want to be one. It would feel so good to be home again. That wouldn't really fix the Finn thing, but Matt and Maggie would know the best way to mend a broken heart.

Rhys wasn't convinced that leaving was the best thing for me, referring to the cut on his eye when he'd been unable to protect me or himself. Reluctantly, I resorted to using my persuasion, but I didn't really have another choice. Besides, I was only convincing him that he didn't need to worry about me.

In the middle of the night, I decided to act. We snuck out of the palace, which was more difficult than I'd expected. Guards and other Trylle walked the grounds in case of another Vittra attack. Even though they thought another one would be unlikely, they weren't taking any more chances.

Rhys and I went through the kitchen and out the back door, to the secret garden that bloomed even in the middle of the night. Scaling the high brick walls that surrounded it would've been impossible if I didn't have Rhys to give me a boost up. Once I pulled him up, we both jumped down on the other side.

Without even brushing the dirt from our clothes, we ran along the wall. Rhys led the way because he knew the area better than I did. We'd nearly made it to the garage when we had to duck behind a bush to wait for a passing guard.

Once the guard moved on, we hurried to the garage. Rhys took his new motorcycle but didn't start it. He pushed out of the garage, leaving the engine and lights off as not to attract attention.

At the end of town was the gate manned by a guard, and I doubted he'd let the Princess through. Rhys had a plan, though. He knew of a weak spot in the fence a ways down the embankment. He'd heard of other mänks getting through it when they ran away.

I had to help Rhys steady the motorcycle so it wouldn't go tumbling down the hill as we made our way through the trees and the brush. The hole in the fence was even worse than it had been before. Apparently, that's how some of the Vittra had broken in, and the Trylle hadn't fixed it yet. They were more focused on securing the palace than making sure the town of Förening as safe.

We were able to get the motorcycle through without much trouble, and it was then as we pushed it up the hill that I started feeling the exhilaration and relief of escape. I ignored any pang of sadness or longing for some of the people I'd met here, and I just tried focus on the fact that I was getting away. I was free.

Once we got to the road, Rhys started the motorcycle. We sped off into the darkness, and I sat on the bike behind him, wrapping my arms tightly around his waist and burying my face in his leather jacket. I could feel his heartbeat speed up every time I squeezed onto him, but I pretended not to notice.

The sky had that eerie blue glow of very early morning when we pulled up in front of my house. Rhys hadn't even turned off the motorcycle before Matt threw open the front door and came jogging down the porch.

Even in the dim light, I could see how stricken Matt looked. I jumped off the bike, and completely oblivious to Rhys, Matt threw his arms around me. He held me so tightly to him, it hurt. I didn't care, though. I buried my face in his shoulder, breathing in his familiar scent and relishing the protection of his arms. I was finally *home*.

There was one other thing. I had a feeling that Finn hadn't stopped tracking me yet. And maybe the only way I could see him again was if I ran away or got into some trouble. If he didn't come after me, that wasn't the end of the world.

But if he did… well, that's just an added bonus, isn't it?

Torn Excerpt

**Read an excerpt from the second book in the Trylle Trilogy –
Torn – available now!**

Finn Holmes stepped into my room with one graceful move, as if
entering through bedrooms windows was nothing out of the
ordinary.

His black hair was slicked back, but he had stubble growing
along his jaw, making him look even sexier. His eyes were so dark
they were nearly black, and he cast one discerning glare at Rhys
before settling them on me, making my heart forget to beat entirely.

Finn Holmes had snuck into my room.

H still managed to stun me the same way he always did. I was so
happy to see him that I almost forget how angry I was with him.

The last time I had seen Finn, he was slinking out of my
bedroom in Förening, per his deal with my mother. Elora told him
that he could spend one more night with me before leaving. Forever.

We had only kissed, but Finn had failed to let me in on Elora's
plan. He didn't even bother to say goodbye. He didn't fight it or try
to get me to run away with him. He just crept out of my room,
leaving Elora to explain to me exactly what had happened.

"What are you doing here?" Rhys asked, and Finn pulled his eyes
off me to glare at Rhys.

"I came to collect the Princess, of course." Finn struggled to keep his expressions and his voice emotionless, but irritation saturated his words.

"Well, yeah, but... I thought Elora reassigned you." Rhys was thrown by Finn's anger, and he fumbled for a minute. "I mean... that's what people were saying around Förening, that you weren't allowed around Wendy anymore."

Finn tensed noticeably at Rhys's words, his jaw flexing, and Rhys looked down at the floor.

"I'm not," Finn admitted once he had calmed down enough to speak. "I was preparing to leave when I heard that you two had vanished in the middle of the night. Elora was deciding who would be best suited to track Wendy, but I thought it would be in her best interest if I went after her, what with the Vittra *stalking* her."

Rhys opened his mouth to protest but Finn stopped him.

"We all know you did a wonderful job of protecting her at the ball," Finn said. "If I hadn't shown up, you might've protected her right into getting murdered."

"I know the Vittra are a threat!" Rhys shot back, sounding perplexed.

Hearing his confusion, I got up off the bed, moving to intercede. Rhys agreed with Finn about the Vittra, which is why he couldn't figure out why exactly he'd let me talk him into coming here.

The truth was, Rhys didn't agree to come here. He wanted to meet Matt, but he was adamant about my safety and had flat out refused to let me leave the security of the compound.

Unfortunately for Rhys, I had *persuasion*. When I looked at people and thought about what I wanted them to do, they would do it, whether they really wanted to or not.

That's how I convinced Rhys to take me with him when we ran away, and I needed to say something before Rhys caught on to what I'd done.

"The Vittra lost a lot of trackers in that fight," I interjected. "They're not eager to repeat it any time soon. Besides that, I'm sure they're sick of trying to get me."

"That's highly unlikely." Finn narrowed his eyes, studying Rhys's bewilderment, and then he looked darkly at me. He'd figured out how I had convinced Rhys to leave. "Wendy, do you care nothing for your own safety?"

"I probably care more than you do." I crossed my arms firmly over my chest. "You were leaving to go onto another job. If I had waited one more day to leave, you wouldn't have known I was gone."

"Is this about getting *my* attention?" Finn snapped. His eyes burned, and I had never seen his anger directed at me this way before. "I don't know how many times I have to explain this to you! You are a Princess! I mean nothing! You need to forget about me!"

"What's going on?" That was Matt, shouting from the stairs.

He'd heard us arguing. If he came up here and caught Finn in my room that would be very, very bad.

"I'll go… create a diversion." Rhys glanced at me to make sure that was okay, and I nodded. He darted out the door, saying things to Matt about how awesome the house was, and their voices faced as they went downstairs.

I tucked my curls behind my ears and refused to look at Finn. It was hard to believe that the last time I had been with him, he had been kissing me so passionately, I could barely breathe. I remembered the way his scruff scraped against my cheeks and the way his lips pressed against mine.

I suddenly hated him for that memory, and I hated that all I could think about how was badly I wanted to kiss him again.

"Wendy, you are not safe here," Finn insisted quietly.

"I'm not going with you."

"You cannot stay here. I won't allow it."

"You won't allow it?" I scoffed. "I am the Princess, remember? Who are you to *allow* me to do anything? You're not even my tracker anymore. You're some guy being a creepy stalker."

That sounded much harsher than I meant it. Not that anything I said ever really seemed to hurt Finn. He just stared at me, his gaze level and unfazed.

"I knew I would find you faster than anyone. If you don't come home with me, that's fine," Finn said. "Another tracker will be here shortly, and you can go with him. I'll just wait with you until he arrives to ensure your safety."

"It's not about you, Finn!" I snapped at him. He played a larger part than I would ever admit to him, but it really wasn't just him. I hated my mother, my title, my house, everything. I wasn't meant to be a Princess. "I'm not going with anyone!"

Finn looked at me for a long moment, trying to understand where this was coming from. I had to fight the urge to squirm as he scrutinized me. His eyes flashed darkly for a second, and his expression hardened.

"Is this about the mänsklig?" Finn asked, referring to Rhys. "I thought I told you to stay away from him."

Mänsklig were the human children taken in exchanged for Trylle babies. They were the lowest on the hierarchy of Trylle, and if a Princess was caught seeing one, they'd both be banished forever. Not that even I cared, but I didn't have any feelings for Rhys that weren't purely platonic.

"It has nothing to do with Rhys. I just thought he'd like to see his family." I shrugged. "It has to be better than living in that stupid house with Elora."

"Good. He can stay here then." Finn nodded. "Matt and Rhys are taken care of. Now you can come home."

"That is not my home. *This* is my home!" I gestured widely to my room. "I'm not going, Finn."

"You are not safe." He took a step closer to me, knowing the effect his presence had on me. He lowered his voice and stared into my eyes. "You saw what the Vittra did in Förening. They sent an army out to get you, Wendy." He put his hands on my arms, strong and warm on my skin. "They will not stop until they have you."

"Why? Why wouldn't they stop?" I asked. "There's got to be Trylle out there that are easier to get than me. And so what if I'm a Princess? If I don't come back, Elora can replace me. I'm meaningless."

"You are far more powerful than you know."

"What does that even mean?" I demanded.

Before he could answer, there was a noise on the roof outside my window. Finn grabbed my arm and threw open my closet door, shoving me inside. As a rule, I don't enjoy being tossed into closets and having the door shut on my face, but I knew he was protecting me.

I opened the door a crack, so I could watch what happened and intervene if necessary. Even as mad as I was at Finn, I would never let him get hurt over me. Not again.

Finn stood a few feet from window. His eyes blazed and his shoulders tensed, but when the figure climbed in through the window, Finn only scoffed.

The kid coming in tripped on the windowsill. He wore skinny jeans and purple shoes with the laces untied. Finn towered over him, looking down at him wearily.

"Hey, what are you doing here?" He flipped his bangs out of his eyes and pulled down his jacket. It was zipped all the way up, and the bottom met the top of his jeans. When he bent over or moved, it rode up.

"Getting the Princess. They sent you after her?" Finn arched an eyebrow. "Elora really thought you'd be able to bring her back?"

"Hey, I'm a good tracker! I've brought in way more people than you have!"

"That's because you're seven years older than me," Finn replied. That made the clumsy kid twenty-seven. He looked much younger than that.

"Whatever. Elora picked me. Deal with it." The kid shook his head. "What? Are you jealous or something?"

"Don't be absurd."

"So where is the Princess anyway?" He looked around my room. "She ran away for *this*?"

"This is my room!" I walked out of the closet, and the new tracker jumped. "You don't need to be condescending."

"Um, sorry," he stumbled, blushing. "My apologies, Princess." He offered me an unsure smile and did a low bow. "I'm Duncan Janssen, and I'm at your service."

"I'm not the Princess anymore, and I'm not going with you," I said. "I just finished explaining that to Finn."

"What?" Duncan looked at uncertainly at Finn as he readjusted his jacket again. Finn sat down on the edge of my bed and said nothing. "Princess, you have to come. It's not safe for you here."

"I don't care." I shrugged. "I'd rather take my chances out here."

"It can't be that bad at the palace." Duncan was the first person I had ever heard genuinely call Elora's house a palace, even though it sort of was one. "You are the Princess. You have everything."

"I'm not going. You can tell Elora that you tried your best, and I refused."

Duncan once again looked to Finn for help. He shrugged at Duncan, and Finn's shift to indifference startled me. I had put my foot down on the subject, but I hadn't really expected him to listen. He seemed to truly believe that I was in danger, even though I didn't.

"She can't possibly stay here!" Duncan moved on to reasoning with Finn.

"You think I don't agree with you?" Finn raised an eyebrow.

"I don't think you're helping," Duncan qualified. He fidgeted with his jacket and continued to try to stare down Finn, a task I knew was impossible.

"What do you expect me to say to her that I haven't already said?" Finn asked, sounding surprisingly helpless.

"So you're saying we leave her here?" Duncan asked dubiously.

"I am right here. I don't really appreciate the way you keep referring to me like I'm not," I said.

"If she wants to stay here, then she'll stay here," Finn ignored me. Duncan shifted and glanced over at me. "We're not going to kidnap her. That leaves little in the way of options."

"Can't you like..." Duncan lowered his voice and fiddled with the zipper of his jacket. "... you know, *convince* her somehow?"

Word of Finn's affection for me must have spread through the compound. Aggravated, I refused to let my feelings for him be used against me.

"Nothing is going to convince me," I snapped sourly.

"Do you see?" Finn motioned towards me. Sighing, he got to his feet. "We should be on our way then."

"Really?" I couldn't hide the shock in my voice

"Yeah. Really?" Duncan echoed.

"You said there was nothing I can do to convince you? Has that changed?" Finn turned to me. His voice was hopeful, but his eyes were almost taunting. I shook my head firmly. "Then there is nothing left to say."

"Finn-" Duncan started to protest, but Finn held his hand up to him.

"It is as the Princess wishes."

Duncan looked skeptically at Finn, probably thinking that this was some sort of trick, much as I was. There had to be something I wasn't getting because Finn wouldn't just leave me here. Sure, that's exactly what he had done a few days ago, but that's because leaving then was what he thought was best for me.

"But Finn-" Duncan tried again, but Finn waved him off.

"We must go. Her 'brother' will notice us soon," Finn said.

I glanced at my closed bedroom door, as if Matt would be lurking right there. The last time Matt and Finn had a run in it had not gone well, and I was not eager to repeat the experience.

"Fine, but..." Duncan trailed off, realizing too late that he had nothing to threaten either of us with. He gave me another quick bow. "Princess. I'm sure we'll meet again."

"We'll see," I shrugged.

Duncan climbed out my bedroom window, practically falling onto the roof. Finn went behind him, helping Duncan through the window so he wouldn't accidentally kill himself.

After Duncan was out, he half-jumped half-fell off the roof. Finn watched him apprehensively for a moment, holding my curtain open, but he didn't follow after immediately.

Instead, he straightened up, looking over at me. My anger and resolution were fading. Part of me believed that Finn wouldn't really leave things this way.

"Once I'm out this window, lock it behind me," Finn commanded. "Make sure all the doors are locked, and never go anywhere alone. Never go any place at night, and if at all possible, always take Matt *and* Rhys with you." He looked past me for a moment, thinking of something.

"Although neither of them are really good for much of anything…" His muttering trailed off and his dark eyes rested on mine once again. His expression was imploring, and he raised his hand as if he meant to touch my face, but he lowered it again. "You *must* be careful."

"Okay," I promised him.

With Finn standing right in front of me, I could feel the warmth of his body and smell his cologne. His eyes were locked on mine, and I remembered the way it felt when he tangled his fingers in my hair and held me so close to him, I couldn't breathe.

He was so strong and controlled. In the brief moments he allowed himself to let go of his passion with me, it was the most wonderfully suffocating feeling I'd ever had.

I did not want him to leave, and he did not want to leave. But we had both made choices we were unwilling to change. He nodded once more, breaking eye contact, and then turned and slid out the window.

Duncan waited by the tree, and Finn dropped gracefully to the ground. Duncan still didn't want to leave, and Finn had to convince him to move away from the house.

When they reached the hedges separating my lawn from the neighbors, Finn looked around, checking to make sure no one was there. Without even looking at me, he and Duncan turned and disappeared.

I closed the window, locking it securely the way he'd said to. I felt a terrible ache watching him go. Even though he had done this kind of thing before, I couldn't wrap my mind around Finn really leaving and convincing Duncan to leave me too. If he was so concerned about the Vittra, why would he leave me so unprotected?

It finally dawned on me. Finn had *never* left me unprotected, no matter what I or anybody else wanted. As soon as he had realized I wasn't going with him, he hadn't wanted to waste any more time arguing. He would wait in the wings until I changed my mind or ...

I shut the curtains tightly. I hated being spied on, but I also found it strangely comforting that Finn was watching over me. After having my window open for so long, my room felt chilly, so I went over to my closet and pulled on a heavy sweater.

The adrenaline rush from seeing Finn had left me wide awake, but I was looking forward to curling up in bed, even if I wouldn't be able to sleep.

I settled into my bed, trying futilely to forget about Finn. Within minutes, I heard a loud banging downstairs. Matt let out a yelling sound, but it was cut short, leaving the house in total silence.

I jumped and ran to my bedroom door. With shaking hands, I opened it, hoping that Finn had tried to sneak back in and had a misunderstanding with Matt.

Then I heard Rhys screaming.

About the Author

Amanda Hocking is a lifelong Minnesotan obsessed with John Hughes and Jim Henson. In between making collages and drinking too much Red Bull, she writes young adult urban fantasy and paranormal romance.

Connect with Me Online:
Twitter: www.twitter.com/amanda_hocking
Blog: www.amandahocking.blogspot.com/
Facebook Fan Page: www.facebook.com/amandahockingfans
Goodreads: www.goodreads.com/amanda_hocking

Other titles by Amanda Hocking:

Trylle Trilogy

Switched

Torn

Ascend

My Blood Approves series

My Blood Approves

Fate

Flutter

Wisdom

Letters to Elise: A Peter Townsend Novella

Hollowland

Made in the USA
Charleston, SC
12 March 2011